SEASONED

DELANEY DIAMOND

GARDEN AVENUE PRESS

Seasoned by Delaney Diamond

Copyright © 2020, Delaney Diamond

Garden Avenue Press

Atlanta, Georgia

ISBN: 978-1-946302-23-6 (Ebook edition)

ISBN: 978-1-946302-24-3 (Paperback edition)

www.delaneydiamond.com

RENEE & CLIVE

1

That darn dog was at it again.

Renee peered out the window of her home office to see her neighbor's German shepherd, Samson, barking as he chased butterflies in her yard. No fence separated her yard from next door's, only a line of bushes that roughly delineated where their property lines met. Which meant the dog often came over uninvited and unwelcomed.

Right now, Renee was working on an editing project. During the summer months when she was off from school, she took on the occasional editing job, and this one was for a former student, a well-known literary author who not only wanted her to edit the book but give her unfiltered opinion as a reader. How could she concentrate on the prose with that dog yelping and running back and forth in front of the window?

Fuming, Renee stood and marched out of the little ranch house and slammed the door.

Samson looked at her, tongue hanging out and tail wagging. She didn't understand why the dog liked her. She was never friendly to it and always took him right back to his owner. Clive Stevenson was the irritating dog owner who'd moved in a year ago and been on her nerves ever since.

If it wasn't the dog coming into her yard, it was the visual mess of car parts strewn all over his lawn and driveway as he worked on his daughter's car, his truck, or the vehicle of one of his many friends who came over to use his services. She'd written eight letters of complaint to the HOA board about his various infractions, and after the last complaint, she hadn't seen any more car repairs in the front of his house.

The nighttime parties hadn't stopped, though. They consisted of a bunch of men drinking, and talking loud as hell late at night, while their cars sat on both sides of the street and made it almost impossible to pass.

Renee took the German shepherd by its leather collar and walked stiffly across the neighbor's yard and onto his driveway where he had a white Dodge pickup parked. The white vehicle was about twenty years old with chipped paint but brand-new tires and a new interior made of supple-looking brown leather. He probably didn't want to get rid of it for sentimental reasons. Her third husband had owned a similar love—an old Mustang he poured thousands of dollars and hundreds of hours into.

More time than he did our marriage, that was for sure, Renee thought bitterly.

In contrast to the old truck, the house was in pristine condition with fresh paint and not a single piece of rotted siding in sight. Mr. Stevenson used to own a small construction company and now worked as a handyman doing odd jobs for some of the neighbors. Renee had barely talked to the annoying man, but she knew a lot about him, thanks to neighborhood gossip.

He was single, kinda-sorta good-looking—if you liked the type of man who was a little rough-looking, unrefined—and the women in Summer Springs couldn't stop talking about him. Of course, they didn't have to deal with his damn dog disturbing their peace and quiet every few days.

Renee rang the doorbell and waited. A few minutes later, Stevenson's granddaughter, Margie, opened the door—an adorable eight-year-old with raven hair styled in pigtail braids.

Her gaze dropped to the dog. "Uh-oh," she whispered, eyes wide.

"Hello, sweetie. Is your grandfather here?" Renee asked as kindly as she could between gritted teeth.

"I'll go get him." Margie ran off, leaving the door open and yelling, "Grandpa, Miss Grumpy is at the door!"

Renee's fake smile fell away and she stiffened. Miss Grumpy? It wasn't her fault she had to keep coming over to bring back their pet.

She heard a muffled conversation in a back room and then Clive ambled to the front door. The moment she saw him, her stomach did a peculiar flip, and her irritation amped up.

Okay, so maybe Clive Stevenson wasn't kinda-sorta good-looking. He was full-on, breath-takingly handsome by anyone's standards. His hair and beard were almost completely white, but his eyebrows and mustache dark, and his tanned skin proclaimed a penchant for working in the elements often. Handsome, yes, but not her type, so she couldn't understand why her belly always did that odd motion at the sight of him. She tended to prefer well-dressed men, suit-and-tie types. This guy was built for manual labor in a pair of worn jeans and a loose-fitting white T-shirt that showed off his barrel-like chest and tattooed arms.

"Damn, did he get over in your yard again?"

His smooth, smoky voice—annoyingly seductive—kept the women in the neighborhood giggling behind their hands and batting their eyelashes. She'd literally seen them do it.

"What do you think?" Renee released the dog's collar and he ran inside the house, his paws tapping on the hardwood floors.

"Sorry about that."

"Are you really? Because if you were, you'd keep him in your yard. To be clear, that's my yard, and this is yours. Keep him tied up. Something. It's dangerous to have him running around. He could get hit by a car or bite someone, and then what? Tie. Him. Up."

Clive sighed and looked past her and up at the sky. "The day is too pretty to argue with you. Anything else?"

"You are very rude."

"So you've told me," he drawled.

His green eyes lowered to hers and caused a wave of heat in her stomach. His eyes weren't just green, they were brilliant. Everything about this man was in-your-face. His devil-may-care attitude, the blatant masculinity in his casual clothes and muscular build, the deep voice that made you want to lean in and bask in the sound, and his eyes—as luminous and as dark as emeralds.

"One of these days I'm going to call animal control and have him picked up."

"You've told me that, too."

"It's not an empty threat."

"Okay." He flashed a grin, which annoyed the hell out of her. "Anything else?"

To make sure he understood she wasn't bluffing, Renee said, "Next time I'm calling animal control."

"You would deprive my granddaughter of her pet?"

"No, that's what you're doing. Keep Samson in your yard. This is your final warning." Renee stalked away.

"Have a good day!" Clive called cheerily after her.

Renee knew he was purposely trying to irritate her, yet she spun in the driveway to look at him. He was tall and the loose-fitting jeans hung low on his hips. She'd seen him shirtless plenty of times, washing his truck or his daughter's car, mowing the lawn or working on some do-it-yourself project in the back yard. Curly hairs sprinkled his chest—some of them already turned gray—as sweat trickled down his tanned skin while he worked.

She'd never met a man who aggravated her more. She'd never met a man who turned her on more. But she was self-aware enough to acknowledge that part of her aggravation stemmed from her attraction to him.

Narrowing her eyes, Renee tossed around a number of tart comments in her head to throw his way but didn't bother. He wasn't worth the effort and she wouldn't give him any more satisfaction in knowing how much he irritated her.

She stepped hard across the grass and once inside her house, slammed the front door shut.

CLIVE STROLLED to the back of the house where the kitchen opened into the den. His granddaughter was lying on the floor, coloring, with Samson right beside her keeping her company.

Margie looked up when he walked into the kitchen. "Grandpa, is Miss Grumpy mad again?" she asked.

Clive grimaced. She must have heard him call her that name when he was talking to his daughter. He'd have to be more careful in the future.

"Maybe a little annoyed. We gotta be careful about keeping Samson in our yard, okay?"

"Okay."

"And no more calling her Miss Grumpy because that's not her name. Her name is Miss Joseph."

"Okay." Margie went back to coloring.

Miss Joseph was sexy as sin but bitter as a lemon peel, and an annoying complication in his life. She was always mad, and she'd been that way long before the problems with the dog. According to the neighborhood gossip, she was a divorcee who'd owned the ranch house for decades and kept it rented for years, finally moving in permanently four years ago. A few of the neighbors had warned him about her penchant for keeping an eye on everyone else to make sure they followed the rules and regulations.

He'd learned the hard way how much she liked complaining. Her letters to the home owner's association had cost him several fines and had landed him on the board's shit list.

Clive turned on the burner under the meat sauce to warm it up for their dinner. His daughter Chelsea always pre-cooked meals he could heat up. She was working tonight, so he was responsible for feeding and getting his granddaughter ready for bed.

Before his wife Margaret died, she used to be responsible for taking care of Margie, her namesake. Their daughter had been living with them ever since she became pregnant and her no-good fiancé had done nothing to help her out. Couldn't hold a job to save his life, and now he was in jail for the next couple of years for stealing a car.

Clive shook his head as he moved around the kitchen, getting plates and glasses ready for their meal. Though his daughter had made a huge mistake having a kid with that loser, Clive wasn't the least bit sorry about his granddaughter. She brought him joy and happiness every single day, and now that he was retired from his construction business, having her around kept him busy when he'd otherwise have to find ways to occupy himself.

Chelsea had her own ideas about how he could occupy himself. She thought he was overdue to start dating, but he couldn't muster the enthusiasm for a long-term commitment at this point. Besides, he wasn't sure what kind of woman he liked anymore. Margaret had been a jewel. As a mother, she'd been patient and affectionate with their three kids. She'd been supportive by working as his administrative assistant and billing department all by herself. And he certainly couldn't have asked for a more perfect wife, one who loved him unconditionally and never failed to lift his spirits with encouraging words. He didn't have high hopes of finding someone exactly like her again.

He did know, however, what he wasn't looking for. He couldn't fathom being involved with a woman like Renee Joseph—miserable, cranky, and in general lacking the joy of life. He'd only seen her smile a few times, and not at him.

Her personality turned him off, but her physical appearance— that was another matter. Her smile, though rare, was pretty and framed by dimples, and she was short, with toffee skin poured over a shapely frame. She taught at the nearby high school and during the school year, always dressed in an understated yet sexy manner in pleated trousers and tailored dresses that made his eyes linger on her breasts and hips.

Her hair was cut in a short, trendy style and jet black. It caressed her face and neck and always looked shiny and soft. On more than one occasion, he'd fantasized about running his fingers through it to test the texture. On more than one occasion, he'd imagined taking a handful and tugging back her head so he could have unfettered access to her angry mouth, her smooth throat, her magnificent breasts.

Shit. Clive shook his head.

"Dinner's ready. Go wash up," he told Margie.

"Okay!" She hopped up from the floor. "Smells good, Grandpa," she said, darting in the direction of the half bath downstairs.

Clive removed the garlic bread from the oven and tossed the oven mitt onto the counter. He shouldn't be daydreaming about that woman. Just his rotten luck, the woman he couldn't stand, and who couldn't stand him, was the one woman he couldn't stop thinking about. No point in thinking about her anyway.

A classy woman like Renee Joseph wouldn't have any interest in a common laborer like him.

2

Renee groaned and punched the pillow. She tossed and turned but couldn't eliminate the noise coming from next door. Loud laughter and talking—at one in the morning! Yes, it was a Friday night, but Summer Springs was a neighborhood, not a local bar.

What were they doing up so late?

Cursing under her breath, she climbed out of bed and walked past the living room and into the laundry room at the other end of the house. She eased the curtain away from the window so she could look into the neighbor's back yard.

Four Black men and a Caucasian man sat outside on the back deck with Clive, all of them around the same age and in the same physical shape. They were guzzling beer and the smell of grilled meat drifted over to her house, along with their loud voices.

Clive often had his male friends over. She'd seen and heard them before, but usually not this late, and not so soon after she had to deal with his dog invading her yard. At least they weren't playing music this time. Their raucous behavior was so inconsiderate, as if there weren't families around and people trying to sleep. She could hear almost every word they said.

"Nah, nah, that was you, bruh," one of the men yelled at Clive, pointing a beer can at him.

Then Clive said something she couldn't hear but which prompted another bout of uproarious laughter from the men. Tonight he wore jeans and a Superman T-shirt that made the muscles traversing the length of his arms look particularly sinewy. A pulse of heat invaded her pelvis as she watched him do what could only be described as a strut across the deck, then he did some kind of wiggle dance and pretended to spike a football. The other men jumped up and cheered, laughing and high-fiving each other as if he'd actually scored a touchdown.

Had he been a football player and these were former teammates? That would make sense.

At that moment, Clive glanced over at her house and seemed to look right at her. Renee gasped and flicked the curtain closed. She clutched her chest. Had he seen her? She hadn't done anything wrong but was embarrassed by the fact that he might have caught her looking at them—and embarrassed by the heated response of her body to his sexy showmanship.

Renee hurried back to her bedroom, where she should have stayed. Instead of trying to go back to sleep, she climbed under the covers and opened her iPad to continue reading the contemporary fiction novel she'd started a couple of days ago.

After plugging earbuds into her phone, she turned on the rain app and settled in to read. But the words swam before her eyes, turning to gibberish as she recalled Clive's tight butt and his silly little dance.

His moves weren't too bad—not bad at all. Sexy, actually. With a body like that, what would his moves be like in bed?

"Renee, what is wrong with you!" she yelled, sinking lower under the covers.

She was disgusted with herself. The man was a nuisance. Not someone to fantasize about. She resumed reading.

A few hours later, she woke with a start. Darn it, she'd fallen asleep.

Yawning, Renee removed the earbuds and only heard quiet. The time on the tablet said four twenty-seven. They must have finally left. She fixed the pillows under her head and settled more comfortably in bed.

One of these days, she was going to call the cops and break up Clive's little late-night soiree.

~

WHAT A NIGHT.

Clive had been too tired to clean up last night, so that was his job today, now that he'd finally gotten out of bed at eleven—much later than his norm.

He surveyed the damage and shook his head but smiled. He loved spending time with his friends, but the cleanup sucked.

"Time to get to work," he muttered.

He gathered up the beer and soda cans all over the deck and tossed the trash in a bin. He cleaned the grill, swept the deck, and then sauntered back inside.

His daughter and granddaughter had already left for their Saturday outing. Because of Chelsea's hectic schedule during the week, she always planned weekend activities for her and Margie, so that meant he had the place to himself for most of the day.

He walked toward the front door and Samson, who'd been relaxing in the hallway staring at the door, perked up.

"Hey guy, want to check the mail with me?"

Samson barked and jumped up, following him outside.

Just his rotten luck, Miss Joseph from next door was walking back from checking her mailbox, too. He almost went back into the house but refused to let this woman's sourpuss attitude dictate his behavior. She glared at him as he made his way down the driveway.

"Good morning!" Clive said cheerily and added a wave, just to annoy her.

She simply stared at him. Samson barked, wagged his tail, and started toward her yard, but Clive whistled at him.

"No, boy, come on, Samson." He patted his thigh and the dog did a U-turn and followed behind him.

He'd picked up the mail and was on his way back up the walk when he realized Renee hadn't moved. His eyes flicked over her attire —denim capris that emphasized her hourglass figure, platform heels that gave the illusion of longer legs, and a white sleeveless top that dipped a little low in the front and showed off the swell of her breasts. With difficulty, he dragged his gaze higher. The only thing marring the delectable package was the frown on her face.

"Do you do it on purpose?" she asked.

"Do what on purpose?" Clive asked pleasantly.

"Go out of your way to aggravate me and your neighbors."

"As far as I know, I don't aggravate my neighbors, just you. But please, tell me, what did I do now? Did I sneeze too loud? Does my laugh bother you?"

She straightened her spine and elongated her neck, as if she could make herself taller.

He chuckled. She couldn't be more than five feet two, tops.

Her eyes narrowed. "As a matter of fact, your laugh does bother me. That and the laughter of your buddies when it happens very loudly at one in the morning."

"Is that why you were spying on us last night?"

"I was *not* spying."

He hadn't actually seen her lurking in the dark, but the curtain in one of her windows had been pulled across, and when he noticed it, it was quickly flicked back into place, which let him know she'd definitely been watching them.

"Looked like spying from my vantage point." Clive pretended to ignore her and flipped through the bills.

"Like I said, I was not spying. The ruckus you and your friends made woke me up out of bed and I went to investigate."

Out of bed?

His gaze lifted to hers and he almost asked, *What were you wearing?*

What did Miss Grumpy wear to bed? He imagined her in pajamas and a long, flannel nightgown, but he'd much rather see that body in a nice piece of lingerie. Pale pink or white would look right against all that brown skin.

His gaze flicked over her again, and his mouth went dry.

He should not be attracted to this woman, but almost every time he saw her, he wanted to knock the scowl off her face and replace it with an expression of open-mouthed, gasping satisfaction.

"Maybe instead of spying you should have come over to join us."

"I wasn't spying! You don't care about anyone or anything, do you? You have no concept of being neighborly. I've heard you and your friends before, but last night was too much, and I've had it up to here with all the yapping and laughing loudly at all hours of the night."

He felt kinda bad that he'd disturbed her sleep, and if he'd disturbed her, he had probably disturbed other people as well. Next time he'd have to make sure to tell the guys to keep down the noise, but he wouldn't give this angry, grumpy woman the satisfaction of knowing he'd change his ways because of her.

Clive folded his hands over his chest. "What exactly are you going to do if you hear us making noise again?"

"Call the police."

"Lady, you have issues. Instead of talking to people, you think the correct way to communicate is to threaten and yell. You've threatened my dog and now you've threatened me."

"Because you don't listen and have no respect for your neighbors."

"That is not true!" Her accusation rubbed him the wrong way.

"Oh, yes, it is, Mr. Stevenson. I'm sending a letter to the board, and if that doesn't stop you, expect a visit from the police the next time you have one of your little late-night parties. This is your final warning." Her eyes flashed angrily at him, and she stomped toward her house.

"Oh great, another final warning," Clive said, walking up his own driveway.

Renee stepped into her house, turned, and yelled, "I'll be sending that letter right away to the board, you asshole!" Then she slammed the door.

"If I'm an asshole, so are you!" Clive yelled at the closed door. He sure hoped she heard him because he didn't usually yell and felt like an idiot. He glanced up and down the street, hoping no one saw or heard him.

Samson looked confused at the outburst.

"She hates me," he muttered, rubbing the dog's head. Now she was going to complain about him to the board, again. She really knew how to make his life a living hell.

"That woman needs to get laid more than I do. If she wasn't such an ornery witch, I'd help her out."

Clive slammed his front door shut.

3

Renee cruised down the street, her gaze swinging left and right, smiling when she saw all her neighbors in compliance with the association regulations. She'd been called a busybody too many times to count, but refused to back down from her role in raising the bar on home ownership. Ever since she started writing letters to the board, there had been a vast improvement in the appearance of the properties in Summer Springs. Landscaping looked better, holiday decorations were taken down in a timely manner, and the exterior design of the homes were more consistent. Frankly, they should be thanking her.

Her smile widened when she thought about her concluded lunch date. She'd taken a former student to lunch and spent two hours giving him advice and critiquing the essay he wrote for his college application. He'd been so pleased, he'd given her a big hug at the end of their visit and promised to update her on the results.

Renee pulled a little past her house and stopped in front of the Stevenson home. That reminded her that she needed to write that letter to the board. She'd get that out of the way today.

She backed into her driveway and was about to pull into the garage when Samson came careening at a high speed from next door and jumped behind the Volvo. She slammed on the brakes to avoid hitting the dog.

"What in the world?"

The crazy dog had absolutely lost its mind. This was exactly what she'd warned Stevenson could happen. The darn dog almost got run over.

Renee exited the car and pointed a finger. "Samson, this is the last time I'm dealing with you. I told your owner that I would call animal control, and that's exactly what I'm going to do because he thinks I'm bluffing."

She reached into the car, glaring at the dog who still hadn't moved, and pulled her phone from the magnetic holder on the dashboard. As she browsed the Internet for the phone number, Samson growled low in his throat. The dog was looking at the house and paced agitatedly. He stopped and growled and then paced again.

Frowning, Renee followed his gaze. "What is the matter with you?"

No sooner had the words left her mouth than the front door flew open and two men ran out! Renee's mouth fell open. The taller man had her television tucked against his chest and the shorter one had her laptop under his arm and a pillowcase in hand that was weighed down with some objects.

They froze when they saw her and the dog, looked at each other, then took off. The dog darted after them.

"Samson!" Renee screamed.

He caught the shorter one by the hem of his jeans and yanked him off his feet. The man toppled to the ground and dropped his loot. Eyes wide, he kicked at Samson but the dog didn't let go. He snarled and tugged on the denim.

"Samson!" Renee screamed again, terrified that one of the thief's kicks might land and hurt him.

She must have gotten through to him because he let go and the man scrambled to his feet and ran after his partner in crime who'd deserted him and disappeared into the trees, more than likely to a car they had stashed nearby.

Dumbfounded, Renee stared after him.

Samson trotted over and sat on his hind legs, looking at her as if waiting to be told what to do next.

"You saved me," she whispered.

Had the German shepherd not been there, she would have entered the house, caught the burglars by surprise, and who knows what they would have done.

Slumped against the car door, she rubbed a hand over the dog's head and then dialed 911. Afterward, she carefully picked up the dropped items so as not to disturb any fingerprints or other evidence. She placed them at the door and cautiously entered the house with Samson trotting along beside her like a security guard.

The house was not completely turned upside down. The men had clearly not spent a lot of time there and only grabbed the first items of value they could find.

They had kicked in the French doors in the living room at the back. The frame had splintered and when the doorknob slammed against the inside wall, it made a hole in the sheetrock and several panes of glass shattered to the floor.

Renee held back Samson so he wouldn't get glass in his paws.

She sighed. "Well, damn."

WHAT IS HE DOING HERE?

Renee watched Clive approaching from the window of her office.

The doorbell rang, and she scurried to the front and opened it.

"May I help you?" she asked.

"Actually, I'm here to help you. My daughter told me what happened, and I spoke to Jim across the street, and he said he helped you secure the back door, but you'll need to replace the door completely, am I right?"

"I will," Renee said slowly, already guessing the direction of the conversation.

"I'm sure you know, I used to work construction. I can help... assuming you want my help." One dark eyebrow lifted in inquiry.

Renee's first inclination was to decline. After all, they hadn't exactly been friendly over the past year, but she saw no point in continuing to hold a grudge. Frankly, if not for his dog, which she now considered a godsend, she might not be standing here today—or at the very least, she could have been hurt instead of only losing a television.

"Actually, I would appreciate your help."

His eyebrows lifted higher, as if he'd fully expected her to decline his offer.

"In that case, I think we need to start over." He extended his hand. "I'm Clive Stevenson. Call me Clive."

"Renee Joseph. Call me Renee." She took his hand.

His rough-textured palm was not unpleasant, and his handshake wasn't the aggressive kind some men liked to use. His was firm, but rather warm—comfortable, even, sending a tingle of sensation up her arm and making the hairs stand on end. When he released her hand, she missed the contact.

She cleared her throat and stepped back to allow him in. "Thank you for coming over."

"No problem."

"They came in this way." She walked him through the house to the living room and showed him the boarded up area. "They kicked in the back door and entered through here."

"You were fortunate not to be home," Clive said grimly, setting down the tool box.

He rested his hands on his hips, and when he stepped closer to examine the damage, she took the liberty of checking him out. Her eyes trailed down the length of his sturdy-looking legs and retraced the path upward to check out his solid-looking back, one of her favorite parts of a man's body and what had attracted her to her second husband. This man was fit.

Renee shook her head to dispel those thoughts. She'd had three unsuccessful marriages. She wanted nothing else to do with men.

Clive turned to face her. "Here's what I suggest. For your next set of French doors, get the ones with impact-resistant glass, and a multi-point locking system. Those include flush bolts that go into the frame and into the floor, making the door harder to kick in. The doors should swing outward, but that can leave your hinges exposed, so I'll install security hinges."

"That sounds...complicated."

"Not really. I can get all the supplies for you, but trust me, it's worth having the extra security. Even with the multi-point locking system, if burglars have something as simple as a hammer, they could release the flush locks at the top and bottom of the door and easily push their way in."

"Even with the deadbolt locked?" Renee asked, alarmed.

"Afraid so, but don't worry about that. I have a neat little trick that stops that problem." His gaze traveled to the hole in the sheetrock. "I can take care of that for you, too."

"Okay. So how much is all of this going to cost me?" Renee braced for the figure.

"Just the door and any supplies I don't have in my shed. Labor's free."

"No." She shook her head vehemently. "I can't allow you to do that. I have to pay you."

"I won't take your money."

"Why not?"

"Call it being neighborly." His gaze rested on her in the silence, and she was reminded of her accusation that he hadn't been neighborly in the past.

With heat warming her cheeks, she said, "That's very kind of you."

"I'm a kind guy." He smiled a little, softening his features in a way that made her heart flutter.

"Thank you," she murmured.

What the heck was the matter with her? It was one thing to find him attractive—after all, she wasn't blind—but quite another to have her heart beating as fast as a hummingbird's wings.

"Would it bother you if I use my recorder? It's easier to get the information I need, and I transcribe the notes later."

"I don't mind."

Clive removed a small recorder from his jeans. He turned it on and then dropped the device into the front pocket of his T-shirt. Then he removed measuring tape from the tool box and spoke the measurements out loud so that the recorder captured the sound.

Afterward, he said, "I can pick up the door, unless you'd prefer to do that...?"

"I'd prefer for you to do it, to be honest. I'm not knowledgeable about that kind of thing, and if you don't mind..."

Clive picked up the tool box. "Don't mind at all. We're all set, then. I'll call you with the details later tonight. Oh, do me a favor, would you?" He pulled a little notebook and pen from his back pocket. "Write down your name, number, and email address for me."

Renee took the notebook and wrote down the information and then handed everything back to him.

He glanced at it. "Perfect. I'll email you the estimate tonight."

Renee escorted him to the door. "Um...thank you. I appreciate your help."

A spark lit his eyes as he smiled at her, and her heart raced a little bit, but she irritably tamped down the excitement.

"Not a problem, Renee. Just being neighborly."

"Neighborly. Right."

She watched him walk back to his house and closed the door. She felt a little something that she hadn't felt in a few years. More than attraction. A type of...longing. A tightening in her chest.

He had a nice smile and seemed nice. He might not be that bad, but she reminded herself that after three failed marriages, she wasn't looking.

"I'm not looking," she said firmly to the empty room.

4

She smelled good today, as if she'd sprayed on perfume right before he arrived. The scent made Clive want to get closer and sniff her skin.

"Hope you don't mind, I brought a helper with me. Margie, say good morning to Miss Joseph."

Because he was working on her repair during the week when he watched Margie, he'd had to bring her with him on the job.

The eight-year-old smiled and said in her most polite voice, "Good morning, Miss Joseph."

"Good morning. And of course I don't mind." Her face broke into a pleasant smile and the dimples appeared, transforming her face and making the muscles in his abdomen contract.

Tools in hand, Clive followed her to the back of the house where the doorway was boarded up. "First, I'm going to remove this and then get the new doors. They're sitting on my truck."

"Do you need me to do anything?" Renee asked.

"Just stay out of the way."

"I can do that." Renee lowered her head to engage his grand-daughter. "How about you, Margie? Can I get you something to drink or a snack?"

Margie shook her head, black pigtails swinging on the sides of her head. "Grandpa gave me cereal, blueberries, and orange juice for breakfast. I'm full!"

Renee laughed. "Well if you change your mind, you let me know, okay?"

"Okay," his granddaughter said with a vigorous nod.

Renee straightened and for the first time, he paid close attention to her eyes. They were a rich, earthy brown. Captivating. Lovely, like her.

"I'll be in my office in the back, down that hall to the right. Call if you need anything."

"I will."

Clive watched her walk away and liked how the white shorts hugged her curvaceous behind and made her hips look wider. "Very nice," he murmured.

"What, Grandpa?"

Startled, Clive cleared his throat. "Nothing. Let's get to work."

"Okay!" Margie said with excitement.

Clive didn't often take her with him on jobs. It depended on the job and the length of time it would take to complete. Whenever he did, she was very excited, taking the role of helper very seriously.

He spent the morning on the door, with Margie helping intermittently. When she wasn't, she played with her dolls. Midway through the morning, Renee came out to check on them and provided glasses of iced tea, which he and Margie gratefully drank. At lunchtime, they took a break and went home to make hotdogs and then returned to Renee's house. It was early afternoon when he finished painting and then called Renee to take a look at the final product.

She stood back with her hands on her hips. "Wow. You did a great job. I'm impressed."

"I'm not sure if I should be flattered or insulted. I've worked in construction for almost forty years—since I was practically a kid and started going on jobs with my father and older brother."

"Take my reaction as a compliment. I'm truly impressed. There aren't a lot of men who are good with their hands."

Mind immediately going to the gutter, Clive raised an eyebrow and smirked. "I have been told many times how good I am."

"I-I mean, able to do this kind of work," Renee said, randomly waving her hand in the direction of the door.

He almost laughed out loud. He'd never see her flustered, and her reaction was adorable. Miss Grumpy might not be as tough as she pretended to be.

"I know what you meant."

She cleared her throat and briefly turned away before facing him again. "Are you sure I can't pay you? I almost feel as if I'm taking advantage."

"You don't owe me anything. I like keeping busy, and I hadn't done one of these doors in a while."

"Well, as long as you don't feel like you're being taken advantage of..."

"I offered to help, remember? By the way, I inserted a screw right here at the flush bolt, so no one should be able to slip the door open."

She stepped in front of him and raised on her tiptoes. Clive got a good whiff of her perfume again, and his breathing became a bit shallow as he let his gaze roam over her body. He was even more tempted to press his face to her skin with her standing directly in front of him, pushing up on her toes as if offering up her body.

"Oh, I see. Is that the little trick you were telling me about?" She turned to face him, and as if suddenly noticing their closeness, her eyes widened and she stepped back.

Neither took their eyes from the other. Her breasts lifted up and down rapidly as her breathing turned as abnormal as his.

"Yes," Clive said thickly.

She'd felt what he felt. A surge of excitement—a sudden uptick in the temperature as the attraction between them intensified and crackled.

"I...um..." She smoothed a hand down her short hair in the back. "I appreciate you doing that."

"Well, we have to be safe out here."

"Absolutely." Her fingers crawled up the front of her throat.

She had pretty hands with short fingernails painted a champagne-brown color. He wanted those hands exploring his chest, running down his thighs, scraping his back.

"Any word from the police regarding the burglars?" Clive asked, voice sounding unnaturally tight.

"Nothing. The detective assigned to my case was very candid and said the chances of catching them was small, but they'd keep working on it." She edged farther away. "Other homes nearby have been broken into in a similar fashion—in broad daylight, kicking in the back door and grabbing whatever they could in a rush, so they think it's the same men."

"Hope they catch them."

"Me, too." Renee rubbed her hands together.

"You know, I noticed there are a few other things that needed to be done around the house. A couple of your siding boards are loose. I could fix those for you and seal them to make sure they don't leak. One of the planks on your deck doesn't seem quite sturdy, and I could replace that too. You know, if you like. If there's anything else you need fixing, I could take care of that, as well."

"You've done enough already. I wouldn't feel right bothering you with more tasks."

"It's no bother. The work will keep me busy, to be honest. Now that I'm retired, I don't have much to do except the occasional odd job."

"How much would that cost?" she asked.

"On the house."

"I should pay you," she insisted.

He didn't want her money, but he did have an idea. "How about you pay me in a different way?" Her eyebrows flew higher and he laughed. "No, nothing like that." Though he wouldn't be opposed if she offered. "I happen to love chocolate chip cookies."

Margie gasped, looking up from playing with her dolls. "I love chocolate chip cookies! Grandma used to make the best ones."

Clive grinned, remembering how the entire house would be filled with the scent of the sweets whenever his wife baked. "She's right. My late wife loved to bake, and her chocolate chip cookies were the best. They never lasted more than a couple of days—sometimes not even that long." He laughed.

"How long has she been gone?" Renee asked gently.

"Four years." Clive brushed away the sympathy in her eyes with a wave of his hand. "We had twenty-six wonderful years together, and I've had plenty of time to grieve and accept that she's gone."

He'd had a hard time at first—a very hard time. The love and perseverance of good friends and his daughter had helped him out of a two-year depression that had sucked the life out of him. Finally, he'd made the difficult decision to sell the house he and his wife had lived in and buy the one next to Renee, allowing himself to start over and heal in the process. He still missed Margaret, but he'd learned to accept her death and cherish the time they'd spent together.

"So, about those chocolate chip cookies—think you can manage that? There's a bakery not too far from here that has some really good ones." He gave her the name of the place.

"Chocolate chip cookies in exchange for home repairs? That's quite a deal. I can handle that," Renee said.

"Excellent. Anything else you need done around here?"

"One little thing. I bought two fans, and they've been sitting in the garage the past couple of weeks. I was going to hire someone to install one in my bedroom and the other in here. If you could take care of that for me..."

"Consider it done. I'll come back on Saturday morning and install them both and work on the other items. I have to meet a friend for lunch, but let me know if there's anything else you need. I don't mind." His voice dropped lower at the end.

Renee licked her lips and his dick jumped. "I will, and I'll do my part and have those cookies for you."

Clive looked down at his granddaughter. "All right, Margie, our work here is done. Let's head home."

"Okay, Grandpa."

She gathered up her dolls in a little carrying case and then Renee escorted them to the front.

"Do you like scrambled eggs?" Renee asked at the door.

"Excuse me?"

"Do the two of you like scrambled eggs?"

Clive studied her for a minute. "Scrambled or over easy."

"Get here at eight on Saturday and I'll have breakfast waiting for you both. Bring your appetites. Toast okay?"

"Eggs and toast are okay with me."

"Me too," Margie piped up with enthusiasm.

"And orange juice for you, right?" she asked his granddaughter.

Margie nodded.

"Okay. You two have a good evening."

She shut the door and Clive and Margie started the walk back to the house.

"Grandpa, your voice sounded funny when you were talking to Miss Joseph."

"Did it?"

"Yes."

"You notice everything, don't you?"

"Yes, I do. Mommy said I should be a detective."

Chuckling, Clive said, "I think your mommy's right."

At the front door, he paused before entering, casting a quick glance at Renee's place.

He was looking forward to Saturday.

5

"I can't believe I'm doing this." Renee stood at the counter in her best friend Adelaide's kitchen, folding chocolate chips into cookie dough.

Instead of going to the bakery, she'd had the idea of preparing a homemade batch and asked Adelaide for help.

Adelaide had dark gold skin and hazel eyes. She was taller than Renee and today wore her long brown hair secured into a bun using hairpins. Six months post-divorce from her husband of twenty-five years, she now had a lot more time on her hands and gladly agreed to help. In addition to being the Mama Bear of their friendship trio, she was also the best cook, whipping up the tastiest dishes with seemingly little to no effort. So far she'd done all of the work on the cookies until Renee, feeling guilty, offered to fold in the chips.

"I can't believe it, either," Jackie said from her perch on a stool at the counter. She sipped lemonade.

She was the tallest of the trio, a full-figured woman, and wearing her short natural today instead of one of her many wigs. She was always talking about financial security and ways to make more money, focused behavior which had served her well as the owner of lingerie and sleepwear stores for plus-size women.

"I'm not as bad as you," Renee said pointedly.

No one expected Jackie to help because, though she could cook, she didn't like to and had a housekeeper who took care of her grocery-shopping and cooking needs.

Renee stopped stirring. "All done, I think."

Adelaide peeped into the bowl. "Looks good. We'll use this scoop so the cookies will be uniform sizes, and we'll place them onto the SILPAT." She held up a small ice cream scoop.

"You are so fancy," Renee teased.

"I can't wait until she starts catering. She's going to make so much money," Jackie said.

"I'm not sure I'm doing that yet. It's just a thought for now," Adelaide said.

"You should," Renee said firmly.

"What if I fail?"

"But what if you succeed?"

Jackie nodded her agreement.

"We'll see." Adelaide placed four equal-sized balls onto the silicone mat spaced evenly apart. "Like that."

"Got it." Renee duplicated what her friend did with the next row.

"Look at you, baking cookies for your man," Jackie teased.

Renee glared at her. "Don't start. Honestly, it's the least I could do. He not only fixed the door, he's hanging my fans and doing some other little things around the house."

Jackie perked up and arched an eyebrow. "Wait a minute, you never mentioned that."

"I didn't?" Renee asked, knowing good and well she hadn't.

Resting a hand on one hip, Adelaide asked, "You have him completing your honey-do list? This sounds serious."

"It's not serious in the least. You guys know how much I can't stand that guy. I've complained about him constantly because he's the worst kind of neighbor, but he's being nice, so I figured it wouldn't kill me to get the cookies he wanted."

"Are you trying to be wife number two?" Jackie asked.

"No. Because that would make him husband number four, and I'm absolutely not interested in getting married again."

"Right, because you've sworn off men." There was no missing the sarcasm in her voice.

Renee stopped working and stared at her friend. "Yes, Jackie, I've sworn off men. I know that's hard to believe, but it's possible."

"Forever?" Adelaide asked skeptically.

"I don't know if it's forever and ever, but certainly for the foreseeable future. I'm fine the way I am and don't need a man in my life right now. Remember what happened with the last man I slept with? The poet, who left me that scathing voice mail about my intimacy issues?"

"That's because you wouldn't let him spend the night after you had sex," Adelaide pointed out.

"You treated him like a whore," Jackie said.

"I did not!"

Jackie raised an eyebrow in rebuttal.

Shaking her head, Renee laughed and continued scooping.

"I was impressed with all the words he used to rhyme with bitch. He's quite talented," Adelaide mused.

Renee shot her a dark look and Adelaide shrugged.

"Did you keep the voice mail? If he's ever famous, that poem could be worth some money," Jackie said.

"No, Jackie, I didn't keep the voice mail," Renee said with a roll of her eyes.

"Too bad. But tell me this, don't you want someone for companionship?"

"That's what you ladies are for."

Fifteen years ago, Renee and Jackie met through mutual friends and became close. Adelaide joined their friendship circle when her daughter was a student in Renee's English class. Adelaide had been an involved parent and the two of them eventually became close friends. The trio shared everything during their get-togethers, squeezing in time for each other between kids, work, hobbies, and other activities to gossip and find out what was going on in each other's lives. At their age—she and Adelaide were forty-seven and Jackie turned fifty-six in the fall—she didn't expect to find anyone else she could connect with as well as she did these women.

Renee looked down at the completed product. "All done."

"Perfect. Now into the oven." Adelaide opened the door and Renee slipped in the baking sheet.

"I give it two weeks," Jackie said with confidence, lifting her glass to her lips again.

"You give what two weeks?" Renee asked.

"Two weeks until Mr. Handyman gets in those panties."

Renee laughed out loud. "And why would I let him in my panties when there hasn't been anyone near this area"—she made a circle in front of her pelvis—"in almost a year?"

If she were going to succumb, it wouldn't be to her neighbor. They were tolerating each other for now, but who knew how long that would last?

"Because, my dear, you can pretend all you want that you're just being nice to the neighborhood handyman, but I've known you too long and I can see right through you. You've been without for a while, and Clive is an attractive man. He's in your house, being all manly and helpful." Jackie shivered. "And he has you baking cookies."

"He doesn't have me doing anything," Renee shot back, annoyed. "It's a payment for services rendered. Can you believe her?" She turned to Adelaide, who silently watched the exchange with a faint smile on her face. "Not you, too, Adelaide?"

Her friend shrugged. "I have to agree, I think you're going to give in. I'm not saying you're going to marry him, but Jackie's right—you're baking him cookies, for goodness' sake."

"They're not just for him. His granddaughter likes chocolate chip cookies, too."

"Mmm-hmm. But you're not baking them for her, now are you?" Jackie arched a brow.

Warmth heated Renee's chest and cheeks. She didn't want to admit it, but her friends were right. There was something about Clive that made this baking exercise seem not only like a nice thing to do, but something she simply wanted to do.

SEATED at the breakfast table in the kitchen, Clive rewound the tape.

"I'd prefer for you to do it, to be honest. I'm not knowledgeable about that kind of thing, and if you don't mind..."

Renee's voice was pleasant to listen to, and the smile she'd given him after speaking those words had tightened his stomach muscles and he'd had to fight the urge to kiss her. Bonus, she kept a clean house. Cleanliness was a big deal for him, and Renee didn't seem to have any problem with that.

"Morning, Dad."

Clive started guiltily and shut off the recorder.

Chelsea yawned as she entered the room, having clearly rolled out of bed only moments before. Her dirty-blonde hair was a rumpled mess with the wavy curls going in every direction, and she still wore her striped pajamas.

"Good morning, hon."

She poured herself a cup of coffee. "Last night was rough. After closing, we had to stock the shelves with the shipment that came in earlier during the day that the first shift hadn't completed. I swear, I don't know why they're on payroll. They never complete their work and then we have to do it." She rolled her shoulders and grimaced.

In addition to working as a cashier supervisor at a department store, she worked three nights a week at a locally-owned hardware store. He'd told her on more than one occasion she didn't have to put in all that work. The house was paid for, thanks to the insurance policy after Margaret died, he had his retirement, and the odd jobs he worked from time to time. But his daughter was proud, and maybe a little bit ashamed that she hadn't listened to his warnings and had to move back home after the sperm donor went to jail.

Clive stood and took his dirty *World's Greatest Grandpa* mug to the sink.

"What are you doing today while Margie and I are gone?" Chelsea asked.

She had a whole day planned. She was driving across the bridge to Coronado Island where she and Margie would go to the beach, have pizza for lunch, and then she was renting bikes for them to take a self-guided tour. His granddaughter hadn't stopped talking about their plans since yesterday when Chelsea announced them.

"I'm going next door to take care of a few extra projects for Renee."

"Oh, that's nice. I'm glad to see the two of you getting along for a change. Did you charge her regular price or a premium because of her attitude?" she asked with a snicker.

"Actually, I'm not charging her."

"Oh."

He could feel his daughter's gaze on the back of his head as he finished washing the cup. Clive wiped his hands in a towel and faced her. "What?"

"Nothing. Nothing at all." Chelsea smirked and lifted the coffee mug to her lips.

"I'm just being neighborly."

"Yeah, like you were neighborly to the couple two doors down the street when you repaired their deck for free...oh, wait, you charged them, didn't you? Let's see, you didn't charge the widow one street over, did you—Mrs. Potter?" Chelsea tapped her chin.

Clive chuckled and shook his head. "You've made your point."

Chelsea stood. "I think it's nice that you're dating again."

"Who said anything about dating?"

"Dad, come on. Don't pretend this isn't part of the courtship. We both know you're not doing all this for her simply out of the goodness of your heart."

"Maybe I am."

"Or maybe you want to spend more time with the woman, which is perfectly fine."

He sighed heavily and scratched the back of his head. "Yeah, maybe."

"What's wrong?"

"I don't know...not only am I out of practice, I'm skeptical that a woman like her would give a man like me the time of day."

"A nice man? A good man? A loyal man? My opinion, she'd be a fool not to."

"You're my daughter, you're supposed to say that."

"I'm being honest. You're a great catch, and if for some bizarre reason she doesn't see it, some other lucky lady will."

"Doesn't matter anyway. Based on how she's treated me since we moved in, I think I'll take my chances elsewhere."

"Sure, Dad."

"I'm serious. She's not my type."

"Mmm-hmm. I heard you." Chelsea kissed his cheek and sauntered from the kitchen.

Clive laughed and shook his head. Okay, fine. Chelsea knew him very well, and yes, he was attracted to Renee. Had been from the minute he saw her, despite their rocky relationship over the past year. He figured he wasn't her type, and she sure as hell wasn't his. Not warm enough, not friendly, and always upset.

But if he had his way, he'd get a shot at finding out if all that passionate anger she exuded could be turned into passionate cries of pleasure.

6

She wasn't trying to impress him. Or was she?

Renee cursed quietly.

Too late now. The scent of a full breakfast filled the house, and Clive would arrive in a few minutes.

Too late to change out of the tight jeans and fitted blouse that showed off what she considered her best assets—her breasts—and she'd already sprayed on her favorite perfume.

When the doorbell rang, she jumped, then laughed at her silly nervousness. They were going to eat breakfast and then he'd fix some things around the house. That's it.

She opened the door and Clive stood outside in a dark pullover and the enticing fragrance of aftershave. Whatever it was, the scent fit the type of man he was—one who was rugged and worked with his hands.

"Smells good in here," he said, stepping across the threshold and setting down his toolbox.

Have mercy, why was a toolbox so sexy? Was she really that hard up for male attention?

"It should. I've been working hard all morning on the food."

"I'm flattered," he said in his warm voice, casting a quick look over her figure and making her skin tingle. The brief spark in his eyes let her know he liked what he saw.

Now that her friends had put the idea of sleeping with him in her mind, she couldn't stop thinking about it. Clive looked like the kind of man who knew his way around a woman's body, and keeping his woman satisfied was not only a task that stroked his ego, it was a task he relished.

"Where's your helper?" Renee asked.

"Chelsea doesn't work on Saturdays, so she took Margie over to Coronado Island. She works so much during the week, she tries to do something once a week where the two of them get to spend quality time together. Margie loves it."

"I can imagine. Well, follow me." She hadn't expected to be alone with Clive, which made her even more aware of him and her attraction to him.

She led the way into the dining room and wondered if he was watching her ass. Her ass did look spectacular in these jeans. That's why she'd chosen them.

When he saw the spread, he stopped in the doorway. "Damn. When you said bring your appetite, you weren't kidding. Is all of this for the two of us?"

The two of us. Why did having him say those words cause her to feel a little breathless?

Renee rested her hands on her hips and shot him a haughty look. "You didn't bring your helper today, so yes, it's for the two of us. I know I only said eggs and toast, but I prepared a little bit extra in case you were very hungry."

"I do have a big appetite," he said, looking at her instead of the food.

Renee blushed, her entire body warming under his intense green gaze as she waved him toward one end of the table. "Have a seat."

Clive sat down and examined the choices.

"There's plenty, so don't be shy. And then you have to tell me how great those eggs are."

"You already know they're great?" he asked in an amused voice.

"Of course. Everything I do is great." Renee sat across from him with a little smile.

Their eyes met for a few seconds, and a bit of tension stretched between them before Renee caught herself and reached for the pitcher of orange juice.

In addition to the bowl of eggs, she set out platters with toast, fruit, waffles, and a fresh pot of coffee along with the pitcher of orange juice. They filled their plates, and Renee sipped her orange juice as she waited for the verdict.

Several minutes passed before Clive looked at her and shook his head. "Mm, mm, mm. These eggs are great, and I do believe these are the best waffles I've ever tasted. Even the toast is special, smothered in butter the way I like. You have magic hands, ma'am."

Renee laughed and then drizzled maple syrup on her waffles. Watching Clive eat was enjoyable, and when he got a second helping and refilled his glass with orange juice, she almost purred. By the way he ate, one would think the poor man hadn't had a decent home-cooked meal in years. Perhaps he hadn't, not since his wife died.

At the end of the meal, he patted his stomach. "I'm completely useless now. That was wonderful. Thank you so much."

"My pleasure. I figured it's the least I could do."

"You sure know how to spoil a man."

His comment took her aback. She didn't spoil people. None of her marriages had lasted very long, and she never had children of her own—or wanted any, for that matter. But her friends were right, there was nothing wrong with male companionship.

Renee dabbed her mouth with a napkin, her mind going in a direction it hadn't in a long time because she considered men too stressful and they never knew what they wanted—a lesson learned after three failed marriages. Clive, however, might get her to change her mind, assuming he turned out to be a different kind of man.

"How is it that you're not married?" he asked.

Once again, he stunned her by asking the one question she hated answering. She immediately started closing in on herself and twisted the paper napkin in her lap. She hated that question. People didn't understand how brutal those words were to a woman with her past.

"Sorry, did I ask the wrong question?"

"No. I mean, yes, in a way. I actually have been married before." She cleared her throat. "Three times."

His eyebrows flew higher. "Oh."

With a pained smile, Renee reached for the orange juice. Now came the judgment. She wished she could banish that question from the vocabulary of everyone she met so she wouldn't have to answer ever again. She considered her failed marriages a stain in an otherwise successful life.

Her first husband had been an ethics professor. Rather ironic, since he'd lost his job and their marriage ended because of an affair with one of his students. Not having learned her lesson, her second husband had been a professor, too. He taught history and they met at a literary event. In retrospect, she'd moved too fast with him, thinking deep conversations about US history and the country's role in shaping politics around the world meant they were compatible. They were not. They married quickly, after only six months. The marriage itself lasted a mere three years, though it had been dead long before they signed the divorce papers.

Her third husband was an attorney, and by the time they split, they were barely on speaking terms. They slept in the same bed, but only mumbled a few words here and there throughout the day when they passed each other in the hallway.

With him, she'd tried. Hard. Over and over again to make the marriage work. When he ignored her, she tried harder. She dressed different, cooked his favorite foods, downplayed her own achievements to make him feel better about himself when he lost his job. When he started spending more time with his cars than with her, no matter what she did, she knew the marriage was over.

Renee really put up with some shit from him. But she'd finally come to the realization that if a man didn't want you, he just didn't and there wasn't anything you could do about it. No amount of trying or changing or cooking or cleaning would make him love you if he didn't.

"Three men managed to snag you but let you go? What are the odds of that?"

She stared at Clive. Had she heard him correctly? There was disbelief, but not condemnation in his voice.

He folded his arms on the table and leaned toward her. "You're not some black widow, are you?"

She'd definitely never gotten that question before. "Not at all. None of my marriages worked out, that's all."

"I hope that you don't let a few numbskulls change you." Definitely not the response she'd expected.

"I won't. I haven't."

"Good for you." He drained his coffee cup. "Guess I better get to work. Can I help you clean up before I get started?"

"Absolutely not. You go ahead, and I'll take care of the dishes."

Sitting back in the chair, hands placed firmly on the arm rests, he looked at her oddly then, as if trying to figure her out. "Thank you, Renee."

"You thanked me already, and you're welcome. Just being neighborly."

He flashed a sexy grin. "Being neighborly, huh? I could get used to this." Seconds ticked by as the words dangled in the air above the table.

She had the same reaction she'd had watching him through the window and when she'd observed him working on the door. Her nipples ached and her loins filled with warmth. Being around Clive Stevenson caused her body to react in ways it hadn't in a long time.

As soon as she thought of a glib comment, he rose from the chair.

"Better get to work," he said, keeping his eyes on her.

She observed him over the rim of her coffee cup—his fit body and the way the sleeves capped around his biceps. Loose-fitting jeans hung on his narrow hips, held up by a firm backside.

When he disappeared, she set down the coffee cup and took a

deep breath. Clive was certainly making it hard for her to stick to her decision of staying away from men.

7

They were both interested in each other. That was fairly obvious, and not even her three marriages had turned Clive off.

Renee tapped a pen on the arm of the chair in her home office, a space simply furnished with a wood desk and chair, a few bookcases stuffed with books, and awards on the walls from her work in teaching.

Last night she'd spent an inordinate amount of time searching the house for additional projects for him to complete, and he was working on those projects now, after tackling the ceiling fans first. Oddly enough, it was nice to have a man in the house. She'd always moved into her husbands' homes, leaving this one rented. It was almost paid for at this point, and with minor repairs and a few upgrades over the years, had served her well. She'd at least had a place to come back to when she decided she was finally and truly done with men.

She returned her attention to the computer and went back to work on the novel she was editing. The book was interesting, flowed well, and only had a few minor inconsistencies. It was an easy job and she'd finish it soon—sooner if she stopped mooning over the virile man busy at work in her house.

Angela Washington was a former student and a successful novelist writing historical fiction with characters who pulled at readers' heartstrings. Though she was published, she never submitted a manuscript without having Renee look at it first. It was an honor to be entrusted with such important work, and Renee didn't take her influence lightly. While she adored Angela's writing, she made sure to critique each manuscript with an unbiased eye.

The hours passed quickly. Clive worked fast and efficiently, left to meet his friend for lunch, and then returned to work on the siding and a few other items he'd noticed needed fixing. By the time he called her to examine the completed projects, the sun was going down in the sky and Renee had completed the edit.

She reviewed the outside projects first. She could hardly tell where the boards had been replaced on the outside of the house. Once the paint dried, they'd be invisible. They then went inside and ended in the bedroom, where Clive showed her the second ceiling fan had been installed.

"Wow, you've done a great job. Once again, I can't find a single fault with your work."

"That's the way it should be."

Having him in her bedroom made her feel all tingly again. Her skin practically jumped at his nearness, and there was a definite tightening at the apex of her thighs.

"Now that I know what you can do, I'll be sure to call you if I need any more work done on the house. And I'll recommend you to others in the neighborhood."

"Others in the neighborhood already know all about my skills," he said with amusement.

"So I'm late to the party?"

"Better late than never," he murmured, his gaze sweeping her figure.

Were they still talking about handyman work?

"So, about those cookies you wanted."

He brought his eyes back up to her face. "You bought the chocolate chip cookies?" He sounded very surprised.

"Of course. That was our agreement. But I didn't buy them. They're homemade."

"I assumed this morning's breakfast was my payment. That's why I didn't mention the cookies."

"Oh no, I pay my debts. Breakfast was me being nice." Renee started out the door.

"You being nice to me? I never thought that would ever happen."

"Careful now, we're getting along. Don't spoil the moment."

Clive's warm laughter filled her ears and tightened her breasts. Darn it, if she could control her body's reaction to him, it would make their interaction much easier.

A plastic container of cookies sat on the counter. She opened it and Clive chose one. As he chewed, he groaned a little.

"You made these?" he asked, picking up another cookie.

"I wish. I can't bake to save my life. I was going to the bakery you mentioned, but one of my best friends loves to bake and whipped up a batch from her own recipe. I helped a little by stirring in the chocolate chips."

"The chips are the most important part," Clive said.

"That means I did the most important part?" Renee asked.

"You sure did. I have to be honest, your friend—and you—did a great job. These are really, really good. They might be better than my wife's." He shoved another one in his mouth and she preened with delight.

"That's quite the compliment."

"I meant it, too. Make sure you tell your friend what I said, and let her know I'd be willing to buy cookies from her."

"I certainly will."

Clive leaned his hip against the counter. "So, did you already put in a complaint to the board about my late-night partying, as you put it?"

Renee raised an eyebrow.

"I only ask because I haven't gotten a warning letter yet." The entire time he spoke, he had a smile on his face.

His words hit her belly with the power of a punch. "That's what this is all about?"

His eyebrows snapped together in confusion. "Excuse me?"

"I should have known you weren't just being nice. You want something, and the something is for me not to file another complaint about you so you can keep breaking the rules. Get your things and get out of my house and leave the damn cookies."

His eyebrows flew upward. "You can't renege on the cookies."

"Oh yes, I can, and I just did." Infuriated, Renee fastened the cover on the container and shoved it into the cabinet. She'd thought they were getting along. She'd thought he actually liked her.

"Lady, you are a piece of work."

"And so are you!" Renee marched to the front door where his tools were located and stood over them.

"I did not help you because I had an ulterior motive. Frankly, I couldn't care less if I get fined again by the board. It would have been less trouble for me to simply pay another fine than spend two whole days helping you."

"You are a fraud, Mr. Stevenson."

"I'm Mr. Stevenson now? This morning at breakfast, I was Clive."

"This morning at breakfast, I thought you were a decent human being, and we could have become friends. Now I know the truth. Have a good day." She looked at his tools and then looked at him, signaling that he should take his shit and go.

"For the record, I'm a good guy. Everybody likes me, except you."

"And I'm sure that gets under your skin, doesn't it? You know what you need? Real friends. Not people who'll come to your house only for loud parties and disturb the neighbors, but real friends who'll tell you the truth about yourself. And the truth is, you are a selfish, overgrown frat boy who thinks the rules of common decency don't apply to him. Well, I'm here to tell you, *Mister* Stevenson, that the rules do apply, and you will abide by them whether you like it or not."

"And do you know what you need? A man, because no one is naturally this bitter and angry."

"Oh yes, I forgot, the white male penis is the solution to all the world's problems."

"What's the matter, never had any white male *cock*? You should try it. We should both try something new, because I've never had any Black—"

Thwack! Renee hit him before she had time to think.

Clive's eyebrows arrowed down and his hand touched his cheek. "Why the hell did you hit me?"

"You are disgusting. Don't talk to me like that."

"Why not? Because then you'd have to pretend you don't like it? Let's lay all our cards on the table, shall we? You want me."

Renee cackled out loud, throwing her head back with exaggerated mirth. "I most certainly do not."

"That's why you're wearing those tight jeans and that tight blouse, leaving little to the imagination. You're wearing sweet-smelling perfume, your hair looks extra good, and let's not forget the feast from this morning. You can deny it all you want, sweetheart, but you most certainly want this white male penis."

"Get the hell out of my house! And when the board meets in the next session, I hope they throw the book at you."

"Well, if I'm already in trouble..." He shrugged and then pulled her against him, pressing his mouth to hers.

Startled, Renee froze for a second and then let out a tremulous moan as his mouth crushed hers and then moved in a seductive slide that made her sex pulse. The hands at her back slipped under her shirt and palmed her skin, sliding up to her bra strap and leaving her shivering in the wake of his touch.

He angled his head to the right and deepened the kiss, flicking his tongue against hers and tilting her backward ever so slightly over his left arm. Her nipples throbbed against his hard chest, and she gripped his big, muscular shoulders, seeking closer contact as she widened her mouth beneath his.

His calloused right hand was rough yet gentle as he shaped her waist, smoothing over her hips and then sliding backward to squeeze her ass. She'd known his touch would make her ache, but this fiery desire was upsetting, insulting in the wake of her anger.

Dismayed by her behavior, she pushed him away. They both stared at each other with heaving breaths, shocked and aroused.

Renee slapped him again. She didn't even know why. She just felt compelled to do it.

"Goddammit, lady, if you don't stop hitting me—"

She grabbed his shirt and tugged him down for another kiss.

8

I n between feverish kissing and fondling, they fumbled their way toward the bedroom. Clive tossed his shirt to the floor and sucked on the side of Renee's neck, deftly unhooking her bra and then flinging both that and her blouse at the entrance to her bedroom.

The rest of their clothes came off fast, and when they were both naked, his mouth crashed down on hers. She met the demand by sliding her fingers into his soft white hair and trembled at the rasping drag of chest hairs over the tips of her breasts and the way his rough hands roamed across her back and over her buttocks. Within seconds, she was on her back and across the width of the bed with one hairy thigh between hers, tipping back her head with a jagged groan as he sank his teeth into her tender flesh.

Renee was on fire, rocking her hips against his hard erection and gripping the back of his hand to prolong the attack on her neck. When his hands cupped her breasts, she shuddered. His thumbs tortured the nipples, teasing until a throbbing ache developed deep in her pelvis.

"I knew you would taste good," he said in a guttural whisper. He kissed between her breasts and around the warm crests, laving his tongue over the soft flesh while continuing to wreak havoc with his hands.

His mouth seized hers again, and their tongues met in a furious tangle of need and pent-up animosity. She boldly moved her lips across his hair-covered jaw and nipped his chin. Meanwhile, her hands roamed freely over his back and ass, exploring the near-perfect masculine beauty of his body.

Renee sank her fingers into his tight behind, and Clive grunted. Calloused fingers tightened on the same breasts they'd been obsessed with for several minutes. The constant touching and squeezing was almost too much to bear. Between her legs was hot and aching.

"Do you taste this good everywhere?" he asked in a gravelly voice, sliding his hand to cup her sex.

Renee didn't have time to answer before he lowered to his knees beside the bed and shoved his face between her legs. She knew it was coming, but was still unprepared for the penetration of his tongue. Twisting in shock, she gasped but immediately recovered and open for him.

Legs spread, one hand gripping the back of his head, she watched as he continued to go to work between her thighs. She'd never experienced anything so good. Her body became attuned to every lick, all the sucking, and the sounds from the back of his throat. He seemed to enjoy the act as much as she enjoyed having it performed on her. He conquered her sex with his tongue, searching out every inch with relish until a pending climax forced her to clamp her thighs around his head and angle her hips higher.

Knowing she was close energized him because his hands gripped her breasts, and his stiff tongue swirled against her clit with increased vigor. Head swimming, Renee hollered for release, finally achieved when he pushed past the slick entrance to her body to taste deeper.

The hairs on his face added to the delicious torture, and as the bottom fell out, she was falling, *falling* into heaven with a cry so loud she surely violated the neighborhood noise ordinance.

His job done, Clive rose slowly to his feet and wiped a hand across his damp beard. He gazed down at her—masculine, almost feral in the way his darkened eyes scoured her body. "You know we're just getting started? The best is yet to come."

Renee pressed a hand to her heaving chest. "My goodness, if that wasn't your best…"

Clive smirked and commanded, "Over."

"Wait, I—"

He flipped her onto her stomach with ease, which she appreciated because her bones had liquefied and she couldn't move. Bent over the edge of the bed with her toes pushing against the floor, Renee felt vulnerable to whatever he planned to do next.

"Spread your legs." From the corner of her eye she saw him retrieve a condom from his jeans.

Renee did as he told her, palms flat on the bed, anticipating his next move. She'd just had an explosive climax but wanted more and arched her butt as an offering. Clive palmed her bottom and smoothed one hand from the base of her spine up into her hair.

"You taste good. You're soft." He lowered onto her and closed one hand around both wrists like manacles, stretching her across the bed.

"What are you doing?" Renee whispered, excited, her breathing turning shallow.

"Giving you something to make you feel good so you'll stop complaining. I think I'll be doing the entire community a great service."

"Maybe I'm the one who'll be doing a—*ah!*"

Her eyes squeezed shut as he entered her with a firm thrust.

He stilled his movement. "You were saying?" he said in her ear.

Renee whimpered, squirming and pushing back. She *needed* him to move.

"You want more?"

She bit her lip and nodded with enthusiasm, without a lick of shame.

"I can't hear you. If I can't hear you, I can't give you what you want." His lips remained next to her head, and his low, smoky voice filled her eardrums.

"Yes."

"Yes, what?"

"Yes, I want more. All—"

Her words broke on a cry of pure and utter pleasure, and her fingers curled into tight balls when his stroking resumed. Steady and strong, he moved with practiced skill, hands still gripping her wrists so she couldn't move. Pinned to the bed, she absorbed his thrusts, moaning into the colorful cotton sheet as they intensified.

Clive slapped her ass and she gasped. The stinging pleasure pulsed between her legs and all lucid thoughts fled her brain. She would let him do whatever he wanted to her—wanted him to do as he pleased.

"You like that, don't you? You like it a little rough." His voice was deep, almost angry with intensity. He slapped her behind again, harder this time, and the sound crashed through the room. "Tell me."

"Yes," Renee hissed, tensing as she anticipated another blow.

He spanked her behind again and again, and she took her punishment. It felt *so good*, being pinned down, totally at his mercy as he spanked her and made her say how much she loved it.

Clive lifted her hips higher, drove harder, and angled his hips deeper. She was so turned on it wouldn't be long before she came again.

He scraped the side of her neck with the edges of his teeth, and that did it.

She came. Hard. Shuddering. Another cry of pleasure bursting from her lungs, intensified by his refusal to release her wrists, his utter control of her body as he rode her from behind. She damn near hyperventilated, gasping as wave after wave of orgasmic pleasure washed over her body.

Clive's hips pistoned against the cushion of her ass cheeks, and his grunts came faster and louder. Within seconds, he lost control, too and loudly muttered a series of curses before collapsing onto her back.

"Damn," he said.

9

Clive lay with one arm folded behind his head, eyes traveling around the room, which contained several pieces of white furniture. They included a large dresser, a five-drawer bureau, and a two-drawer table beside the bed with an iPad and a couple of books on top.

She lay on her side, facing away from him. He wasn't sure if she was sleeping, but she was awfully quiet and hadn't said a word since their sweat-drenched bodies separated.

Drowsy, his eyes slowly closed. He'd take a quick nap and see if Renee was up for another round in a bit.

"My second husband was white."

His eyes opened at the sound of her voice, and he turned his head in her direction. "Who was better—me or him?" he asked.

"My ex-husband."

"Damn."

Her laughter shook the bed, and when she turned to face him. "I don't kiss and tell, Clive."

"Oh, I'm back to being Clive, huh?"

She shrugged, humor in her brown eyes and a contented expression on her face that tightened his chest. Her normally perfectly coiffed hair was in disarray, and she'd sweated out her curls. No matter if the ex was better or not, she was satisfied.

"I have a question," she said.

"Shoot."

"Were you ever an athlete?"

"I was. My father played football and baseball. I was only ever good at football—started in the peewee league, played all through school and got a scholarship to play in college. The guys that come over to my house every couple of weeks are former teammates from back in college. Hell, we're brothers at this point, after everything we've been through over the years."

"Your house is the central location where everyone hangs out?"

"Yeah."

"I have a similar situation with me and my two closest girlfriends. We usually go to Adelaide's house. She's the who baked the cookies. I've known her and Jackie, my other best friend, for years. I'd do anything for those women."

"Guess we're both lucky in that respect." Clive smoothed her hair back from her cheek. The strands were soft as feathers. She briefly closed her eyes, as if that simple touch brought her pleasure. "What do you do all day, now that you're out of school?"

"I edit manuscripts for writers. It's a side gig to make a little extra money, nothing serious. I only work with a few clients each year and don't advertise. It's fun and a way to exercise my mind. I get to read interesting stories and shape them in my own little way. One of my clients is Angela Washington. Ever heard of her?"

He shook his head. "I'm not much of a reader."

"She writes engrossing historical fiction and is a former student of mine. She's doing a reading this summer and invited me to attend. She's published four books so far, and I helped her with each one."

"I thought publishing companies supplied editing services to their authors."

"They do, but Angela is a perfectionist and likes having another set of eyes on her work before she submits. In all honesty, she's so good I have very little work to do on her manuscripts."

"You're smiling a lot. You must love the work." His eyes focused on the curve of her lips. He'd enjoyed sucking and licking the fuller bottom one.

"I do."

Clive tugged down the sheet and exposed her breasts—dark skin capped by darker nipples. She was confident in her body. Not the least bit shy, which he appreciated.

The darkness of her skin was marred only by a pale line about two inches long on her left side. He'd noticed the scar when they were making love. He traced the mark with the tip of his finger. "How'd you get that?"

"I was in a fight in high school. This girl kept picking on me. An all-around bully, but I'd learned to fight because I had two older brothers and a mama who didn't take no mess. I couldn't come home and tell her anyone was picking on me and I didn't stand up for myself. One day I told that bitch to meet me outside. We fought, but when I got the upper hand and got her down on the ground, she pulled out a knife and stabbed me."

"Damn, that's awful."

"It wasn't as bad as it could've been. I went to the hospital and she got expelled."

Clive looked at her in amazement. "You're either a badass or crazy."

Renee laughed. He really liked the sound of her happiness, and her entire face brightened—especially her dark brown eyes, which captivated him with the way they lit up.

"Maybe a little bit of both. When you're short, you learn real quick to stand up for yourself or get trampled on. I'm a teacher, and I try to pass on the same lessons to my kids that my mother taught to me. I make sure they know they need to stand up for themselves."

"What grade do you teach?"

"Tenth-grade A.P. English and literature. Let me show you something."

She reached over him, her breasts and chocolate nipples gliding over his chest. The lower half of his body contracted but he maintained his control, watching as she pulled a card from the top drawer of the nightstand.

"Read that."

"Can't. I don't have my glasses."

"I didn't know you wear glasses."

"I'm supposed to," Clive said with a shrug.

"Why am I not surprised you're vain?" Renee shook her head.

He laughed.

Renee leaned back against the pillows and read the card. "To the best teacher I've ever had. One day when I'm a famous writer, I'll shout you out in all my interviews. Thank you for your encouragement. I learned to soar because of you." She wiped the wetness from the corner of her eyes. "I received this from a student before the end of the school year. This is why I do what I do. I'm going to miss those kids when I retire."

Clive wished he'd had a teacher like her when he was growing up. "Even the bad ones?" he asked.

"*None* of them are bad," she said in a hard tone. "Some are misunderstood. Some are troubled. We don't know what their home life is like. So many factors can determine how they behave, and I believe in all of my students and don't allow them to give up on themselves or sell themselves short thinking they can't succeed because of personal limitations. I make sure they know anything is possible if we work hard enough."

Her passion and optimism made her sexier. Maybe she wasn't as bad as he originally thought. "Your husbands were fools," he said.

"You think so?" She handed him the card, which he tucked back into the drawer.

"I know so. Why did you marry those men?"

The question seemed to take her by surprise, and she thought for a moment, staring up at the ceiling.

"At the time, I thought I loved them," she said honestly.

"So what went wrong?"

"Different problems with each man. They changed. Or maybe I ignored who they really were until I had to face the truth in our marriage. My first husband was a professor and cheated with one of his students. My second husband was also a professor. He wanted kids even though I was clear that I didn't want children before we got married. The third—I'm not sure what happened, but I desperately wanted that marriage to work because it was my third marriage and frankly, I was embarrassed."

"What type of work did he do?"

"He was an attorney. We drifted apart. A few years into the marriage, he became obsessed with his collection of cars and paid more attention to them than he did to me. By the time he lost his job, we were already teetering on the edge of divorce, barely speaking to each other. That pushed him over the edge. He couldn't handle me being the sole breadwinner, so to speak. We split shortly after that." Sadness filled her voice.

"Who initiated each divorce?"

"I did."

"I see," Clive said slowly.

"What is that supposed to mean?" Renee asked.

"Don't get offended, but what you said has me thinking that maybe all along you were looking for something each time you got married."

"Aren't we all?"

"I suppose...to some degree, but you clearly didn't find what you were looking for. In all honesty, I'm doing some looking myself."

"I'll be candid with you, the way you were with me. I'm set in my ways, and I'm not going to change. I'm not looking for another husband, either."

Clive laughed and shook his head.

"Why are you laughing?"

"I was thinking about how much I enjoy your honesty. It makes it easier for me to be forthright. I'm stuck in my ways too, and I've had my kids—three total and my granddaughter. You've met Chelsea. My oldest son is in Japan, madly in love with a co-worker and planning an elaborate proposal. My younger son plays minor league baseball in Florida. I'm certainly not looking for more children. I don't work anymore, but I have a nice retirement, so I won't feel threatened by the nice retirement I'm sure you have. Most of all, I'm not interested in turning someone into something they're not."

"Good. As long as you're clear on that."

"Something else I should make clear, is that everything about you drives me crazy. Your lips especially, when you're angry."

"You like to see me angry?"

"Absolutely."

Renee angled her body toward his. "What else?"

"Fishing for compliments?"

"A little."

His forefinger traced a line from the bottom of her jaw, over her neck to her shoulder. "This spot right here has been causing me problems. This collarbone. These cheekbones. These eyes."

She breathed slowly as his hands caressed her skin after each accusation.

"Any other parts of me you find intriguing?"

"I'm trying to be polite."

"Don't be polite," she said quietly.

He silently assessed her. "Where do we go from here, neighbor?"

"I don't know. What do you want to do?"

"We could order dinner and watch a little TV. Then have some more sex."

"More sex?"

She arched an eyebrow but didn't appear at all turned off by the suggestion. Matter of fact, her torso arched ever so slightly toward him. He was certain she didn't even notice.

"More sex," he confirmed.

He pulled her naked body atop his, and she slid a leg between his thighs. Her skin was so smooth and soft, he groaned.

"I realize I have more work to do. I'm not just trying to be the best white man you've ever had. I want to be the best sex you've ever had."

"That's going to take time and effort," she said, running her fingertips through the hair at his temple.

"Guess what?" he whispered, pushing his thick fingers into her short hair.

"What?" she whispered back, eyes locked on his.

"I've got plenty of time, and I'm willing to put forth the effort."

Tightening his fingers in her hair, he gently tugged back her head, and she moaned as his mouth connected with her arched throat.

10

Renee locked her front door and started the short trek across the grass to where Clive stood waiting, leaning against the passenger side of his truck with his feet crossed at the ankles. He looked absolutely scrumptious all dressed up—wearing dress shoes and tan slacks.

Since the first night they slept together, they had slept together three more times, but tonight he'd said he wanted to do something different. He invited her out to dinner. He wanted to go to his favorite burger joint—Stanley O's Burgers near Ocean Beach. She'd tried to coerce him into visiting her favorite Mexican restaurant, Habanero, which she hadn't been to in a while, but finally gave in because he spoke so highly of the burger place.

As she walked across the grass, he watched with a faint smile on his lips as if he couldn't tear his eyes away and made her feel—not simply like an object of lust—but like a person who was deeply desired. Someone he wanted to spend time with. After three divorces, she wondered if there was something inherently wrong with her, but doubts about her appeal to the opposite sex wavered in his presence.

"I'm gonna have to beat off all the men in that place," he commented, pushing off the truck.

Renee glided into his open arms and accepted his kiss. That was another thing about him. He was very affectionate, which she had to get used to. He thought nothing of reaching to hold her hand or dropping a random kiss to her neck. Men were usually affectionate in the early stages of a relationship, but she hadn't been in the early stages of a relationship in quite a while—thirteen years, at least. So Clive's behavior felt new and foreign, and she still wasn't accustomed to it.

"And why is that?" she asked.

"Because you look so good and smell so good." He twisted them around so that she was against the truck, and pressed his face to the crook in her neck. Doing a combination sniff-and-kiss, he made her skin tingle.

"Should I be worried about this wonderful burger joint you're taking me to? We can still go to Habanero."

"The minute you used the word fusion and paired it with the word Mexican, I knew that place wasn't for me."

"But the food is delicious," she said, leaning toward him and pressing her hands against his chest.

"Uh-huh. Authentic, too, I bet."

She shot him her signature look of disapproval usually reserved for her students. "The food is excellent and you'd know if you tried it."

He leaned closer, casting a shadow over her and placing her in a little cocoon of heat. "Get in the truck, Buttercup. I'm starving, and when I get this hungry, I'm liable to eat anything in sight."

His nostrils flared ever so slightly and the temperature in their little cocoon increased by fifteen degrees.

"You are so filthy."

"I know. Don't you just hate it?" His smoky voice dropped lower and his signature smirk appeared.

He dipped his head and she lifted her lips. No hands. No pressing against each other. Their connection was more erotic because they didn't touch. The torture of deprivation enhanced the kiss as their mouths moved with familiar ardor against each other.

Finally, Clive groaned and yanked her flush against his body. He lifted his head and their breaths merged in the tiny space between.

"You know, we could put off eating and go back to your place," he said in a husky, hungry voice.

Renee laughed shakily to dispel the haze of lust that had temporarily consumed her. "You promised me the best burger in San Diego, and I'm ready for it."

Clive groaned. "My ability to sell has done me in again."

Laughing with genuine humor this time, Renee climbed into the truck, and he shut the door. He paused for a moment outside, and time stood still as they looked at each other through the window. There was a tiny shift that she couldn't quite put her finger on but recognized in that brief moment. Their relationship had changed. They weren't just sleeping together. This was their first date, and the magnitude of this moment was not lost on her, and apparently not on him either.

Clive rounded the front of the truck and climbed in. Once he hit the road, he placed a hand on Renee's knee, demonstrating his affectionate nature once again. Holding her breath, Renee placed her hand over his, doing her best not to live up to the accusation of her last lover—that she had intimacy issues.

He turned away briefly from the road and smiled at her, and she relaxed, smiling back and absorbing the silence of riding in the comfort of the truck's cab, on the way to dinner with her man.

When they arrived at the restaurant, Clive came around and opened her door and also held open the door of Stanley O's Burgers so she could pass in ahead of him. They walked up to the counter and perused the options. The restaurant contained eight tables sprinkled around the small dining room, and dimmed bulbs that offset the glare of the street lights coming in from the wall to ceiling windows. Behind the counter was a chalkboard with the handwritten specials of the night, as well as a permanent board that listed all the regular menu items.

"Know what you want?" Clive's left arm snaked around her waist, and she leaned back into the strength of his chest.

Renee shook her head. "What do you suggest?"

"I always get the same thing—the American cheeseburger, which comes with bacon."

"Hmm. I'm going to get the California, with the guacamole, and the sweet potato fries."

"I'm sure you will not be disappointed. What do you want to drink?"

"Tonight's drink special is a root beer float, so I'll have one of those."

"I missed that. I'll have one, too." Clive slipped away to pay for their meal and took the numbered flag, which he placed on the table when they sat down at a table near the window.

"How did you find this place?" Renee asked.

"My daughter found it, actually. One night after she and her coworkers left work, they stopped in here on a whim. She and her friends all enjoyed their meals, so she told me about it because she knows how much I love a good burger."

"How did your son's proposal go?"

"She said yes." Clive grinned.

"That's wonderful! You're about to have a new addition to your family."

Clive laughed. "She's a great girl. When he called and asked for my opinion, I wasn't sure he'd go through with the proposal. I'm glad he listened to his old man."

"There was no way for you to know that she would say yes."

"And there was no way for him to know that she'd say no, unless he asked. If you want something, you gotta go after it. I learned that playing football."

"How long did you play?"

"Until I busted up my knee in college and couldn't play anymore, but it was fun while it lasted." He shrugged dismissively, but she saw the disappointment in his face.

"I'm sorry to hear that. Were you planning to go pro?"

"I was never good enough for pro," he said with a shake of his head. "But I had a great time. Enough about me. What made you want to become a teacher?"

Renee was surprised by the quick change of subject, as if he didn't want her to learn any more about him. Which was odd, since she considered him one of the most open people that she knew.

"My mother was big on giving back. She required my brothers and me to do volunteer work, whether it was in the community, at church, or both. During the holidays we volunteered at the food bank and the homeless shelter. During the school year, I had a part-time job but managed to squeeze in tutoring elementary school kids a couple of times per week. One of the instructors told me I was a natural and suggested I go into teaching.

"At the time I wasn't sure what I wanted to do. I thought something in business administration or even nursing. I literally had no clue what I wanted to be when I grew up." She laughed at her naïveté at the time. "But when she made that suggestion, something clicked, and I knew I was meant to be a teacher. English was my strongest subject. From then on, I worked my butt off and always earned A's. Now, here I am, twenty-three years later, and I'll be retiring in a couple of years."

Clive had listened closely while she talked and now asked, "What will you do when you retire?"

"I don't know. I might work harder to turn editing into a real business. Or maybe I'll just lounge around the house like my neighbor, Clive."

He chuckled. "Being able to relax does have its advantages."

The food arrived ten minutes later and Renee bit into the burger. It was juicy, the guacamole clearly freshly made, and the toasted bun was just the additional added detail to make the meal even better.

"Well?"

Renee swallowed and shook her head in disbelief. "You were right. This is one excellent burger."

"Don't ever doubt me again," he said, and bit into his burger.

"Promise me something."

"Anything."

"Next time, we'll go to Habanero. I think you'll like it." She'd experienced a bit of nerves as the sentence left her lips because it meant she saw them doing more of these kinds of activities.

"I promise to consider it," he said.

"Thank you," Renee said.

Then she enjoyed the rest of her burger.

11

She was either a new fool or an old fool. Either way, Renee was a fool for enjoying the time she spent with Clive way too much.

Covering her nakedness with a robe, she slid her feet into fluffy pink bedroom slippers. In a few minutes, Clive would exit the bathroom and she'd escort him to the front door. That had been their routine for the past couple of weeks.

Tonight they'd gone to the burger joint again. He loved to eat there and she had to admit the food was good. On each date she was surprised by his chivalry. She'd come to expect men to be the opposite of chivalrous, and as a woman who made her own money and took care of herself, it was a nice change to be taken care of.

Renee was smiling to herself when Clive exited the bathroom.

"Guess I'll head out," he said, lifting his white shirt from the foot of the bed.

"Got to go home for the girls?"

Clive buttoned his shirt. "No. Margie's spending the weekend at her cousins' house, and Chelsea went out with her coworkers."

"So you don't have to go home yet?"

"Not really." Clive paused, eyeing her with something akin to suspicion. "Why do you ask?"

"I thought if you wanted to stay and watch a movie or something..." Renee shrugged.

"Or something?" He cocked an eyebrow and a lascivious smile spread across his lips.

Renee rested her hands on her hips. "We already did something. Maybe we can watch a movie. Of course, if you'd rather go home to an empty house..." She shrugged again.

Actually, she didn't want to stay alone in *her* empty house. She wanted Clive to stay. They'd become much more relaxed in each other's presence, and on the days they didn't see each other—she hated to admit—she missed him.

"My house isn't empty. Samson is there. But, I don't have anything else to do. To be clear, are you inviting me to spend the night?"

"You might as well."

"Is that a request or a demand?"

"Call it whatever you want," Renee said.

"Can't bring yourself to say it, can you? That you want me to stay. That you want to spend more time with me."

"Do you want to spend the night or not?" Renee asked with an exaggerated sigh.

Clive chuckled. "Only if I get to choose the movie. Something with lots of shooting and fighting and explosions."

"Oh, goody, a movie with a bunch of macho men blowing things up. Sounds like fun."

"You like macho men," he said.

She did now. "Huh. Whatever."

With a knowing smirk, he strolled over to where she stood and leaned toward her. "Tell the truth, I'm much more fun than those stuffy men you've dated in the past. And whether you want to admit it or not, my movie choice will be more entertaining than what you had in mind, which was probably a movie about feelings or something equally boring."

"Oh, look, you just reminded me that I don't like you."

He laughed. "I'll find something on TV. Hurry up." He gave her a kiss and then a swift pat on the butt.

Renee grabbed her bottom even though the blow didn't hurt. "Would you please stop smacking my behind."

"Why? It's so smackable." He flashed a grin that made her want to grab him for a longer kiss. "Oh, that reminds me, I'm having friends over for the Fourth of July. There'll be plenty of food and drinks. You should come."

"I usually spend the Fourth at Adelaide's. She always prepares a nice spread and has friends over."

"Come afterward. We'll be partying all night."

"I'll only come if you promise to keep the noise down."

"I'll do my best, but let's be real, on the Fourth there will be plenty of noise all over the neighborhood."

Renee arched an eyebrow at him.

"I won't promise something I can't deliver," Clive said.

"At least keep your guest cars on one side of the street and be respectful of our neighbors. If you like, some of your guests can park in my driveway."

"That's awfully nice of you. Does that mean you're coming?"

"I guess," Renee said airily.

"You know you want to come."

"Oh, you think so?"

"Just say yes."

"Fine. Yes."

"Thank you for gracing us with your presence. While you get dressed, I'll go check on our movie options." Clive started out the door.

"Wait a minute, I have a question. Why did smacking my butt remind you of the Fourth of July barbecue?"

"Oh, because of a conversation I had with one of my friends—Jayson—who you'll meet on the Fourth. Months ago I told him that you had a bad attitude but a great ass, and it was posing quite a dilemma for me." He flashed another sexy grin and left.

Renee stood there in shock, knowing she should be upset, but feeling oddly pleased by the backhanded compliment.

TODAY WAS an exercise day with the girls. Wearing shorts, tennis shoes, and a T-shirt, Renee moved briskly with her friends as they walked through Adelaide's neighborhood.

"So how are the kids doing?" Jackie asked Adelaide. They both wore joggers and tank tops.

Having wanted children for years, Jackie was constantly asking about someone else's kids. If she were in the vicinity of a baby, you could be sure she'd find a way to get the little bundle in her arms.

"They're great. Junior is loving his photography work, and Karen found a part-time job to help supplement the income she lost when her temp assignment ended." Karen was an actress, currently in New York trying to find work in the theater.

"It must be so tough being in a new city, trying to make ends meet."

"But she also has Hector and Adelaide to fall back on," Renee reminded Jackie.

Jackie laughed. "True. Wish you guys were my parents. My parents soundly discouraged me from starting my own business, which in fact forced me to want to do it even more."

"We can always trust you to do the exact opposite of what you're told," Adelaide said.

They laughed and kept up the pace. As they passed by one of Adelaide's neighbors working in the yard, they all waved at him. He was one of their favorite parts of the neighborhood when they went on their walks. In the summertime, he was always outside working in the yard, shirtless. Today was no different. Holding clippers, with bulging muscles and a slim waist, he trimmed the hedges in front of his house with his dark brown skin glistening with sweat.

"God broke the mold when he made that man," Jackie murmured.

"Amen," Adelaide and Renee said at the same time.

Once again, the ladies cracked up.

"What's the latest on the adoption?" Adelaide asked, directing the question to Jackie.

"Still going through the assessment process. They told me it could take up to six months, but I thought that was a conservative estimate. Seems like it really will be the full six months."

"What happens after that?" Renee asked.

"Then I get to choose my kid." Jackie grinned. "I'm annoyed by this whole process, but I know it'll be worth it once I find my child. I just feel weird about going online and looking through the photos—as if they're in a catalog."

"I understand your discomfort, but I think it would be harder on the kids if you had people coming in and looking them over like cattle."

"Good point," Jackie said.

They moved into single file to accommodate one of the residents walking her dog. Another resident that knew Adelaide honked at them, and she waved in return.

Back in formation, Renee said, "I have some news about me and Clive."

"With that wide grin on your face, it must be really good," Jackie said.

Feeling a surge of exuberance, Renee pumped her arms harder. "He asked me to spend Fourth of July with him. Oh, and we've been sleeping together."

Adelaide stopped in the middle of the sidewalk and Jackie followed suit. Renee swung around and looked at them.

"Way to bury the lede. We've been walking for almost twenty minutes, and you're only now telling us that you'll be spending the holiday with your new lover man?" Adelaide asked.

Pumping her arms, Jackie walked in place. "Let's keep moving, ladies. Remember, walk and talk."

She took off and her friends fell into step beside her.

"Details," Adelaide said.

"Where do I begin? We hardly have anything in common. I mean, he's blue-collar and a former athlete—exactly the kind of man I've avoided all my life. Look at who my husbands were. Yet...I really like him. And he's such a gentleman. He opens doors and insists on paying for dinner when we go out. A lot of men don't do that anymore, especially when they find out you have your own money." Not to mention he didn't judge when he found out that she had been married three times.

"True." Jackie nodded.

"I really couldn't stand the man before, but now I'm sleeping with him—literally sleeping with the enemy. Can you believe it? I don't know how that happened."

"Girl, you are way too old for that. You know how it happened," Jackie said dryly.

"Thank you for your commentary," Renee said.

"I'm just saying, that didn't take long."

Laughing, Adelaide shook her head as she pumped her arms and kept pace with them. "So, what's this about the Fourth of July? You're dumping me this year?"

Renee groaned and grimaced guiltily. "I'll still come by earlier in the day and then head over to Clive's later. He's having friends over and asked me to join them."

"The same friends that you always complain block the street and are way too loud?" Jackie peered around Adelaide to look at Renee.

"The same ones. He said he'd try to keep the noise down," Renee said defensively. "Adelaide, would it be too much trouble for you to make a dessert for me?"

"What did you have in mind?"

"How about a lemon cake with glaze? The one you made before was absolutely delicious."

"Oh sure. That's pretty easy. You can pick it up when you come over during the day."

"Perfect."

Renee noticed Jackie watching her from the corner of her eye. "What, Jackie?"

"Nothing. It's good to see you getting back out in the dating game after being gone for so long. Welcome back." Her friend smiled, clearly happy for her.

Renee laughed. "You know what, it feels pretty damn good."

12

————

Standing in front of Clive's door, Renee took a deep breath and slowly released it. The lemon cake in her hands felt like an anvil, and her pulse beat an erratic rhythm beneath her skin.

Tonight was momentous. This wasn't simply a Fourth of July barbecue. This was a barbecue at the home of the man she'd been sleeping with for weeks, and she'd be introduced to his friends.

She rang the doorbell and Chelsea opened the door with a bright, welcoming smile, looking very patriotic in jeans, a T-shirt with the American flag on the front, and a red, white, and blue-striped ribbon holding her hair in a ponytail.

"Hello, Miss Joseph, come on in."

"Thank you." Hiding her nervousness, Renee gave her best smile.

"Oh, what's that?" Chelsea asked.

"Glazed lemon cake. Your father told me I didn't need to bring a dish, but I didn't feel comfortable coming empty-handed."

"You baked this?" Chelsea asked, taking the covered dish.

"I wish. I have a friend who loves to cook and bake. I asked her to make a dessert for this evening."

"Nice friend. Everyone is in the back. Follow me."

Renee did just that, taking stock of the inside of the house as she did. Despite their budding relationship, this was the first time she'd been inside Clive's home. In the past, she'd only seen the interior from the outside as she brought back his dog.

They walked through the spacious living room with walnut floors and heavy furniture dominating the space. The dining room was smack-dab in the middle of the path to the kitchen and contained a long table that seated eight and a china cabinet that actually contained a chinaware set that might have belonged to his deceased wife.

The house looked as she'd expect a contractor's house to look— with upgrades of crown molding, fairly new-looking carpet, and modern appliances in the kitchen.

Still balancing the cake dish in her hand, Chelsea led Renee out the back door. "Renee's here," she announced, making eye contact with her father, who held court with a can of beer in his hand and his back against the deck railing.

Chelsea dipped back into the kitchen and left Renee hovering near the door.

There was a bigger group tonight. Eight guys and four women sat outside on the deck. In the yard, Margie ran around with a dog and a biracial-looking boy and girl who appeared to be a year or two younger.

"You made it," Clive said, pushing away from the railing. He looked extra sexy tonight in a short-sleeved Henley and jeans. An easy smile crossed his face and he came over to where she stood and slipped an arm around her back. "Everybody, this is Renee, my neighbor."

Her cheeks heated at the attention.

"Oh," a few of them said.

"Uh-oh," someone muttered.

By their responses, they all knew she and Clive had had problems in the past. They'd probably heard the *Miss Grumpy* moniker a time or two.

"Don't worry, I'm not here to break up the party. Clive and I are friends now. I even like the dog," she said.

Her words broke the ice, and they all started laughing.

One of the men, a tall man with mahogany skin who looked more like a basketball player than a football player, stood. "Hi, Renee. I'm Jayson."

"Hi, Jayson. Nice to meet you."

He motioned to the chair he'd vacated and she sat down.

"Thank you."

Everyone introduced themselves, and Renee learned the parents of the kids playing with Chelsea were Jayson and a blonde woman named Sasha who had a tight body and appeared significantly younger than most of them at the party. She looked about twenty-eight.

Renee hadn't eaten much at Adelaide's but brought home a plate so she'd have food for tomorrow, which meant she was now hungry and gladly filled her plate with some of the offerings on display. There were hamburgers and hotdogs, but she selected what turned out to be a delicious grilled chicken breast, grilled veggies, and grilled fruit for dessert. The meal was a lot healthier than she'd expected, but maybe not so surprising, considering all the men had been athletes.

Clive went back to his position at the railing, and Renee sat near him with the plate on her lap, listening to the interesting stories the men told about their playing days in college. Clive had been a tight end and one of the best until his knee got busted up in a freak tackle that twisted it in at an odd angle and ended his college playing days in his sophomore year.

They joked about stories that—interestingly enough—they all remembered differently. One guy, a light-skinned man with dark eyes, talked about his amazing tackle that saved the game, but no one else remembered the play. Another man, dark-skinned with a lisp, had been the quarterback and reminded everyone of some of his great throws and how he'd broken the school record. There were some arguments about that as well. Renee couldn't help but laugh, but maybe the different versions were to be expected since those events took place over twenty-five years ago.

They weren't always in disagreement about past events. A few memories that came up had them very animated, yelling and laughing so loud they scared the dog and made the kids holler that they should keep down the noise.

During a lull in the conversation, Sasha—currently seated on Jayson's lap—asked Renee, "What kind of work do you do?"

"I teach high school A.P. English and literature, but I'll be retiring in a few years."

"How did you manage to land her?" Sasha asked Clive.

"Don't start with me, Sasha, I already know how lucky I am," he said, eyes crinkling in amusement as he took a sip of his beer.

Clive didn't correct the assumption that they were a couple. Renee's eyes lingered on him, and his eyes lingered on her. The message within let her know quite clearly that they were, in fact, a couple, and he was happy with her.

A wave of heat swept over her skin. What an odd experience. For the past year, she'd wanted to throttle him. Now she wanted to jump his bones and wished for this get-together to wrap up quickly so she could do just that.

"I'm going to get some water. Anyone want anything?" Renee stood.

They all shook their heads, so she went inside and found the cooler with iced water on the floor near the door. As she picked a bottle, Chelsea entered the kitchen.

"You're having fun, I hope?" she asked.

"I am. That's an interesting bunch. I'm not sure what to make of them." Renee sipped her water.

Placing her hands on her hips, Chelsea laughed. "They're good guys, I promise."

"I'm kidding, they seem to be. I'm so impressed with the friendship they've maintained all these years—for decades! That's impressive."

"Yep. They stayed friends after my dad dropped out of college a couple of years in, when his knee got messed up."

"He dropped out?" Renee asked in shock.

Chelsea nodded. "He started working construction full-time, and that's the field he stayed in until my mom died. He loves working with his hands."

Leaning her hip against the counter, Renee was enthralled by the new information from Clive's daughter. She didn't speak because she didn't want to interrupt the flow of information.

"That's how he met my mom. Her father ran the construction company he worked for, and she worked in the office. They started dating, but my grandpa didn't approve. He thought my mother could do better." Chelsea rolled her eyes.

"But love prevailed," Renee said, her heart tightening with sympathy for Clive. She couldn't imagine how that must have made him feel, and she realized she'd had her own reservations because he didn't fit the mold of the type of man she'd envisioned herself being with.

Chelsea's face brightened. "It did. My mom left the company, she and my dad got married, and Dad opened his own construction company. Mom answered the phones, did all his paperwork—everything she used to do for grandpa. Those guys out there stood by his side when he married my mom, and...when he lost her. That was a tough time for all of us." Her voice throbbed with pain at the end.

"You don't have to talk about it if you don't want to."

"No, it's fine." Chelsea played with the ribbon in her hair and took a deep breath to corral her emotions. "After she died, Dad was devastated. That's how these get-togethers started. I know the noise bothered you, but they started because, when my mother died, my father was in a dark place. She was his everything, you know? And he became very depressed, couldn't get out of bed. He forgot how to enjoy himself. Jayson—God bless him—suggested a few of them come over to cheer up my dad, and they started visiting regularly to get him out of his funk. That's when we lived in the old house, and they continued the tradition even after he was okay. These barbecues and guys' nights out keep them connected, and they help each other. They helped when Dave and Misty lost their son and when Gary, who's not here tonight, had a cancer scare. Only six of them from the original team still live around here and come over, but Dad keeps up with some of the guys in other parts of the country, too. "

"That kind of friendship isn't easy to come by," Renee said softly.

"No, it's not. Anyway, I've said too much." Chelsea gave an embarrassed laugh. "I just wanted you to know how important those guys are to him. How important they are to each other."

"I understand, Chelsea. Believe me, I understand."

13

The guests had left an hour ago after they all watched an impressive fireworks display in the distance, courtesy of the Port of San Diego. Cleaning up took Clive, Chelsea, and Renee about forty-five minutes before they completed all tasks and had the house back in order.

Chelsea yawned exaggeratedly, covering her mouth and then lifting her arms upward into a stretch. "Guess I'll head upstairs and join Samson and Margie." The lateness of the evening and running around for hours had caused Margie, with little prodding, to go upstairs earlier, her eyes drooping so low they'd almost closed entirely. Samson had followed her up to her room.

"It was good talking to you tonight, Renee."

"Nice talking to you, too," Renee replied, appreciative of the insight she'd gleaned into Clive's past.

"Don't be a stranger." Chelsea made eye contact with her father and sent him a silent message. "Good night, Dad."

"Good night." After she left, Clive added, "That's my daughter. Real subtle."

Renee giggled.

Clive glanced around the kitchen. "Thanks for staying behind and helping out. You're a guest and shouldn't have had to clean up. I owe you one."

"Please, you don't owe me anything. It's only a fraction of what you've done for me at the house."

"I hope you don't feel like you owe me anything," Clive said with a frown.

"Absolutely not."

"Although if you want to pay me back..." he said with a leer, wiggling his thick eyebrows.

Renee placed a hand on her hip. "I said, absolutely not."

Clive let out a throaty laugh that made her smile. She couldn't imagine this man depressed and struggling to get out of bed.

"Care for another drink?" Clive asked.

"I could use a beer, if you have any left."

"Sure do." He grabbed two bottles from the refrigerator, opened both bottles, and handed one to her. "Let's go outside." He slipped his hand into hers.

On the deck, they stood close, leaning against the railing as they overlooked the yard. They sipped their drinks in silence. The sounds of laughter and music came from a couple of doors down, and the sound of firecrackers popped in the distance.

"Chelsea told me how difficult life was for you after your wife passed."

He glanced at her. "You feel sorry for me now?"

"I'm sure you're fine, but I can't help feeling a bit sympathetic. I've never known that type of loss—that kind of love where losing the other person could thrust me into a depression." What did loving someone like that feel like? What did being loved like that feel like? She'd been married three times and had never known that type of emotional attachment.

"It was hard." He took a sip of beer and then set the bottle on the railing.

"Is that why you left the construction business?" she asked.

His jaw tightened and he didn't speak for a while. Renee rubbed her thumb over the condensation on the bottle, hoping she hadn't gone too far with her questioning.

"She was my best friend, my business partner," Clive said in a grave, quiet voice.

Was he still in love with his wife? She hoped not. Renee swallowed the lump of jealousy in her throat.

"Shutting down the business was the best decision. I couldn't do it on my own. It wasn't the same without her. Nothing was the same without my Margaret." Clive balled up the fingers of his left hand.

Renee covered his oversized hand with her palm. "I didn't mean to upset you."

"I'm fine," he said gruffly.

She squeezed his tight, tension-filled fist. "Hey, I have an idea. How about we dance?"

"Dance?"

"Yes, dance. I learned something new about you today, and now you can learn something about me. You already know I love reading and going to literary events, but I also love to dance."

Renee went back inside and retrieved her purse. When she came out, she removed her phone and pulled up one of her many Spotify playlists. She hit play, and the first song was "Use Me."

"Bill Withers," Clive said, the furrow of his brow loosening. He pulled her into his arms.

"What do you know about Bill Withers?" Renee teased, tilting her head back and admiring the strong angles of his jawline.

"Have you seen the men I hang out with?"

They laughed as he pulled her closer, and they turned in a circle around the deck. Renee draped her arms over his shoulders and relaxed in his arms. As they danced, she smoothed her hands over his biceps, reveling in the strength exuded by the muscles beneath his shirt.

"I haven't danced in a long time," Clive said.

"You're doing a pretty good job," Renee said.

Clive turned her in a slow spin and she shook her hips.

"Wait a minute now," he murmured, pulling her back against him.

Laughing, Renee tossed her head back and settled against his chest. With the deck lights breaking up the shadows across the back yard, they swayed together in time to the music, like one unit, as if they'd always been together.

Renee realized with deep sadness that there hadn't been many moments like this in her marriages. Her second marriage in particular had been more like a business arrangement, two people proud of the fact that they could talk about the intersection of politics and education at cocktail parties and education summits.

But no dancing. No laughter. No fun.

"I think it's time for us to go to bed, don't you?" Clive asked. He was already hard against her bottom.

Renee rubbed her ass harder against him and he groaned.

"Do you want to go to bed, or do it out here?" Clive whispered huskily. He cupped her breasts and squeezed. "Hmm?" Nuzzling her neck, he moved her toward the railing.

"What are you doing?" she whispered.

"I thought I could bend you over this railing..."

She gasped. "I'm not tall enough."

"I can make it work." His hand slid between her legs.

"Behave."

Renee slapped away his hand and shoved back with her bottom. Clive groaned again, grinding hard against her ass this time.

"Here or in the bed. Make a decision."

"In the bed."

Renee turned and nibbled on his lips a little bit because she simply couldn't help herself, before they both went back inside and eventually exited the house, locking the door on the way out. They made their way to her house next door and once inside, kissing and touching, moved to the bedroom.

As Renee was undressing, Clive laid back on the mattress on his elbows.

"You are absolutely stunning."

Renee stopped moving. She was half naked, wearing a lacy white bra and panties, both put on because she had anticipated making love with him tonight. The heat in his eyes, the thickness in his voice, tightened her chest with emotion.

"Keep talking like that and you'll get laid." It was supposed to be a joke, but neither of them laughed. They simply looked at each other.

Renee straddled Clive's thighs and he sat up, cupping her bottom with his hands.

"Are you still in love with your wife?"

His eyebrows flew higher. "No. Why would you ask that?"

"Because I had to know. Our conversation tonight made me wonder."

"I told you before, I loved my wife dearly, and we had a wonderful marriage. But I've moved past the pain."

"Good, because I want to share everything with you, and I don't want there to be any barriers between us."

"There are no barriers. I promise."

She kissed him gently, softly. "Remember I told you about one of my author-clients, Angela Washington?"

He nodded. "The one who has the event coming up?"

"I'd love for you to attend with me."

"A reading?" Clive wrinkled his nose.

"Come on, it'll be fun."

"A reading?" he said again.

"Yes!"

"I'll be bored out of my mind."

"Oh, come on. I came to your cookout."

"And had a great time, I might add." He laid back on the bed and pulled her with him.

Renee nestled against his hard-on, nudging the hardened length with her leg. He grimaced.

"You know that feels good," he murmured, running his hands up and down her spine.

The soothing motion warmed her skin and her nipples tingled.

Renee kissed his neck, caressing his chest as she did so. "Come on. If you hate it, I'll never ask again." She sucked his earlobe.

"You drive a hard bargain." Clive rolled her onto her back and settled between her thighs.

The fullness of his erection and his hard thighs made her squirm and thread her fingers into his soft white hair.

"Is that a yes?"

"You promise, if I don't like it you won't insist I attend another event like that with you?"

"I promise."

Clive slid his hand under her panties and into the slick evidence of her desire. Renee sucked air hard between her teeth and arched her back, pressing upward into the single digit he used to tease her.

"Okay, I'll come."

"Just for that, you get a very special reward."

With a saucy grin, Renee began undoing his belt buckle.

14

"I'm almost ready!" Renee yelled from the bathroom.

Seated on the edge of her bed, Clive shook his head. He'd been waiting ten minutes already while she rushed around getting dressed for the event tonight. At this rate, he'd have to drive like a bat out of hell to get there on time.

Renee came out of the bathroom in a black dress with a bejeweled neckline and the same design around the ends of the three-quarter-length sleeves. His mouth went dry as he scanned the way the dress hugged her curvy body and showed off her cleavage.

"How do I look?" She did a quick spin on three-inch patent leather pumps.

"Beautiful, like I told you eight minutes ago before you changed into this outfit."

"I know you're annoyed, but I want to look my best." She held up two sets of earrings, one in each hand. "Which ones do you think? Diamonds or pearls?"

"Diamonds," Clive answered.

Renee stood in front of the mirror and held one earring up to her ear, then the other earring up to her other ear. Shaking her head, she said, "No. I think the pearls go better with this dress."

Clive didn't say a word. His wife used to ask his opinion about outfits, shoes, and jewelry, but ended up doing whatever she wanted anyway. He was fairly convinced that women only asked those questions so they knew which items not to choose.

After inserting the earrings in her ears, Renee smoothed her hands over her hips in the fitted dress. She turned to the left and then turned to the right, checking her appearance before finally taking a deep breath. "I'm ready."

Clive stood, but she wasn't actually ready. He groaned quietly as she dashed over to the walk-in closet and came out hopping on one foot while slipping on a different black heel on the other. Finally, she took another deep breath and stood erect. "How do I look?" she asked again.

"Fantastic. Can we go now?"

Strutting over to where he stood, she cupped his face and planted a kiss on his hairy jaw. "Thank you for coming with me."

"I'm starting to wonder if this was a good idea. I thought this was your student's event, but you're so nervous I have to wonder if it's really yours."

She walked to the dresser and picked up her black beaded clutch. "It's because I've known her since she was a fifteen-year-old kid in my class, and we've worked together for years. This is a big deal for her, and I guess in a way for me, too. Watching her grow and become the success that she is makes me so proud. I kinda feel like a mama."

"Why didn't you have kids of your own? You obviously have a tender spot for the young people you teach."

Renee paused, a thoughtful frown coming over her face. Finally, she said, "I do love children, young people in general. But not everyone is supposed to be a mother—and liking young people is not enough of a prerequisite to be a parent. My calling was not to be a mother. My calling was to be a teacher. And I'm a darned good one. Besides, I never needed children of my own. Not when I've had the privilege of molding the lives of thousands of kids over the years."

She often amazed him, but now Clive was actually proud to walk in with her on his arm. He took her hand. "Let's get out of here and go see your kid do her thing."

They left the house in Renee's Volvo, with Clive driving. Amazingly, they arrived at the boutique hotel on time with one minute to spare. Outside the room where the event was taking place, the person at the door greeted them with a smile and escorted them to two reserved seats three rows back from a stage where two comfy-looking chairs faced each other. The audience chairs were arranged theater-style with only a few empty spots.

"Full house," Clive whispered out the side of his mouth as he settled on the seat.

Renee crossed her legs and leaned toward him. "I've been to other author events and they're not usually this crowded, but Angela has name recognition. She also hardly ever does events, so a lot of people are attending tonight because they don't know when they'll see her again."

As the lights lowered, a hush fell over the crowd. A young man with a low Afro in a navy suit stepped onto the stage holding a sheet of paper.

"Good evening," he said.

The audience murmured their response.

"I said, good evening," he repeated, voice louder.

"Good evening!" the audience greeted him back.

He went into the reason why they were there, to hear a reading by Angela Washington from her latest work, *Fire in My Heart*, a fiction novel that explored the tense relationship between a woman, her mother, and the Black man they both fell in love with during the height of the Civil Rights Movement. He provided information about her background, previous works, and accolades before stating, "Please hold your questions until after the reading. Now, without further ado, I present to you the reason we're all here tonight— Angela Washington!"

Angela walked out—a slight-looking woman, dark-skinned, with shoulder-length black hair and thick glasses. Clive sensed her nervousness as she waited for the thunderous applause to end.

Finally the audience became silent, and a bright smile stretched across her face, as if she suddenly realized she was worthy of the praise.

"Look at all of you here tonight. Don't you have anything better to do?" she asked.

The crowd laughed.

"Thank you all for coming. I was blown away by all the wonderful things Thomas said about me. Is he really talking about me, I wondered?" More laughter trickled through the crowd. "As you can tell, my life as an author is still surreal, and I couldn't be here without each and every single one of you. Before I begin reading the passages I've picked out, I want to give a special thank-you to someone in the audience—someone who encouraged me when I doubted myself. Someone who not only pushed me to dig deeper in my writing, but who helped me improve my writing. She didn't know I was going to do this tonight, so she'll probably kill me, but is Renee Joseph here?"

Angela looked a little anxious as she searched the crowd, and Clive could well imagine her as a shy but brilliant writer who, thanks to the nurturing and encouragement from Renee, became the best-selling author that she was today.

Renee raised her hand, and Angela's face lit up.

"Miss Joseph, please stand."

Slowly, hesitantly, Renee stood and all eyes turned to her.

Angela continued. "I don't mean to put you on the spot, but I had to let everyone know that the reason my books exist is because of you. Miss Joseph was my tenth-grade English teacher. She refused to let me doubt myself. With tough love, encouragement, and well-needed critique, she elevated my writing and brought me out of my shell so much that I decided to become an author, and I know I wouldn't be here without her because I've never submitted a work without letting her review it first. I've thanked you profusely in private, and now I want to thank you publicly. Thank you, Miss Joseph. For everything."

Angela clapped her hands, and the audience joined in the applause. Renee blew a kiss to her former student, and as the clapping died down, she took her seat.

Clive slipped an arm across her chair back and squeezed her shoulder. She smiled at him, blinking back tears as Angela took a seat on the stage and joined Thomas in a conversation that began by giving background information about the book.

Clive half-listened as Angela read the first passage. He couldn't stop thinking about how many lives Renee had impacted—lives she didn't even know she had because not everyone was vocal about their appreciation. Not everyone recognized how much she influenced their writing and their life.

Renee was an amazing woman. One who deserved to be with an amazing man.

So what in the world was she doing with a man like him?

15

here in the world is he?

Antsy, Renee stepped away from the group and took another look down the hallway. The reading had finished and most of the crowd dispersed. Only a few stragglers remained behind. Angela, her assistant, Thomas, and three of Angela's personal guests hovered together chatting.

Renee and Clive had been in that group talking about the book, the themes, and writing in general until he stepped away to use the bathroom.

Angela touched Renee's arm. "We're going to the restaurant upstairs. They're open until midnight and have the best appetizers and a great wine list. Would you and Clive like to join us—my treat?"

"That would be lovely. As soon as he gets back, I'll let him know."

"Perfect."

Angela rejoined the group, and Renee cast another look in the direction of the restrooms.

Finally, Clive appeared and she hurried toward him.

"Hey, what took you so long? Angela invited us to join them for appetizers and wine in the restaurant upstairs. I almost left without you," she said with a teasing smile.

"Now?" He frowned.

"Yes." He'd been acting strange ever since the event ended.

"It's kind of late to be eating, isn't it?"

"Since when do you turn down a meal or care about eating late? We're not eating a full dinner and maybe having just a drink or two."

Clive rubbed the back of his neck. "I don't know, I hadn't planned on doing anything else except attending the reading. Now I have to go eat and drink wine, too? I don't even like wine."

"Then order a beer or some other drink. I only mentioned the wine because Angela said they have a great selection. Listen, I have two words for you. Free. Food." She was starting to get annoyed.

"I'm not in the mood, Renee. Why don't you go ahead with Angela and Thomas and the rest of them. I'll head home."

"I want you to join us."

Clive shook his head. "It's not my thing."

"What's not your thing? Eating, drinking, and having a conversation? We did that a couple of weeks ago at your Fourth of July party. You included me in a part of your life, and I don't want to exclude you from this part of mine."

"You're not excluding me. This is my decision because I'm honestly not interested in talking about books and eating a bunch of expensive, fancy food. That's your thing."

Renee's jaw locked in anger. "Should I be offended?"

"No," Clive said wearily.

"Well, I guess I'll remember this the next time you ask me to participate in one of your events. I believe we were going fishing next week?"

When she'd told him she'd never gone fishing before, he invited her to join him and his granddaughter. Despite her reservations, she was excited about spending more time with him and being included in yet another part of his life. But why didn't he want to be included in hers?

"Renee, don't act like that." He reached for her, but she stepped out of his reach.

"Go. I'll call you later," she said, voice frigid.

"You're upset, but I told you from the beginning this wasn't my thing."

"Of course I'm upset, Clive. I like spending time with you doing a variety of activities. But so far we've only ever done what you want to do. I went to your favorite burger joint. We watch the movies you want to see. I attended your holiday barbecue. Tonight was the one time I've asked you to do something that I like, and you act as if it's too much. You're actually going to back out."

"It's one event," he said through his teeth, as if he had any right to be upset with her.

"It is not one event. You know what, never mind. I don't have time for this. Take the car back, I'll catch an Uber home. See you later." She walked away.

"Renee."

She pretended not to hear him.

When she reached the group, she said, "I'm ready."

Angela peered behind her. "Clive isn't coming?"

"No, he's not," Renee replied with a tight smile.

Thomas clapped his hands together. "Okay, everybody, follow me."

As they turned away, Renee peeked over her shoulder and saw Clive walking toward the exit. Hardening her heart, she stepped onto the elevator with the rest of the group and refocused her energy on the conversation and the good vibes she'd been experiencing beforehand. If Clive hadn't come with her, she would have been just fine, so why did she even care that he wasn't there now?

Because in a very short while he'd become an important part of her life, and the aching in her chest reminded her of how important he'd become. Not wanting to be rude, she eased her phone from her purse and, holding it in her lap, tapped out a quick text.

Renee: Please come get me so you and I could have a conversation about what happened tonight. I promise I'm not mad. Call me when you get here.

He couldn't have gone far. They'd only been upstairs for a few minutes, and it would have taken him a few minutes to exit the hotel, go to the car, and get on the road. He should get back to her shortly, and then they could have a real heart-to-heart conversation.

HE NEVER CAME. She couldn't believe he never came and couldn't believe the ridiculous message he'd sent back.

Clive: Just now seeing your message. At home now. Talk in the morning.

Standing in the driveway behind her car after the Uber driver dropped her off, Renee glared at the light in the window in the upstairs bedroom next door. Clive's bedroom, which meant he was still awake. She debated whether or not she wanted to confront him, but truly, there was no way she could sleep tonight without giving him a piece of her mind. And it would have to happen in person, not over the phone.

She strode across the grass to his front door and rang the doorbell. She only hoped she didn't wake Chelsea or Margie.

After a few minutes, Clive appeared at the front door.

"Can I come in?"

"Of course," he said in a tired voice.

Renee stepped across the threshold. "What the hell happened to you tonight? Not only do you run off and leave me, but then you send me that lame message, which was petty and inconsiderate."

"Petty?" Clive demanded. "I didn't see the damn message until I got home. I don't text much, in case you've never noticed."

Renee pointed a finger at him. "You have no right to be angry. You bailed on me and then didn't pick me up."

She was shaking now. What was happening to them? One minute everything was fine—the next, he was losing his temper and they were arguing like a couple who couldn't stand each other. She'd been here before, but this time—this time the panic gripping her insides tightened with viselike precision that left her consumed with the fear of losing him.

"What do you want from me?" His green eyes flashed at her, his anger so unprecedented she couldn't speak at first.

"I want a little consideration. I want my needs to matter in this relationship. I want you to do things I want to do, too." This always happened. Something always changed. Was she too demanding. Too easy-going? She didn't have a clue how the night spiraled out of control.

"And I did, but I didn't want to hang out and talk for God knows how long with a bunch of people I just met. I missed your message. I'm sorry, okay? If that's not a good enough answer, then too bad. I can't help you. I told you a boring literary event wasn't my idea of a good time, but you still insisted that I attend."

Her face burned from humiliation. He made her sound needy—something she prided herself on not being. "I did not insist. That's so unfair."

"Sometimes the truth hurts."

"Is this really what you want? This is how you want to end the evening?"

"I didn't start the argument, you did coming here in the middle of the night to yell at me."

His face was so hard, so unyielding. She'd never seen him like this and didn't like it, but there was nothing she could do. He didn't see anything wrong with what he'd done.

Throwing caution to the wind, she asked, "What did I do wrong?"

"I..." He shook his head, but no answer came.

The silence hurt more than if he'd given her a ten-bullet-point list of all her faults. Maybe he simply didn't care. Maybe he got tired of her and she wasn't worth answering.

"I'll just go home, then."

She opened the door, leaving it open as she walked on legs so tingly and rubbery she was certain she wouldn't make it through her own door. Despite the hurt feelings and the anger at Clive's behavior, she wanted him to stop her. She wanted him to call her name and tell her to get her butt back there. At this point, he didn't even have to apologize. She just needed to know that he cared.

But neither of those things happened. He didn't call her name. He didn't tell her to get her butt back there. He didn't care enough.

He just let her walk away into the night.

16

With heavy feet, Clive climbed the stairs, thoughts so consumed by the argument he didn't notice his daughter at the top of the stairs until he was on the second-to-last step. She leaned against the wall in her robe, arms folded over her chest.

"What?" he asked irritably.

"You need to tell her."

He and Chelsea had this conversation the other night when she realized he was getting serious about Renee. He didn't like it then and he didn't like it now.

He started toward his room. "She'll be fine. We'll be back to normal soon enough." He said the words but wasn't so sure. He hurt Renee tonight, and this probably wouldn't be the last time he'd hurt her.

Chelsea followed to the doorway of his room, a frown marring her face, as if she were the parent and he were the child.

"Until another incident comes up. You're hiding very important information about yourself."

"Women like Renee Joseph don't go for men like me."

"That's not true. You and Mom were happy together. She loved you, because you're a good man."

"Your mother was the exception to the rule. She was one of a kind."

"So no other woman could meet your standards?"

Clive laughed. "You've completely missed the mark. *I* don't meet *their* standards. After the event tonight, I listened to Renee and the author and some other people talking. Discussing book themes and tie-ins with other books that I've never read—never even heard of! I couldn't contribute a single sentence to the conversation."

His only contribution was laughing when they laughed and an occasional head nod, pretending to understand what they were talking about, the whole time wishing for an escape. Wishing he and Renee could drive away and he'd be back at her house watching television, a less stressful situation.

How could a woman like her possibly be happy with him? What did he have to offer? He'd simply embarrass her or make her friends uncomfortable. They'd have to dumb down their conversations for him.

"Dad, whatever your differences, you guys are great together, and pushing her away without an explanation is wrong."

"I didn't push her away. We had a fight."

"You and I both know you didn't only have a fight."

His jaw hardened in annoyance. His daughter knew him way too well. "Go to bed, Chelsea."

"Dad—"

"Go to bed, Chelsea," he said in a firmer tone of voice. "Clearly you've forgotten, you're the child, I'm the parent."

"You'll always be miserable unless you're honest with your partners—whether it's Renee or someone else in the future. Mom wasn't the only one who could love you, and what you've done to Renee is unfair." She stomped away in a huff.

Clive waited in silence for a while before he closed the door and then sank onto the bed. He buried his face in his hands. The frustration overwhelming, weighing him down.

"Dammit, Renee."

He already missed her, but how could he tell her the secret he'd kept for most of his life?

How could he tell her that he couldn't read?

"Boy, did you fuck up," Jayson muttered.

Fishing with Clive at Cesar Chavez Park Pier, he spoke softly because Margie stood nearby with her own rod and reel.

Clive knew Jayson would give him the unvarnished truth and he needed the verbal flogging because the mental flogging he'd given himself hadn't been nearly enough.

Jayson leaned closer and whispered, "Please tell me how you got here. You told me you were falling in love with Renee. So how in the world did you go from falling in love and spending so much time together to not speaking for days? You know what you have to do."

The thought of taking the additional step of being completely honest with Renee made Clive's abdominal muscles clench.

"You're a fighter, Clive. I've known you for over twenty-five years, and I've never known you to give up on anything."

Gazing out at the water, Clive said, "Not true. After my injury, I gave up on school because I couldn't hack it."

"You know I think you made a mistake then, too. Just tell her, man."

Clive shook his head. "And deal with her disdain when she finds out that I can't read? Deal with the disdain that I've had to deal with from people like Margaret's father? No thanks. Renee is an intelligent, accomplished woman. I already knew that when she and I got involved, but the night of the literary event made me fully understand her level of intelligence. Listening to her talk to those people about topics that I knew nothing about... I didn't belong there with them."

"BS. You belonged there because she invited you. She wanted you there. Tell her the truth—tell her everything."

Clive remained quiet, listening to the sounds of the water and the conversations of the other anglers around them. His gaze landed on his granddaughter—adorable in denim shorts, a unicorn T-shirt, and a wide-brimmed hat to protect her from the sun. So happy to be by his side. No judgment. She simply admired him.

But not once had he been able to read her a bedtime story. He hadn't been able to read them to Chelsea, either. He could barely read the invoices that he gave customers when he owned his own business.

Margaret used to handle all the paperwork. How could he explain to Renee that the reason he dissolved his business—the job that he loved—was because of his lack of ability to read? He could make out words here and there, stumbling through if he used phonetic pronunciation. But he was functionally illiterate.

"Do me a favor," Jayson said.

"What?"

"At least look into the adult literacy classes I told you about. Those folks are patient and will help you."

"I don't know... I tried before and it was hard as hell."

"That's when you were with Margaret, and you gave up because she was alive and able to do everything for you. Now you've got Chelsea, but how much longer do you think she'll be there? At some point, she's going to get her own place and move out with Margie. Then you'll be alone."

Of course he knew Jayson spoke the truth. Eventually he wouldn't have the crutch of another person to help him. The night Renee sent the text, he waited until he arrived at home so Chelsea could help him send a reply.

"I'll think about it," he said.

He'd missed out on opportunities over the years because of his limitation, such as opportunities that would have afforded him the chance to grow his business. Something had to change. If he didn't make the effort now, he'd miss out on other opportunities, including one that was about to slip through his fingers.

Finding love again.

RENEE SAT QUIETLY in Adelaide's sunny den on the sofa, appreciative when her friend brought over a cup of coffee and set it on the table in front of her.

"I can't believe he still hasn't called," Adelaide said, settling beside her.

Adelaide was in full Mama Bear mode, which was why Renee was glad she'd come to see her. She needed her friend's soothing voice and calming words to get her through the rest of the week. The past few days had been difficult. Not a peep out of Clive, though she'd spotted him a couple of times through her office window as he drove out of the subdivision.

A perpetual numbness took over her body, and she remained stunned and confused. What happened? What could she have done differently? But he would have to reach out, not her.

"Maybe I shouldn't have pushed him to attend the reading with me. He told me he didn't want to go."

"Don't do that. You had every right to expect the man you're involved with to attend an event with you. If he can't make small concessions, then he won't be able to make big concessions. Relationships involve compromise, otherwise why bother? You'll always be bumping heads."

"You're right. I'm just trying to make sense of what happened." Renee sipped the coffee.

"Did you actually break up, or are the two of you simply not speaking to each other?"

"I have no idea." Renee shrugged.

"I know you really care about Clive and this situation is upsetting, but you're a great woman. You're a strong woman."

"No." Renee's voice cracked and she couldn't speak for several seconds. When she spoke again, she appealed to Adelaide with tear-filled eyes. "I don't want to be strong. Why can't I feel weak and vulnerable and tired? Do you know what I want? I want to be liked. I want to be loved. Why can't I find a man to love me?"

Three failed marriages. Over and done. A new relationship that she thought—hoped—was going in the right direction, over. The common denominator: Renee. There was no one to blame but her, and she didn't know what she'd done wrong, so she couldn't fix the issue. Her heart ached for Clive—with his rough edges and macho attitude, tattoos, a pickup truck, and worn jeans. None of those things had appealed to her before, until he came along.

Adelaide took her right hand in both of hers. "You're a generous spirit, and they don't know what to do with a woman like you."

Renee wiped a tear from her cheek. "Or maybe they don't want a woman like me. Independent. Outspoken. Accomplished. I intimidate them."

"So what are you going to do? Your first two husbands were professors and the last one a corporate attorney. This man is a retired contractor. You've been in serious relationships with men in academia, a white-collar man, and a blue-collar man."

"So then it's me?" Renee said.

"*No.* You can't change. You'll find someone who appreciates you the way you are, and you'll be fine. Please don't contort yourself into someone else to fit a blueprint that frankly doesn't exist."

Renee rested her head on her friend's shoulder and sighed. "What do I do in the meantime? I miss him, and he's right next door."

A single woman raising three kids on her own, her mother always told her: *"You don't need no man."* Because of her, Renee and her siblings learned to be independent and care for themselves while their mother worked.

She didn't need a man, but she wanted this one.

Adelaide patted her shoulder. "He might come around, and remember, you don't know what he might be going through. But whatever you do, give yourself time to heal, okay? No matter how good being with Clive felt, he might not be the right man for you."

"He sure felt like it," Renee whispered.

"Time. Give yourself some time," Adelaide said.

17

C live regretted taking advantage of being alone in the house. He sat in the quiet kitchen, staring at the workbook he pulled out of a box in the closet upstairs. He couldn't remember the last time he'd looked at it, and the past hour reminded him of why. The harder he tried, the more difficult reading the words became.

Would he ever get it? Would he ever get past these moments of complete and utter frustration?

He slammed his fist on the table. Slammed it again. Then he stood and upended the table in anger. It crashed to the floor, scattering the workbook and pencils with it. Chest heaving, he wondered why none of his teachers had expressed the same care and consideration for him as Renee did for her students.

As a lifelong athlete, teachers had always let him slide, pushing him through to the next grade because he scored touchdowns or ran for record-breaking yards on the field. Few people cared about his academics when his physical prowess meant trophies and championships.

Clive stepped away and braced his hands on the kitchen counter.

Success seemed so far away. The same thoughts flooded his brain that had appeared for years.

Learning to read was too hard.

I'm too old.

I'll never be able to get this.

He stared down at his hands gripping the counter, so hard his knuckles turned white. Slowly, he loosened his grip and remembered the helpless feeling he'd experienced the other day when he went fishing with Jayson. The longing to be able to—just once—read a book with his granddaughter.

Frustration built inside him until the pressure mounted behind his skull. Clive rubbed a hand across his forehead and let out a heavy breath of resignation.

How many more regrets was he destined to have in life? Despite the excellent work he did, his construction business had never grown beyond him and Margaret. Opportunities to expand had passed him by because of the fears caused by his limitations.

Then of course, there was the current situation with Renee. Another opportunity lost, another regret. He still wasn't sure how to repair that fractured relationship. Tell the truth or stick to the bull-shit explanation he'd given her about not being interested in the event?

Clive righted the table and picked up the workbook and the pencils. He took the educational supplies into his bedroom and placed them back in the box.

He could no longer let pride and embarrassment keep him from reaching his full potential. He recalled Renee's words from a while back: *anything is possible if we work hard enough.*

Clive needed help to get the work done, and he knew where to find it.

He found the number in his wallet that his daughter had given him a few days ago. He stared at it for a minute, still unsure. Still petrified of failure.

After dialing the number, Clive pressed zero to bypass the main menu recording.

A cheerful male voice came on the line. "Hello, San Diego Adult Learning Center. How may I help you?"

The sound of the welcoming voice eased his anxiety, and Clive loosened his grip on the phone.

"Hello, my name is Clive Stevenson. I heard you have literacy classes."

"We sure do. Would you like to sign up?"

His gut tightened, but he forced out the words. "Yes, I'd like to sign up. I...I want to learn to read."

SAMSON HAD RETURNED.

He ran back and forth in front of the window as if trying to get Renee's attention, though she was looking right at him. She and the dog had become good friends ever since he saved her from potential bodily harm by the burglars. But he hadn't come over in a while, ever since she and Clive had the fight.

Ten days had passed since that night, but if she didn't know better, she'd say one hundred days had passed. She missed him so much—literally ached with the need to talk to him, to understand what had happened.

She was angry, too. Angry that he hadn't reached out or apologized or properly explained. The more she thought about the abrupt way their relationship had ended—because clearly it had ended—the angrier she became. He should have never kissed her in her home. He should have never given her hope that she could have a different kind of relationship—one filled with humor and hot sex and comfortable nights sitting on the sofa watching TV.

Renee collected a couple of dog treats she now kept on hand. When she exited the house, Samson raced over, tail wagging, and eagerly accepted the snacks. She scratched behind his ear and rubbed on his head and sides, working up the nerve to take him next door.

Across the street, Jim stood at his mailbox and waved. "Hey,

Renee, I'll have this grass cut soon. Lawn mower's not working. Thought I could get it fixed, but the guy at the shop said there's no saving it, so I'm going to pick up another one this weekend."

She hadn't even noticed the overgrown grass. "Get to it when you can."

His mouth fell open and he stared at her. "Are you sure?" he asked slowly.

"I'm sure, Jim. Have a good one." She grasped Samson's collar and headed over to Clive's.

She rang the doorbell and Margie opened the door, welcoming her with a wide grin. "Hi, Miss Joseph."

"Hi, honey. Is your grandpa home?"

Margie nodded vigorously, opening the door wider. "Come in."

Renee shook her head. "I'm going to stay out here. Would you call him for me, please."

"Okay." Leaving the door open, Margie hurried off with Samson in tow.

Renee lifted her head higher and straightened her back as she waited for Clive to come to the door.

When she saw him coming toward her through the open door, a little whimper of pain escaped her throat. No man had a right to look so good in a snug-fitting black T-shirt and a pair of jeans that hinted at his powerful thighs.

"Hi, Renee," he said quietly. He stepped out and closed the door. Now that he was closer, she saw bags under his eyes, and his normally vibrant green eyes appeared dull and lifeless.

"Hello, Clive." Clenching her fingers at her sides, she fought the urge to reach for him.

He studied her with something akin to concern in his eyes, which irritated her.

"There's no need to be worried about me. I was fine before you came into my life, and I'm fine now."

"I know that, and I've been meaning to talk to you."

"There's nothing for us to talk about, so don't bother with your lame excuses. I'm a person who likes closure, and this is how I'll get it, by telling you what I think about you. You pretend to be all macho and strong, but you can't even speak to me after our fight. I've been waiting for you to say something—something meaningful. Then it dawned on me. You're not going to, because for whatever reason, you can't handle a woman like me. I thought you were different, but you're not. You're a numbskull—your words—like my ex-husbands were.

"I'm not what you want, and that's fine. But you know what, that's your loss. I'm a good person. I'm kind, smart, loyal, funny, and generous. And if you don't like any of that, then too bad. I'm going to find someone who does. Goodbye. For good."

She swung around and started toward her house.

"Renee, wait!"

He grasped her arm and she slapped away his hand.

"Do not touch me." Her voice vibrated with anger and pain. She took off again toward the house.

"I'm sorry. Let me explain."

"The time for explaining is over." She opened the door and turned to face him. She didn't want to break down in front of him, but the crushing loss of losing him was almost unbearable. "Get the hell out of my yard, and keep your damn dog in yours!"

She slammed the door in his face.

18

D espite the proud tilt to her head and the firm words, Clive heard the tremor in her voice and saw the pain in those beautiful brown eyes.

To think he'd caused that pain not only shamed him, but caused him pain, too. The last thing he had ever wanted to do was hurt Renee. Equally painful was knowing she thought he didn't appreciate the type of woman she was, when in fact he did. Hell, he didn't deserve her.

He flattened his palm on the door. "Renee, hear me out. Please."

The only response was silence.

"Renee!"

Nothing.

He knocked and rang the doorbell.

Still nothing.

Knowing Renee, she'd leave him out there all night without a second thought, but she couldn't stay inside forever.

Clive went back to the house. He'd catch her the next time she left.

The opportunity arrived less than two hours later while he was at the mailbox getting the mail. Her garage door slowly lifted, and he seized the opportunity.

Clive shoved the mail back in the box and hurried over to stand in front of the car. He was taking a huge risk. She might very well run him over.

She rolled slowly forward and honked the horn, but he didn't move. His stomach tightened as she edged closer, but he didn't move, staring right back at her as she glared at him.

Finally, she slammed on the brakes, the car jerking to a stop only inches from his knees. Clive let out a relieved breath.

Renee leaned out of the window. "Get out of my way!"

"Not until you hear me out."

"You've had plenty of time to talk and you didn't."

"I want to talk now."

"Well, I don't want to talk."

"Well, I'm not moving."

She stared at him through the windshield, and he folded his arms and waited. Rolling her eyes, she shifted the car into park and stepped out.

"What do you want to say?"

"Not here. Let's go inside."

"No. I don't have time for that. I'm very busy. Let's get this over with right here."

"Renee, if you don't go inside with me willingly, I'm going to lift your ass up and take you inside. And we both know I can carry you with no issue."

She tightened her lips and cast her eyes downward, but he didn't miss the brief flash of heat that sent a pulse of awareness through him. He wanted to take her in his arms, kiss away the hurt and beg for forgiveness, but he knew their reconciliation would not be that easy. At the very least, he had to take a chance that she would under-stand his predicament and forgive him for being a coward.

Without a word, she grabbed her purse, locked the car, and led the way back into the house through the garage. The entire time, he fixated on the way the cream linen pants fit over her hips and complemented the shape of her ass. She wore a gold link belt, gold sandals, and a burgundy blouse.

She'd had a haircut recently. Her hair was tapered extra short in the back and stacked in shiny, lustrous curls. He missed messing up her hair with his fingers or having her sweat out her neatly arranged style. Whether she was freshly dressed and put together like now, or laughing as they lay in bed together—her hair flat and face makeup free—Renee was a sexy woman.

He couldn't let her go yet. Seeing her up close and hearing her voice again had reminded him of how much he needed her and how empty the past couple of weeks had been without her.

Clive trailed Renee into the living room. "Where are you headed?"

She tossed down her purse and rested her hands on her hips. "None of your business."

"You look amazing."

"Don't try to flatter me," she said in an arctic tone.

Fair enough. He had work to do.

"I'm sorry I left you at the hotel restaurant, but there's something you should know. I didn't respond to you because I...uh...I didn't, I couldn't, read the text."

"What do you mean you couldn't read the text? You got it, didn't you?" she asked irritably.

"You don't understand." He took a deep breath, closing his eyes and then opened them again to look at her. "I couldn't read the text, Renee."

"I heard you the first time." Her eyes widened. "Oh. Are you saying...?"

"Yes, that's what I'm saying," he said harshly.

Her mouth fell open. "Clive, why didn't you tell me?"

"If you were me... No, if our roles were reversed, would you have told me?"

She remained silent.

He exhaled and pulled in a little more courage with the next inhaled breath. "I can read a little bit, but not much. Struggled in school my whole life, but because I was an athlete, they let me sail through. I never wanted you to find out and figured I could delay that as long as possible. But the night of the reading event, it hit me how much more educated than me you were. So that's it."

"That's why you use the recorder. That's why you had me write down my name and number."

He nodded, heat burning his cheeks. When she looked at him with sympathy-filled eyes, he snapped, "Don't do that! I'm not stupid!"

"I never said you were. I don't think you are."

They were both silent for a few seconds, neither looking at the other until she asked softly, "Does anyone else know?"

"Very few people," he admitted. "Sometimes I can figure words out, but it's a struggle. I want to be able to read stories with my grand-daughter and help her with her homework when Chelsea's at work, but sometimes I think it's too late. I don't have the brain necessary to learn what I need to. I'm too old."

"You're never too old. Have you considered taking classes?"

"I signed up for classes at the Adult Literacy Center. I've signed up before and didn't do well, but I decided to try again."

He hoped the classes weren't a waste of time again, but one thing he did notice, there were a lot more people than the first time he tried. Maybe the stigma was disappearing from illiteracy, but he saw all ethnic groups, young, old, and in-between.

"I can help, if you want," Renee said gently.

"I couldn't ask you to do that."

"You didn't. I offered."

"No."

"I'm a teacher, for goodness' sake."

"I need to do this on my own, once and for all."

She rubbed her hands together. "Thank you for telling me. My opinion of you hasn't changed. If you'd told me in the first place, I would have offered to help then. You don't have to hide who you are from me. I like you the way you are."

He smiled in relief. "You're an amazing woman, Renee. I like you just the way you are, too, and I'm damn sorry I didn't have the courage to tell you sooner. I've gotten so used to hiding my limitations over the years, I naturally did it, even after we became closer. Matter of fact, the closer we became, the more amazing I realized you are, and the more I wanted to hide that part of myself."

"I don't want you to hide any part of yourself."

"I don't want to, either. I promise to work hard as hell when I'm in these classes. Something has to change, and a wise woman once told me that anything is possible if we work hard enough."

Her lips broadened into a smile. "Sounds like something I would say."

He moved closer. "Is it? I'm not sure where I heard that."

She tilted her head back to smile up at him. "I'm pretty sure I'm the wise woman you heard that from."

He chuckled, pulling her soft body against his and sliding his arms up the curve of her back. "I missed you. Damn, I missed you."

"I couldn't tell," Renee said with a pout.

"I was still deciding whether or not I was going to tell you the truth. Time slipped away from me, but don't doubt that I missed you. You really are an amazing woman, and if you didn't know already, I'm falling in love with you."

Her eyes widened and she bit her bottom lip. "I'm falling in love with you, too, and I absolutely didn't expect it."

"Well, that's because I'm so lovable."

She threw back her head and laughed. He squeezed her closer, kissing and then sucking the tender skin of her neck as he inhaled her intoxicating perfume.

"That you are," she said softly.

ADELAIDE & HECTOR

1

"Honey, I'm fine. Your father and I have been divorced for six months. You don't have to keep checking on me." Adelaide held the phone to her ear, a tote bag of groceries on her shoulder as she entered the house through the door leading from the garage.

Her only daughter, Karen, was on the phone. She'd gone to New York after college to start a career in theater and been out there for a year but hadn't had much luck so far. She was certainly talented, but there were thousands—possibly millions—of Karens in the Big Apple with the same talent, drive, and hunger for success.

"I check on you and Dad because I want to make sure you're both okay. My new roommate, Monica? Her parents divorced after years together, too, and four months later her father ended up with a shiny red Corvette and an Instagram model. Her mother wound up following the rock band Imagine Dragons across the country."

"Sounds like fun," Adelaide joked as she plopped the bag on the counter.

"Not funny, Mom. I want you and Dad to be normal, please."

"We'll be normal, I promise."

"Okay, fine. I'll stop worrying. Maybe. Have you heard from Junior?"

Karen's twin, Hector Jr., was a wildlife photographer and currently on location in Botswana.

"We talked a few days ago, and he emailed a link to pictures he uploaded to the cloud. You didn't see them?"

"No. Why doesn't he send a text, like normal people? Oh, I know, because our parents prefer to use email like it's the Stone Age."

"I see you haven't lost your charm."

Karen laughed. "By the way, Monica wants to know if you'd like to adopt her. The carrot cake and cookies you sent last week have convinced her to sever ties with her own family to join ours."

Monica had only been living with Karen and their other roommate for a few months, ever since the last young woman gave up on her entertainment dreams and moved back home. Since Monica moved in, Adelaide had sent cookies, chocolate cake, and an apple crumb cake as well. She was used to this type of reaction because few things gave her as much pleasure as cooking and baking, and she was gifted at both.

That's why, on a whim, she'd stopped on her way home and picked up a multi-page brochure from the School of Culinary Arts. The school offered classes for newbies and seasoned cooks. She toyed with the idea of starting her own catering service and having a diploma would give her credibility. She placed it on the counter with the intention of reviewing it later.

Adelaide pulled pasta and fresh tomatoes out of the bag. "Tell Monica I'm sorry, but I'm not looking for any more children at the moment. Well, I might be in the market for a new daughter if my current daughter doesn't act right and stop calling me with unwarranted concerns about my mental health."

"Ha, ha. I call because I love you."

The chime of the security monitor snagged her attention. Adelaide set the tomatoes in a bowl on the counter and checked the screen. "Danny's here. He's parking his car."

"Let me talk to the little knucklehead."

"Hold on."

Daniel was home for the summer and would be entering his sophomore year once classes resumed in the fall. Exiting the gray Nissan, he looked dispirited with his shoulders slouched, hands shoved into his jeans, and his head bent. His head full of curly hair appeared much more disheveled than when he'd left the house earlier to go see his girlfriend.

He entered the kitchen.

"Hey, honey."

Dull eyes met hers. Something was wrong.

"Hey, Mom."

"Karen's on the phone. She wants to say hi."

Adelaide handed over the phone and proceeded to finish unpacking the groceries while listening to Daniel's end of the conversation and keeping an eye on him. He only offered monosyllabic responses to Karen's enthusiastic chatter, and their conversation ended around the same time she finished putting away the groceries.

"What do you want for dinner? You can have meatloaf or meatloaf." She grinned, expecting her attempt at humor to elicit a smile, but none came. Sad brown eyes met hers. "Honey, what's wrong?"

"Promise you won't get mad."

Conversations that started with those kinds of requests were not a good sign.

"I can't promise that."

"Never mind then." Daniel ducked his head and turned to walk away.

Adelaide quickly closed the distance between them and grabbed his arm. "Danny, what's going on? Are you in some kind of trouble?"

"I don't want to talk about it," he mumbled, attempting to squeeze past her.

Adelaide blocked his escape and placed a hand on her hip. "Well, we're going to talk about it. What don't you want me to get upset about? Look at me."

He lifted his gaze and his jaw settled into a firm line. He looked so much like his father then—a younger, darker version with curlier hair, but the same mouth, nose, and brown eyes.

"Nothing. I'll figure it out myself."

Right then, Adelaide decided that whatever the problem, she'd do her best to help him through it. Her voice gentled. "Danny, if you're in some kind of trouble, you need to tell me so I can help."

He blinked rapidly and then roughly wiped his eyes with the sleeve of his denim jacket.

"Please, what's wrong, baby?" She placed a comforting hand on his shoulder.

"I messed up, Mom." He lifted his gaze.

He'd messed up before, and she hoped they'd be able to overcome this particular screwup—whatever it was—like they had all the others.

"It's okay. We'll figure it out. How did you mess up?" Her stomach tightened as she waited for his answer.

"Jamie's pregnant," he whispered, dropping his gaze to the tiled floor.

Adelaide gasped and her heart sank. "Jamie's what?"

"Pregnant. Please don't tell Dad." He looked up at her with pleading eyes.

Adelaide pressed a hand to her forehead. "Oh, my goodness, Danny. Of course I have to tell your father. This isn't exactly something I can keep from him."

"But he'll get upset and yell at me."

"That's not a reason for me to keep the news from him. He'll find out eventually. The sooner the better." She didn't think it was possible, but his shoulders slumped even more, but his sadness was not enough to quell her anger and disappointment. "What were you thinking?"

He shrugged. "I guess I wasn't."

"No, you weren't." Adelaide crossed her arms and paced past him to the window overlooking the back patio. She pivoted and faced him. "You are a nineteen-year-old college sophomore who is having a baby with a girl who just graduated high school. What about your future? What about hers? How are you going to support this child? Did you think about any of this while you were being careless?"

"Mom!"

Startled out of her tirade, she saw tears in his eyes.

"Not now. Please." Daniel swallowed hard.

She was a hypocrite, reaming him out when she and Hector had only been a year older than him and unmarried when they got pregnant with Junior and Karen. Right now he did not need her anger. He needed support. The type of support she and Hector hadn't received when they were having their babies.

Remembering how hard that period had been, Adelaide opened her arms and Daniel rushed over. She enclosed him in her embrace. "We'll figure it out," she whispered.

She couldn't hear him crying, but felt the tears where he'd pressed his face against her neck.

"But you have to tell your father."

Daniel lifted his head and swiped at his tear-streaked face. "Would you talk to him for me, please? He's gonna kill me."

Nothing so dramatic would happen, but she understood why he was worried. Hector had not been pleased with Daniel the past few years. Neither had she, but her ex-husband was much more vocal. During Daniel's last year in high school, his grades had fallen off, and he'd started getting into all sorts of trouble.

"Danny, you need to tell him yourself."

"He's going to be so disappointed."

"Of course, but that doesn't mean you shouldn't tell him."

"I can't." He shook his head vigorously.

"Honey—"

"Please, Mom, could you tell him for me? Please?"

His red-rimmed eyes made him look very young and softened her heart. She cupped his face. "Fine. Yes, I'll tell him."

He let out a sigh. "Thanks, Mom."

He gave her a tight, grateful hug, but minutes later Adelaide was all alone in the kitchen, contemplating the conversation with her ex-husband. She'd only talked to Hector once in the past six months, and the conversation had been brief. This should be interesting.

She picked the School of Culinary Arts brochure and thumbed the pages. No rush. She'd have time to work on this later. Right now, her son needed his mother. Her kids were her life. She hadn't failed them in all these years, and she was not about to start now.

She opened one of the drawers and tossed the brochure inside.

2

Hector parked his gray Jeep Cherokee in the driveway next to his son's Nissan.

Stepping out of the vehicle, he loosened his tie, which suddenly felt restrictive. It was the end of the work day and he still wore a suit and tie after a day spent in meetings. He had rushed out of the last one so he wouldn't be late.

The very quiet Bayview subdivision contained mostly one-story homes with three-car garages, and nothing had changed in the six months he'd been gone. All the houses were still well-maintained by their owners who had neatly trimmed lawns and bushes. Except for their house, which stood out like a sore thumb with its too-long grass. He'd have to find out what was going on. Technically, the house was no longer his business, but maybe Adelaide needed help.

He strolled to the front and let his gaze travel over the burgundy door. The original color had been gray, but Adelaide had wanted a different color, so he spent one Saturday morning painting the door and shutters the more vibrant color.

Scrubbing a hand over his face, he pushed away the memory and rang the bell. Seconds later, the door opened and he was gut-punched by Adelaide's soft, hesitant smile.

"Hi," she said.

"Hi."

Damn. She looked like...his Adelaide. Often mistaken for a woman in her thirties, she was sexy and beautiful in a pretty blouse splashed with dark and light flowers all over it and dark jeans that enveloped her hips and hugged the lines of her waist. She wore her long hair in a ponytail, which perfectly displayed the beauty of her round face, bright and pretty hazel eyes, and a mouth that was wide and full and inviting.

Hector hadn't seen her since they signed the papers in the attorney's office and went their separate ways in the parking lot, like strangers. They talked once in the interim because she had a question about the mechanic who'd worked on her car before. He used to be in charge of taking their cars in for repair, so he had easily answered the question and wished he could have kept her on the phone longer.

Adelaide stepped back. "Come in."

The bitter taste of irony forced a wry smile to Hector's face at the realization that he had to get permission to enter a house he thought he'd grow old in. The home he still thought of as *their* home.

Inside, he was immediately hit by the inviting scent of pineapples. Adelaide believed their house should smell good, and she achieved that with air fresheners in every room.

He followed her to the bright kitchen that opened into the great room. She'd added yellow pillows to the two white sofas. The gold and white curtains covering the sliding glass door and large windows were open to give an unobstructed view of the covered patio.

A few years ago they'd added the covering. He set up a gas grill, bought a table, chairs, and a sofa, and *voilà*—Adelaide had an outdoor space to spend time with her friends and for the few times a year they entertained. They'd remodeled the kitchen the same year, opting for white appliances and white cabinets with nickel knobs. Everything looked pretty and shiny, conveying the message that all was well in the Flores home, when in reality it hadn't been.

Hector sat on one of the backless stools at the kitchen counter.

"Okay, I'm here. Care to tell me what's going on? You were mighty secretive about why you wanted me to come over."

Adelaide walked to the opposite side of the counter. "Would you like something to drink? Water? Lemonade?"

"I don't want anything to drink. I want to know what's going on, and why you needed me to come over to talk about 'something important.'"

He wasn't upset, but maybe a little worried. Was there something wrong with her? The kids?

"I'll tell you in a second."

She pulled a jug of lemonade from the refrigerator and he watched her backside in the snug fitting jeans. Erotic memories fast-tracked through his brain—his dedication to her pleasure and her cries of passion when he succeeded. Overcome by the need to touch her, his eyes dropped to his clenched fingers on the granite counter-top. Before he moved out, he'd experienced the same painful need to touch her but stayed away as if she'd been wrapped in a blanket of thorns. He still wasn't sure how they'd gotten to that point in their marriage. No touching. Barely talking.

Hector loosened his fingers. They'd done what they had to do. They'd drifted apart and divorce had been the right decision.

Adelaide placed a glass of lemonade in front of him. "I'm sorry for all the cloak-and-dagger, but this wasn't something I thought we should discuss over the phone. It's about Danny. He was very upset yesterday when he came home and told me what was wrong." She took a deep breath and Hector's abs tightened. "Jamie's pregnant. She's three months along, and the baby is due—"

"Pregnant!" This news was better than an illness, but not much better.

"Hector, calm down."

He stood and braced his hands on the counter. "He's out of control! He keeps screwing up. He made shitty grades the last year of high school, scraping by in math and science—classes he used to breeze through and could practically do in his sleep. He got in that fight and got suspended, and then the foolishness with spray-painting foul language on the outside of the school with his friends and getting caught as they left the school grounds. What's wrong with him? Matter of fact, is he here?"

"Yes, but he asked me to talk to you," Adelaide said, an exceptional example of calm compared to his intensely agitated reaction.

"So he couldn't tell me himself? He let you do it?"

She gestured at him. "Look at your reaction. Do you blame him? He needs our support, not condemnation."

Hector laughed and rested his hands on his hips. "Support. So what about school? Is he going to finish? And what about Jamie? What are her plans now that she'll be a mother in about six months? They're both kids, Addie." He cursed and stalked away, too wired to stand still.

This was not the path he'd wanted for his son, to make the same mistake he and Adelaide had made decades before. The boy had been making bad decisions for a while but this—this was too much. He and Adelaide had managed—together—because they'd been older and in love and wanted their kids. Were Danny and Jamie in love? What were their plans? How were they going to support a child?

Adelaide silently watched him.

"Does he plan to get a damn job? Does he have any plans at all? Babies are expensive."

"You and I both know that, and I think he and Jamie can learn from what happened to us. We need to help them."

"Are you suggesting we financially support them?"

"They're going to need help," Adelaide said, sounding frustrated and in disbelief that he didn't understand that point.

"I'm not parting with a dime, except a few gifts for the baby. Danny can get a job." Hector cursed under his breath.

"So we should turn our backs on them?"

"That's not what I said, but when you make adult decisions, you deal with the adult consequences, and come up with adult solutions."

Adelaide stared down into her glass of lemonade on the counter.

"I'm not wrong, Addie."

Her gaze met his. "Do you remember what it was like for us? How hard it was that first year without any help? We both had to leave school."

When Adelaide became pregnant, she'd been frantic, but Hector had been excited and insisted they get married. She'd been hesitant and put him off, unsure if marriage was the right decision for them because they'd been together less than a year by then. Plus, she'd had her family to contend with. Her father was a workaholic and her mother found solace from her miserable marriage inside of a gin bottle. Because her father's ambition meant getting transfers to accommodate his promotions, Adelaide lived in four states and seven cities from the age of ten until she graduated high school.

As the oldest of four, she became the default babysitter and surrogate mother who whipped up delicious meals for her younger siblings. When her parents learned she was pregnant at twenty, they had both expressed their disappointment and said they'd 'expected more from her.'

After the kids were born, Adelaide took them to see her parents, but Junior and Karen were almost eighteen months old before they saw them again in person.

"That was a decision we made together. I promised you if you stayed home and took care of our kids, I'd make sure you didn't have to work. Even if it meant working ten jobs, I'd do whatever I had to do to make sure we—our family—was okay." A man took care of his family. That lesson had been drilled into his head by his father.

Adelaide placed a hand on her hip and her lips tightened. "I know you don't want any of our kids to go through what we did. Yes, Danny has been screwing up and hasn't exactly lived up to the ideal we set for all our kids. I get it, Hector. But I'm his mother, and this is where we are. I'm not going to throw him in the middle of the ocean and tell him figure out how to swim, and I know you won't, either. That's not the type of man you are."

Dammit. Hector gritted his teeth.

Adelaide could always break him down with one of her calm, no-nonsense speeches. She was a natural caretaker, always looking out for others. Maybe because she didn't have that type of support and love growing up.

After a resigned sigh, Hector muttered, "I do remember what it was like to be in this very situation."

He had to admit that when he learned they were having twins, he'd experienced a moment of panic. One child would be tough, but two? His family in Mexico hadn't been able to offer any help, and her family had offered no help.

The moment of panic was fleeting. He'd already known he would marry Adelaide, and the thought of starting a family with her only made him more determined to get started on the life he'd been planning. She'd been the one since he saw her in a crowded movie theater sitting alone.

Hector took a seat and sipped the lemonade, wishing it was a double shot of whiskey.

"What's our next step?"

3

"How do you think that went?" Adelaide thought the conversation went well but was curious to hear Hector's opinion.

Surprisingly, he had held his temper in check and talked calmly to their son. She believed his self-control eased Daniel's fears, because after a hesitant start, the three of them sat around the coffee table in the living room and their son opened up. They discussed options and came to the tentative resolution that Daniel would leave school, get a job, and stay with Adelaide to save money.

They also called Jamie and talked to her grandmother, whom she had lived with since she was eleven. Hector and Adelaide let them both know they were ready and able to help Jamie, emotionally and financially.

After a few words, Daniel went to his room to continue talking to Jamie, and Adelaide walked Hector out to his car.

"Good. Definitely could have been worse," Hector replied.

His voice sounded grim and she glanced at him. He'd draped his jacket and tie over his arm. Over the years, he'd changed a lot and yet only changed a little.

The dress shirt hugged his tight body and the waistband of the black trousers emphasized his narrow waist. His hair was still the same midnight color it had been when they met, and his face still carried the perfect symmetry of a square jaw, an aquiline nose, and the piercing dark brown eyes of the man she'd married. But there were lines around his eyes now and a somberness in their depths that never used to be there.

He had the same physique, his body a tight mass of muscle that hadn't softened much since their twenties. She could barely look at him without thinking about running her fingers over his hard body or climbing on top of him as his long-fingered hands gripped her hips.

Or—she swallowed as heat swept her skin—her favorite position, where she lay on her back and those same hands gripped her wrists above her head as he used masterful strokes to bring her closer to an earth-shattering climax.

She missed their lovemaking, but she also missed him. God, how she missed him. In all their years together, she'd never slept apart from Hector. Even when they were angry with each other, they shared the same bed. She never sent him to sleep on the couch, and he never went to sleep in another bedroom. Maybe it was habit, or maybe just the comfort of knowing that no matter what happened, even when they were mad, they'd still lie side by side. They were still husband and wife.

Arguments, cold shoulders, and a separation disrupted the harmony in their marriage. The divorce made the changes final. She'd be sleeping alone for the foreseeable future.

Adelaide crossed her arms and forced her thoughts into the present. "I'm a bit concerned about Danny leaving school. He doesn't have to do that if we're helping him."

"I don't like it, either, but you should be glad that he's being so responsible."

"He's still a baby," Adelaide murmured.

"Our baby is about to have a baby."

Adelaide frowned. "Why are you so hard on him?"

"Why are you so easy on him? He's nineteen, not nine. It's time he learns to be responsible and understand that Mommy and Daddy are not always going to be here to help him. What better time to learn that than when he's about to have a child himself? Danny has never had to be responsible for anything."

"That's not true."

"Karen and Junior had part-time jobs and summer jobs while in high school, and they both worked while in college. Danny had a summer job mowing lawns and quit because it was too hard. He's lazy."

Adelaide faced him fully. "He is not lazy. It's just that we provided everything for him."

"We?" Hector chuckled softly and gazed across at the street at the neighbor's house.

"What are you trying to say?"

His dark eyes slid back to her. "You provide for all of his needs and indulge all of his whims."

"Are you suggesting that I'm a bad mother?" Adelaide whispered, aghast.

"Of course not. You're a terrific mother. But you've gotta give our kid a chance to grow up. Let him breathe."

She crossed her arms and glared at him. He was belittling her one accomplishment—being a mother. "Excuse me for wanting our kid to be okay. He's not like Karen and Junior. Different children require different rearing, even if they're in the same family. I'm sorry if my parenting skills are not up to your standards."

Hector muttered a curse and ran his fingers through his hair, a sure sign of his frustration. She could always tell if he had a good day or bad day at work by the condition of his hair when he walked through the door.

"I don't want to fight with you," Hector said wearily.

"I don't want to fight with you either," Adelaide snapped, not sounding at all sincere.

Tightening her arms around her torso, she refused to look at him. Being around him for the first time in months had her...itching for something. A fight, or something else, she wasn't sure. There were so many things she wanted to say—to yell at him. She wasn't sure what those words would be exactly, but it was a long list if she ever put it all together.

"What's going on with the lawn?" Hector asked.

Surprised by the change in topic, Adelaide's gaze swept the front of the house. "Sam moved away. I received recommendations from two of the neighbors, but when I called, the guys said they can't take on any more customers." She shrugged.

"How long has Sam been gone?"

"Almost a month."

She avoided looking at him, like before the divorce. Classical conflict avoidance. Avoid looking. Avoid talking. Avoid touching.

Adelaide rubbed the back of her neck. She was ready for him to leave, yet she couldn't walk away because she wanted him to stay. She was a mess.

"Danny hasn't offered to cut the lawn for you?" Her eyes finally met Hector's pensive gaze. Hector believed a man should work, and he had worked since the age of fourteen.

"He just got back from school." She shot him a look that warned he should drop the subject. Of course he didn't pay attention.

"This is what I'm talking about," he said, gesturing with his hand. "He's here, he's not working, our son can absolutely help you with the lawn, at the very least."

"Or I could just as easily have done it myself."

"You? The woman I was married to for twenty-five years, who I happen to know hates yard work? Danny and I will take care of the lawn. He'll cut, I'll edge."

"What?" His offer to help surprised her. "You don't have to do that."

"I know, but it needs to be done."

That's the kind of man he was. A gets-things-done kind of man. From the moment she'd told him she was pregnant, he started planning their future, and she went along with his every decision—confident and secure she was in good hands. After all, she had no one else.

A year after he moved out, she still didn't know what to do with herself.

Hence, the culinary arts course. It would be hers, and she'd be damn good at it. If she ever got the courage to actually sign up for the classes.

Hector looked up at the sky and then checked his watch. "If we start now, we can finish before it gets dark. I'm going to get Danny."

He didn't wait for her response. He went into the house, and Adelaide stayed outside.

She should have told him no. She'd find someone to cut the grass or she'd do it with Daniel. But she'd remained silent. Because in addition to missing him in her bed or hearing his comforting voice in the house, she missed the little things she'd taken for granted when they lived together.

Something as simple as fastening a bracelet on her wrist had become an effort in acrobatics, and there were so many other tasks he used to take care of. He took out the trash the night before pickup. Washed her car. For years she'd never had to put gas in her car because he made sure she had a full tank when the gauge dropped below the halfway point.

He was old-fashioned, but she didn't mind. They both had their roles, and they willingly and happily filled them. Delineating tasks worked for them.

That's what that itchy, uncomfortable feeling meant. Having him here reminded her of how much she missed...and needed him.

4

Adelaide went out into the front yard carrying two bottles of ice-cold water.

"Thanks, Mom," Daniel said, taking one.

"Thanks." Hector's fingers grazed hers as he took the second bottle. The shock of touching her skin, even for that brief moment, was so great that he almost dropped the bottle. She stepped away quickly, almost too quickly, and put their son between them.

Hector took an appreciative swig of the water.

"What do you think, Mom?"

"It looks like a brand-new lawn," she gushed.

Adelaide had a way of making you feel as if the simplest accomplishment was a feat of gigantic proportions, but the yard did look 100 percent better. He and Daniel gave the front and back yards a facelift. With the work they'd done, they could easily be in contention for the neighborhood beautification award.

Adelaide ran a hand over their son's head, playing with his curls until he squirmed out of her grasp. "Quit, Mom!" He swatted away her hand and dodged when she reached for him again.

They both laughed, as if Hector wasn't there. How ridiculous that he was jealous of this moment between his ex-wife and his son, but the need to be touched in the same way—letting her fingers run through his hair like they used to—the need to receive her playful smile—burned bright inside him.

Hector finished the water with two huge swallows.

"I'm going to take a shower before I head over to Jamie's. See you later, Dad."

"Bye, son."

They bumped fists and Daniel entered the house, which meant once again he and his ex-wife were all alone. Adelaide's gaze followed their son.

"He's going to be fine," Hector said.

"I know. I can't help but worry, though." She sent a tentative smile in his direction. "Can you believe we're going to be grandparents already? We used to joke about wanting a bunch of grandkids in our golden years."

"Yeah, but I figured I'd be a little more golden than this," Hector said.

"Me, too." Adelaide laughed, and seeing that smile on her face lifted his spirits.

"About the meeting with Jamie and her grandmother, we should get on the same page before we meet with them."

Adelaide nodded. "Agreed."

"So we should probably discuss strategy at some point."

"This isn't a business meeting, Hector," she chided lightly.

"I know, but you know how I get."

"Yes. You're already figuring out how to tackle this problem."

He laughed, unable to deny the truth of the words. *Dios,* when was the last time he'd laughed? Really laughed like this?

"Thank you for helping out today. I appreciate it," Adelaide said quietly.

Their eyes met for a few seconds, and a twist of longing tightened his chest. He enjoyed spending time with her, feeling useful again, appreciated, needed. If this was all he could have right now, he'd take it until the feeling of loss faded and he could be normal again. He hadn't been happy in so long, he'd forgotten what that felt like.

"You're welcome. Any time."

HECTOR WALKED SLOWLY up the walkway to his ground floor apartment and turned the key. He was home, but received no pleasure because the woman he'd loved for the better part of his life was not here.

"Yoohoo, Hector, how are you today?" The woman in the apartment next to his had peeped her head out the door.

He sighed internally. "Great, Rita, and you?"

"Oh, taking it one day at a time. I'm going to my ballroom dancing class tonight. You're welcome to come if you like. You'd actually be doing us a favor because we have a shortage of male dancers." She smiled.

She was a little plump, with a ready smile for everyone, and brunette hair cut in a pixie style that accentuated her features. Not bad-looking, either. They'd slept together once, and he'd felt like a jerk for pushing her firmly back into the friend zone afterward, but he simply didn't have any interest in getting involved with anyone right now. He'd learned very quickly that jumping back into the dating game before he was ready was a terrible idea.

"Thanks, but I'll have to pass tonight, too. I have a lot of...business to take care of."

"Suit yourself. The offer remains open until whenever you choose to accept it."

Hector nodded and slipped into the apartment before she could say another word.

Rita had been friendly from the day he moved in and before sleeping with her, he'd made the mistake of accepting a casserole from her the third week he lived in the apartment. He should have turned her down, but he didn't know how to cook shit except French toast and eggs and had been tired of eating out. Frozen dinners had lost their charm. He'd been desperate for a home-cooked meal.

Adelaide had spoiled him. She'd done his laundry and every day he had come home to a hot meal. There were always leftovers in the refrigerator for him to snack on or eat late at night. She mended his clothes, organized and paid the bills. Kept the house clean and smelling good. In addition to missing her, he missed all those things she used to do to take care of their family.

Hell, he even missed the five thousand pillows she kept on the bed. He used to grumble about having to transfer them to the basket against the wall just to take a nap, but now he'd give anything to have that minor inconvenience again. Where would he find another woman he'd have that kind of synergy with?

Hector tossed his keys in the bowl at the door and stood in the living room of his one-bedroom apartment. Resting his hands on his hips, he wondered how he got here—a divorced man of forty-seven who was still in love with his ex-wife. Not a position he'd expected to find himself in this late in life.

Snorting with self-disgust, he went into the simply decorated white kitchen. Everything in the apartment was simple because he didn't want to spend more than he should, and he needed to support two households—his and Adelaide's.

He grabbed a beer from the fridge and sipped it while staring out the window at the parking lot. He'd pretty much fallen for Adelaide when he saw her enter a crowded movie theater and squeeze into one of two empty seats in the middle. He'd sat at the back with friends, watching and waiting to see if anyone else joined her. He finally worked up the nerve to stroll down the aisle and ease over to her.

"Is anyone sitting here?" he'd whispered.

Soft hazel eyes looked up at him and he lost his ability to speak. She responded in a sweet voice, "No, you can sit there."

Her hair was the same length now as back then, falling between her shoulder blades. After three kids and more than twenty years, her figure had changed. She'd put on a little weight and her body was fuller and more rounded. But she was still his Adelaide, the woman he'd watched in that crowded theater before ditching his friends and taking a leap of faith.

They became lovers right away, rushing headlong into a serious relationship that took them both by surprise. Like fireworks, they were explosive and hot from the start—almost obsessive in their need to be together all the time.

When she became pregnant, getting married not only seemed sensible, it was the logical progression of their relationship. He couldn't imagine spending his life with anyone else, and living alone had been hard as hell once he met her.

He couldn't stop thinking about her or stop the yearning that engulfed him when he laid in bed alone at night. It was downright brutal to come home to an empty apartment instead of the scent of air freshener and the sound of her sweet voice.

The oddest things made his chest hurt. Like the scent of vanilla or lemon. Those fragrances reminded him of the vanilla-lemon lotion she used to rub into her feet and hands every night. Even when they argued or got on each other's nerves, one of the few constants was lying in bed next to her and smelling her lotion. That's how he'd fallen asleep every night. But not anymore.

He supposed there were worse things in the world than being in love with your ex-wife.

But right now, he couldn't think of any.

5

"What are you doing?" Adelaide asked her reflection.

She was being silly. Hector was coming by to talk to her about Danny and Jamie and their next steps, not to take her on a date.

They'd talked a couple of times since he came to the house, and at the end of every conversation, she had the uncontrollable urge to scream and yell and kick in frustration. But during today's phone call, he stated that he was stopping by after work and had taken Adelaide by surprise, throwing her into a tizzy.

She critically assessed her appearance. She had let her hair fall across her shoulders in loose waves and applied a little bit of lipstick. She wore a dress she hadn't worn in a long time, a spaghetti-strapped maxi that skimmed her body and flowed loosely around her ankles.

Would he notice the way it fit? She was almost embarrassed to admit that she was trying to get his attention. Maybe make him regret the divorce? Hell, if she couldn't get his attention when they lived in the same house, she sure as hell couldn't capture it now that they were apart.

Living apart for a year hadn't diminished her feelings for Hector one iota. In fact, she was almost certain they'd intensified. She still loved her ex-husband, but she had asked for a divorce because in her mind, their marriage had ended long before.

Annoyed and frustrated, Adelaide tossed the dress on the bed and pulled on a pair of jeans and a black T-shirt. She couldn't remove the perfume she'd spritzed on, but did wipe off the lipstick and give herself a quick pep talk.

"You're attractive, even if your ex-husband doesn't think so."

The doorbell rang and she jumped. A fist of nerves pounding in her stomach, Adelaide went to the front of the house and opened the door.

"Hey there." Hearing his warm, accented voice brush over her skin, the bundle of nerves tightened in her belly. He had removed his jacket and wore the blue and gold tie she'd bought him two Christmases ago tugged loose around his neck. His dress shirt and pants were a little wrinkled, but they flattered his muscular build.

"Hi."

Adelaide wanted to do much more than give that simple greeting because he looked so handsome standing on her doorstep. One of his comforting hugs would be perfect right now, but she restrained herself from rushing into his arms by squeezing the doorknob tight.

"What's that?" She pointed to the white paper sack in his hand.

"I stopped at our—er, at Mona's Restaurant and picked up some tacos and a couple of quesadillas since you said you hadn't eaten yet. You still haven't eaten, right?"

He had almost said *our favorite restaurant,* but stopped himself. Funny how certain words automatically wanted to leave your mouth and you literally had to train yourself not to use them.

"So that's why you asked if I'd eaten dinner?" Adelaide opened the door wider.

"Yes. When you told me you hadn't had dinner and you were going to eat crackers and hummus, I figured since I was stopping to get myself something to eat, I'd pick up dinner for you, too." His warm voice sounded directly behind her.

"I'm glad you did. Thanks."

"Good. I'm a hero." Hector smiled and set the bag on the counter. "You don't cook much anymore, I take it?"

"I do but I don't. It's hard to cook for myself, so a lot of times I order in. Even though Danny's here, he's gone quite a bit with Jamie, so it's just me." She shrugged, hoping she didn't sound too pathetic, living the life she'd been afraid of—a life without purpose—worse because she was no longer married.

"I know what you mean. The owners at the Chinese restaurant down the street from me already know my name."

"How many times have you had the Mongolian beef?" That was his favorite meal to order at Chinese restaurants.

"This week or since I moved into that apartment?"

"I'm not going to ask about since you moved into that apartment. I'm sure you don't know because that number would be too high. So let's stick with the statistics from this week."

Hector let out a laugh. He was always so serious, but when he laughed, it was the best sound. Rich. Hearty. Nipple-throbbingly sexy.

"I feel like that's a jab at me, but I'm going to pretend I didn't notice."

"If you're going to pretend you didn't notice, then you shouldn't mention it. See how that works?"

He laughed again, harder this time, and that brought a smile to her face but a pinch of pain in her chest.

"Fair enough. I ordered the Mongolian beef three times this week."

Adelaide shook her head. "They might as well set up a standing order for you every day."

She reached into the cabinet and pulled down dishes. When she turned around, Hector's gaze quickly flicked up to meet hers, and her breath caught. Had she caught him looking at her ass? She couldn't be sure, but she was almost certain that's what he'd been doing.

"Need some help?" he asked.

"Um, no, I have it."

"How about we do this. Dinner first, then we get down to business?"

"Sounds good to me."

They ate in the dining room. Initially, conversation was a bit awkward, but then they both gradually relaxed.

Hector told her his aunt, the one he'd lived with when he moved to the United States as a teenager, was going back to Michoacán. Adelaide made a mental note to call her. They hadn't talked in a while, but she wanted to visit and wish her well before she left. Now that her kids and grandkids were scattered around the country, Adelaide understood why she wanted to return home.

She told Hector the latest news in her family—weddings, deaths, and caught him up on news about mutual friends. She had always been better at keeping up with the happenings among their friends, reminding him about birthdays and other special events.

The conversation was friendly and they laughed a few times from shared memories. It was nice having someone to talk to in the house.

After the meal, they took the dishes to the kitchen and then settled in the living room where Hector placed his laptop on the coffee table and opened an Excel file. "I worked on a budget and a checklist for Danny and Jamie. It's just the beginning, but I wanted to get them thinking about what their responsibilities would be regarding this baby."

Seated on the other end of the sofa, Adelaide angled her body toward the screen. "What do you have?"

Hector moved closer and Adelaide tensed. She caught the scent of him. A musky odor. Not a bad smell, but one that came from working all day. Unique to Hector. No one else smelled like him, and she became a little breathless at the memory of how his scent would be painted into her skin after they made love.

He scrolled through the spreadsheet and Adelaide stared at it with raised eyebrows. He'd listed everything that could possibly be listed, from before birth to when their grandchild started kindergarten. The costs included food, a car seat, strollers, diapers, clothing, health insurance, and even the hospital stay when Jamie delivered.

"Jamie needs prenatal and postnatal care," Hector said, pointing to cells highlighted in yellow. "They'll also need to start a college fund and Danny needs life insurance, because if anything happens to him—"

Adelaide placed a hand on his forearm and they both froze. Heat filled her palm and his muscles tightened. They stared at each other, and she forgot why she'd touched him in the first place. When her memory came back, she calmly eased away her hand.

Clearing her throat, she said, "If you're trying to scare them, you've done a great job."

"Not scare them. I want them to understand the gravity of becoming parents."

"I'm sure they understand."

"This will bring it home. They need to take this pregnancy seriously."

Adelaide opened her mouth and then closed it again, wondering about the best way to tactfully let him down easy. He'd done a lot of work. "I don't think we should overwhelm them like this," she said gently.

Silence filled the air between them.

Hector closed the laptop and rested his elbows on his knees. "This isn't what I wanted for him. He was supposed to finish college and get a job or start his own business. Eventually he'd get married and have a couple of kids."

"I know. But the current situation is not the end of the world. We're both here and able to help him and Jamie, which is better than the situation you and I were in. I believe they'll take this seriously. This is all good information, but the baby isn't here yet, and it's...a lot."

"Too much?"

"Too much," Adelaide confirmed with a nod.

"Yeah, maybe I went too far with the college fund information."

Trying to fight a laugh, Adelaide ended up snorting and Hector glanced at her.

"I'm sorry," she said, covering her mouth. "But I'd forgotten how much you liked to be prepared."

A smile broke out on his face, then he laughed, too. Falling back against the sofa, he ran his fingers through his thick dark hair. "Shit. What am I doing?"

Adelaide spoke quietly to him. "What you always do. Take care of a problem. There's nothing wrong with that, but the kids will be fine."

She ached to run a hand over his head the way she used to, to reassure him when he was worried about work or starting the business, or whatever else plagued his mind. But she kept her hands to herself, her palm still burning from when she'd touched him moments before.

"You always could rein me in when I got out of control." He touched her finger and their eyes met in the ensuing silence.

"We balance each other."

The next move she half-expected. His eyes became hooded and she knew that look, so when he leaned toward her, she leaned toward him, too.

6

The second Adelaide leaned toward him, Hector was on her. Quick and harsh, his mouth covered hers, his libido breaking through what little restraint he'd managed to keep in place while talking to her. Laughing with her. Fantasizing about taking her against the counter when she bent to put the dishes away.

The taste of her was like the top shelf whiskey that he couldn't get enough of. He was drowning in the sensation of the kiss. His dick thickened and his blood pulsed hot as he pushed her back against the arm of the sofa. She tasted like heaven, and when her tongue touched the edge of his mouth, he groaned and sucked that pink tease between his lips.

Her fingers weaved into his hair, as if she'd simply been waiting for an excuse to grab it. And he kissed her throat, tasting her sweet skin and filling his nostrils with the heady scent of her perfume.

One hand cupped her breast and squeezed, while the other smoothed up her throat and closed. He held her in place as her nails scraped at his back, and the urge to claim tightened his neck muscles as he devoured her lips. She moved under him, legs opening, hips tilting up to his and grinding in a frantic show of wanton need.

He wanted to fuck her so bad he couldn't think straight. He pushed the T-shirt higher, anxious for a glimpse of rosy brown nipples. When his lips covered one breast through the sheer lace, she gasped and bowed her back, pushing harder against him.

"Hector," she whispered.

"I know. I know."

His voice was hoarse against her breasts, his need untenable as he sucked the thin material and her nipple transformed into a tighter bead in his mouth. Her bra became soaked as he continued to feast and his hand held her arched throat so she couldn't move from under his control.

Kissing his way down her belly, Hector marveled at how her skin was so damn soft, and she smelled so good.

With a rough tug he unsnapped her jeans and—

The front door slammed. Everything came to a halt.

He lifted his head and met Adelaide's wide-eyed stare.

Hector swore and they moved at the same time, scrambling apart like guilty teenagers, their breathing shallow like marathon runners.

"Mom!" Daniel called.

Adelaide tugged down her shirt and fastened her jeans with trembling fingers. "I'm—" She cleared her throat and jumped up from the sofa. "I'm in here. W-with your father."

She took several steps away and shot a glance at Hector before turning toward the open doorway.

Elbows to knees, Hector felt his erection die a slow death. Pressing his face into his hands, he fought back his body's demand to drag Adelaide into the bedroom and finish what they'd started.

Daniel entered the room. "Hey, what are you guys up to?" he asked.

Hector dropped his hands and looked at his son.

"We were talking about you and Jamie," Adelaide answered.

Hector still couldn't speak. His gaze dragged over his ex-wife's bottom and he bit back a groan at the way her nipples had felt in his mouth. Hard and downright delicious as he sucked them through the sheer material of her bra. He wished he'd taken her bare flesh into his mouth and had the full pleasure of that tight peak against his tongue.

This damn boy...

"I'm sorry." Daniel shoved his hands in his pockets. "I know you guys are worried about us, and I feel awful about it, but I don't want you to worry."

Hector forced himself to concentrate on his son's crestfallen face.

"I went looking for a job today, but then I had a thought." He glanced at Hector. "Dad, I was wondering if you and I could talk?"

His request surprised Hector and he frowned in confusion. "Sure," he said, standing.

"Outside. No offense, Mom. This is a man-to-man conversation."

"Oh." Adelaide looked between them. "Go ahead."

"I'll, uh...call you later about what we were talking about," Hector said to Adelaide.

She nodded vigorously and didn't quite look at him. "Of course. Sounds good."

Hector picked up the computer and she stepped aside, giving much more room than he needed. He followed his son out to the driveway and put the computer in the car. Then he leaned back against the driver door and folded his arms. "What's going on?"

Daniel inhaled and released a deep breath. "I've been thinking about all my responsibilities now that I'm going to be a father. I definitely need a job, and I was wondering...if I could come to work with you."

"With me?"

"Yeah. I mean, I need a job." Daniel bit into his bottom lip.

Hector had always wanted his kids to show an interest in his business, but none of them had. The two oldest chose artistic pursuits that had taken them away from the family. But Daniel, the one he thought would be the least likely to work with him, unexpectedly expressed an interest.

"You understand that if you work with me, I expect you to work?"

"I know."

"And other than mowing lawns, you've never had a job before."

Daniel stood up straighter. "I know, but I'm ready to work. I want to. I want to...work with you."

"Work with me?" The conversation had gone in an unexpected direction.

"I've kind of always wanted to, but I didn't think you would want me to."

Hector unfolded his arms. "What makes you say that?"

Daniel scuffed his tennis shoes against the driveway. "I know what you think about me, Dad. You think I'm lazy and I screw up all the time."

"Danny..."

"No, you're right. I have been kinda lazy, and I have screwed up. I disappointed you and Mom, and I feel bad about that. But the truth is, I was always kinda interested in Solar Beams, but I didn't know how to tell you. And honestly, I figured you would say no if I asked to come work with you."

"I had no idea you were interested in working in the business with me."

"I kind of hinted at it, but you didn't pick up on my interest," he said, looking a little embarrassed.

Hector laughed a little. "Son, I'm not good with hints. You have to come right out and tell me something if you want me to get it. A lot of times, I'm in my own world because I'm so busy."

Daniel nodded. "True."

The way he said that one word gave Hector pause. "What does that mean?"

Daniel hesitated at first, then replied, "Well, I was thinking about you and Mom. How things were before you split, you know? She was lonely, but I could tell you didn't notice. I don't know if she always was, but I noticed it the past couple of years for sure."

"What do you mean your mother was lonely? She had you at the house, and I was home every night."

"Come on, Dad, you didn't know she wanted to spend more time with you?"

"What the hell are you talking about?"

"It was obvious to me, but not to you, I guess. She said certain things that made me realize how she felt. Like, if you came home late and she'd cooked a nice dinner, she'd say something to me like, 'Well, at least I get to see you appreciate this meal.' Or if I ended up playing checkers with her, 'Your father and I used to play checkers, and he absolutely hated to lose.' I felt kind of bad leaving her alone when I went off to school—with the two of you getting separated last summer and that whole empty-nest thing. Then you got divorced, and I knew it would be really hard on her."

Had he really been that obtuse? Did her withdrawal happen because he ignored her? This was definitely news to him. He worked a lot, yes, but that was to provide for his family. Besides, he and Adelaide had been married long enough that she knew to be direct with him. If she wanted something, she told him outright. Not only did he not like hints, he didn't have time to play games.

"You've given me a lot to think about," Hector said. His eyes trailed back to the house where he'd spent several glorious minutes kissing and humping his ex-wife.

"So, about the job?" Daniel looked expectantly at him.

"Listen, if you're going to work with me, I need to discuss this with Martin first. We're equal partners. If he says it's a go, we'll start you small. Working on the sales floor and maybe shadowing the guys when they go out on installs."

"Cool." Daniel's eyes brightened.

"How long have you wanted to work at Solar Beams?"

Daniel shrugged. "A while."

Silence fell between them for several seconds.

"Danny, I want you to work with me. But I need you to take this seriously."

Daniel straightened like a soldier in front of a commanding officer. "I will. I promise, I won't let you down."

"Okay. No special treatment."

"I don't expect any."

It dawned on Hector that he'd never seen him so ready to tackle a task in a long time. If his son really had wanted to work with him for a while, he regretted not noticing sooner. He was a firm believer that his kids should go to college, and he wasn't completely on board with Daniel choosing to leave school. But working at Solar Beams might not be so bad. Major changes were coming to the company. They were opening another store and Hector was planning to buy out his partner Martin's share of the business so Martin and his wife could move to Jamaica to look after his mother-in-law.

Hector squeezed his shoulder. "All right. I'll call you tomorrow with our decision."

"Thanks, Dad." Daniel grinned.

"By the way, do me a favor and help out your mother around the house, all right?"

"I will. I promise."

"Good. I'll see you later."

Hector waved goodbye as he backed out the driveway, his head fixed on thoughts of his son...and his ex-wife.

7

"What are you doing?"

Adelaide loved the sound of his voice, and after their make-out session earlier today, that enticing bass brought a smile to her face. He'd made her feel alive again. Got her blood pumping. The short time they spent together had been unexpectedly thrilling, and her body still throbbed with the memory of that kiss. The heat between them was still very much alive.

"I just finished rubbing lotion on my feet and hands," she answered.

"Vanilla-lemon lotion?" Hector asked.

"Yes." Adelaide slid under the covers and rested against the pillows.

"My favorite. I can smell it now."

She smiled. "What are you doing?"

"Thinking about you and our kiss earlier. How far would you have let me go if your knucklehead son hadn't shown up?"

She let out a laugh and stretched her legs. "He's your son, too, you know."

"I know, but that tendency for knuckleheadedness comes from your side of the family."

Adelaide scoffed. "Nice try. I remember the stories Papi Flores told me about your behavior growing up, and you were a headache. That's why he sent you to live with your aunt, to keep you out of trouble."

"Keep me out of trouble, yes, but I never interrupted him and my mother getting busy, I can tell you that. After all these years, Danny's still cock-blocking. He's the reason I had to pay my cousin and his wife to keep the kids the weekend of our sixth anniversary. Just to get away from his constant interruptions."

"You paid your cousin to keep the kids that weekend?"

"Of course. You know Manny never does anything out of the goodness of his heart. He's always got to find a way to hustle money out of someone."

Adelaide laughed because that was the perfect description of Manny. "It was an expensive weekend, then. You paid Manny, and you paid for our getaway to Vegas."

"Worth every dime," Hector said in a soft voice.

Adelaide smiled at the fond memories of their escape to Vegas. "That was a really nice weekend. No kids, just the two of us. It was a good idea and a nice break."

Hector had splurged on a suite with a private pool. They gambled, ordered room service, swam naked in the pool, and made love whenever and however they wanted with no interruptions.

"So, back to my original question...how far would you have let me go if Danny hadn't interrupted us? Would I have been able to take off your bra?"

"Yes, definitely."

Hector groaned. "Damn, Danny."

Adelaide cracked up at the pain in his voice.

"Maybe we can try again," he suggested.

"I don't hate that idea."

"No?" He sounded surprised that she'd actually agreed.

Adelaide smoothed her hand over the geometric pattern of the quilt on the bed. "I'm open to revisiting that moment if you are," she said quietly.

"I'm definitely open to that. I want to see you again, but not because we have to work on getting Danny and Jamie ready to be parents."

Adelaide could hardly breathe. Her feelings didn't die simply because their marriage did, and clearly Hector felt the same way.

He continued talking. "Could I swing by Friday night?"

"You're not free any other night this week? I'm going out Friday night." She hadn't seen Joseph in a long time, and he'd promised her a good time, so she was looking forward to the night out. She was getting her hair done and meeting Jackie to go shopping for a dress.

"No, I have a pretty full schedule all week because...well, I might as well tell you my great news. Martin and I are opening a third location in Carlsbad, so I'll be traveling back and forth for the rest of the week, checking on the progress, meeting with the contractors and handling paperwork, that kind of thing. Which means I'll be getting back later than usual, and I might stay out there a couple of nights."

"Hector, that's wonderful! You've wanted to open another location for a while."

"And we're finally in a position to do it. Cash flow is good, business is on the rise, and since we revamped the website a couple of years ago, mail orders have picked up. Solar Beams is growing!"

Hearing the pride in his voice and listening to him talk about their plans for expansion made her want to share, too.

"I have some news, as well. I'm going to cooking school! I start in September, and I'll receive my diploma next summer and then I plan to start catering."

After becoming pregnant, Adelaide dropped out of college. Years later she started taking cooking classes and loved them, but the hectic schedule with three children and a husband forced her to table the idea of getting her diploma.

A few years ago, with Danny nearing his senior year, she'd mentioned to Hector she wanted to start them again, with the idea that she could start catering, but hadn't seriously considered that option until they separated last year.

"You're back to that idea?" His words stung, his voice lacking the enthusiasm she'd hoped for. "You're not worried about having to study again or the time that will take away from other activities?"

Adelaide remembered her trepidation at contacting the admissions office to ask a few questions. Nothing—including Hector's lackluster response—could squash the intoxication of knowing that once she completed her course work, she'd have a diploma, proof that she was trained in the art of cooking.

"Going back to school will be a challenge, but it's a challenge I believe I can handle."

"Good for you." His voice lacked emotion and was not encouraging.

"I went shopping the other day, looking at backpacks. I'm not sure I'll use one." Adelaide laughed at herself.

"It's late. I have to be up early, so I'm going to bed now. Congratulations. It was good talking to you. I'll call you again tomorrow, if that's okay?"

"I would like that. Have a good night, Hector."

"I will now. Good night, Addie."

Adelaide hung up the phone but stared at it for a while, a mixture of happiness and sadness in her spirit.

"I can't believe you told our neighbor that," Adelaide said.

Night number three of her daily conversations with Hector. He'd just told her that he warned away their neighbor who used to live across from them in the apartment complex they lived in when they first got married.

She settled on the couch with the phone wedged between her ear and shoulder while balancing a bowl of vanilla ice cream in her hands.

"I did. I knew he was interested in you by the way he looked at you. You didn't notice?"

"I thought he was a little friendly but harmless. Why would he be interested in a woman who had a husband and two toddlers, for goodness' sake?"

"Because he wanted to be your husband and replace me as Karen and Junior's father."

Adelaide spooned ice cream into her mouth with a laugh. "I doubt that's true. He'd have been crazy to want to get with me while I had two rambunctious kids in tow. I'm sure all the neighbors knew what a handful the twins were. Getting them in and out of the car was like herding cats."

"I'm just telling you what I noticed, so I had to set him straight."

"Poor guy. That explains why he stopped being friendly after a while. Well, I guess since we're being honest, I should come clean about something I did, too."

"Uh-oh. What did you do?" Hector asked in an amused voice.

Adelaide set the bowl atop a magazine on the coffee table and shifted so one leg was beneath her and the other dangled off the edge of the sofa. "I'm a little embarrassed to tell you now."

"You brought it up, so you have to finish, otherwise I'm not going to let up until you tell me."

"Okay." She let out an exaggerated sigh. "Do you remember a very helpful staff member at the Chuck E. Cheese that had blue hair?"

"Blue hair?" Hector said slowly. "I kind of vaguely remember someone like that when we took the kids there. What about her?"

"She and I had words."

"What! You never told me that."

"I didn't tell you because there was no reason to tell you. I took care of the situation. She was always overly friendly to you, and I remember one time she was laughing all up in your face and touched your arm. When she saw me approaching, she pulled back immediately, which said to me that she had bad intentions. You don't remember any of this?"

She could practically hear him thinking in the pause between her question and his answer.

"No, I honestly don't."

"She might not have made an impression on you, but I definitely remember her. When you went to the bathroom, I pulled her aside and told her she needed to back off, and that I thought her behavior was inappropriate. I didn't say anything to you back then because I didn't want you to say I was overreacting, but she really, really bugged me."

Hector let out a laugh of disbelief. "My sweet Addie confronted someone?"

"I didn't feel very sweet that day."

Hector's voice dropped. "I'm a little turned on by the badass version of Adelaide Flores."

Adelaide let out a loud laugh. "It was a long time ago and I was hardly badass."

"I like the idea of my woman getting jealous and keeping other women away."

"Don't expect me to do that anymore. Enough of that, how is the progress on the building?"

"Looking good, and my meetings are going well, too. Everything is on schedule so far."

"I can't wait to see the finished product."

"I can't wait for you to see it, either. I'll take you out there one day."

"I'd like that."

They were getting closer. Talking and sharing in a way they hadn't in a long time. What had happened to them? Where did they go wrong and drift apart?

"I better get off this phone. I'll call you Saturday. Have fun Friday night."

"I will. Good night."

8

Hector hung up the phone.

"You've been smiling more than usual lately."

The comment came from the doorway where Martin, his best friend and partner at Solar Beams, stood. They founded Solar Beams fifteen years ago. After a rocky start, their hard work and sacrifice paid off when they became the largest installation service in the county.

Hector grabbed his jacket from the back of the chair and walked toward his friend. "Life is good. I'm on my way out for drinks with my best friend and partner. What's not to smile about?"

Martin raised his eyebrows and followed him out of the office. "I like this new Hector," he said with a laugh.

They drove separately to Seaport Village, a dining and shopping complex near the waterfront. Hector hadn't been there in a long time —last time with Adelaide, a date night of salsa dancing, chips, and one too many margaritas.

They found a seat at one of the bars and ordered beers, wings, and calamari.

"I really needed this. I didn't realize how long it's been since I've gone out for drinks," Hector said.

"I hear you. It's been a minute." Martin clinked his glass filled with rum and Coke against Hector's whiskey and took a sip. Then he let out a satisfied groan.

Martin was a fun guy with dark brown skin and a big personality. They met in the early years of Adelaide and Hector's marriage. At the time, Hector had been working two jobs. During the day, he worked at a solar installation company with Martin, installing solar panels and selling solar-powered lighting and other items. At night, he stocked shelves in a department store.

Martin had come across as having a rather devil-may-care attitude, and Hector didn't think they had much in common. Martin was always joking around and was the loudest guy on the sales floor, but every month he landed at the top or near the top of the sales charts.

Hector always made his quota but was more interested in being an entrepreneur and usually had his head stuck in books on the subject of business ownership. One day, Martin stopped by his desk and asked about the textbook he pored over during lunch, and they hit it off when they learned they were both newlyweds and had babies at home.

"Paula told me she spoke to Adelaide the other day and mentioned you're going to be a grandfather. Is that why Danny needed a job?"

"Yeah, and I'm still getting used to the idea that my kid's going to be a father."

Martin adjusted the black-framed glasses on his nose. "When's the baby due?"

"Less than six months."

Martin shook his head. "I know it's not easy coordinating something like that while you're newly divorced."

Hector shrugged. "We've been good, actually."

"Oh yeah?"

Hector nodded. "I helped her out with the lawn the other day, and now we talk all the time."

"No shit."

"It's no big deal." He didn't want to disclose how much the conversations with Adelaide meant to him. He felt lighter, as if wings had grown on his shoes and kept him elevated above the negativity his life had become. "You know, I've been meaning to ask you, how did you and Paula manage to get back on track?"

Martin had at one time mentioned he and Paula were headed for divorce, and he had thought about moving out of the house, but something changed. Martin stopped sulking when he arrived at work, and he no longer complained about his wife.

"Paula dragged me kicking and screaming to a therapist."

"You never told me that." He could imagine Martin doing exactly that, too—kicking and screaming.

"Turns out it was a waste of time." He sipped his drink.

"How could it be a waste of time if the two of you ended up working things out? From what I can tell your marriage is stronger than ever. You're still thinking about moving to Jamaica, right?"

"Yep, if you ever buy me out," Martin said pointedly.

Hector chuckled. "I'm working on it."

He had to make a decision soon or Martin would sell his interest to someone else, which could be problematic. He and Martin had made a great team for almost two decades, and he didn't know if he'd have the same easy-going relationship with anyone else.

"Back to your question—my marriage to Paula is stronger than ever, but not because of the marriage therapist. A friend of hers recommended a book called *The Five Love Languages*. Ever heard of it?"

"No."

The bartender set down Hector's order of wings and Martin's order of calamari.

"I'm telling you, it changed our lives and improved our relationship." Martin dipped some calamari in the marinara sauce.

Hector laughed. "Come on, are you telling me that you read a book and that's what saved your marriage?"

"That's exactly what I'm telling you." Martin finished chewing his food. "I thought it was bullshit, too, but the book explains that there are five ways people express and receive love. Every person has their preference. I see that skeptical look on your face, but listen to what I'm saying. I thought it was corny as hell, too, but Paula was adamant that we read the book. So we did. I figured, what the hell, it was cheaper than the therapist. There's also some exercises that you can do that the author created to encourage you to better communicate with your spouse."

"Sounds like some new-age crap that somebody made up to make a ton of money." Hector ate a piece of chicken.

"I would agree with you, except that it absolutely works. At least it did for us."

"Okay, so what did the book tell you to do that was so wonderful?"

"Okay, basically the author says we all speak in different love languages. For instance, my wife's language is she likes to receive gifts. When I give her gifts, it makes her feel good."

"Wow, what a revelation," Hector said sarcastically. "What person doesn't like to receive gifts?"

Martin laughed. "It's actually more than that. The thing is, I thought that by providing for her and the kids, that was enough. But she really enjoys getting gifts from me. They don't have to be anything extravagant. The occasional flowers, a piece of jewelry." Martin leaned closer, really getting into the story. "One of the things the book taught me was to really pay attention to her and her needs. Instead of doing what I thought she wanted, I did what she actually wanted. I also paid attention to the things she liked, in a way that I did when we first started dating but had slacked off on as our marriage progressed."

"So what, you just started buying her a bunch of stuff?"

"Yes and no. It was a little bit more calculated than that, and at first it felt awkward and cheesy. I struggled with what to get her because the truth was, I hadn't really been paying attention to her needs for years. But we did the exercises included in the book, and as time passed it got easier to show her love in the way that she appreciated. So now I do shit regularly. Like the other day, I bought her flowers for no reason. I was driving by the flower shop and saw a sunflower bouquet in the window, and it caught my eye. Honestly, in the past I would've never noticed anything like that, but she loves sunflowers and because we're on this new path, I pulled over and went in and bought the bouquet. When I got home, I gave it to her and said something like, "To the prettiest woman I've ever known. These flowers don't compare to your beauty." And you know what, I meant it. That's the thing about learning to speak someone's language. It's better if it's more authentic, and it was authentic because to me she's still that girl I spotted across the supermarket parking lot and ran over to speak to because I couldn't let her get away."

Hector digested his friend's words. "That's nice. I'm happy for you. But I don't see Adelaide doing any exercises with me."

"You can do the exercises yourself. You said you guys still talk, right?"

"Yeah."

"So, all you have to do is pay attention to what she says. Think back to your marriage. What were the complaints that she used to have about you?"

"That's the thing, she never complained. And then one day, she just asked for a divorce." He hated the sound of bitterness that crept into his voice. Cracking his knuckles, he added, "She gave up on us, after twenty-five years and three kids."

"Nah, I doubt that's how it happened. Even if she didn't outright tell you what her needs are, she let you know. Women are like that sometimes. She probably didn't want to nag you, and so she let you know in other little ways what she wished you were doing. You just weren't in the right frame of mind to listen. But now, maybe you should try."

Hector expelled a deep breath as he recalled the conversation with Daniel in the driveway.

Come on, Dad, you didn't know she wanted to spend more time with you?

"What did you say the name of this book was?"

His friend smiled. "*The Five Love Languages.* You can find it anywhere. In the bookstore or order it online. If you follow the steps,

I promise it'll change your relationship with Adelaide, and you might win back you wife—assuming that's what you want."

Hector didn't reply, but he thought deeply about what his friend said. Maybe he should get the book.

After all, what did he have to lose?

9

Hector threw his head back and drained his second beer. Time to get out of there. He waved at the bartender, who was in the middle of taking another order but nodded his acknowledgment.

A couple of seats down, a woman with black hair held his gaze for a bit before looking away.

"Did you see that?" Martin asked.

"Yeah, I did." Hector lifted off the seat and pulled his wallet from his back pocket.

"Nothing, huh?" Martin asked.

"Not a thing."

The woman was pretty enough, but he wasn't tempted to ask for her number. He'd had one hookup since the divorce and found it sorely lacking, evidence that he wasn't ready to start dating again. The sex had been mechanical and lacking passion, devoid of the emotional euphoria he'd grown accustomed to. The complete knowledge of someone else's body and their complete knowledge of yours had been missing.

Making love to Adelaide had been easy, seamless. Downright

intuitive. During the encounter a few months ago, he kept comparing poor Rita to his ex, which was completely unfair.

Anyway, dating was different nowadays. According to Junior, everyone dated online, but Hector was turned off by the whole process of uploading his photo and writing out a list of his attributes. It was worse than trying to get a job. Like putting himself on the auction block.

"Hey, is that Adelaide?"

Hector swung his head in the direction of Martin's line of vision and sure enough, passing by was Adelaide, strolling along the waterfront with another man.

He sat up straight. Time suspended and the air around him contracted.

Adelaide. With another man.

She looked so different, but in a good way. He hadn't seen this side of her in years. Certainly not for him—walking with confidence in a pair of heels and a stunning red dress that opened at the back and showed off the lines of her body and clung to her hips, waist, and bouncing breasts. He sure as hell didn't remember that dress. Had she bought it to impress that man?

Had she colored her hair, too? It was a subtle lightening, but he recognized right away that it was browner than usual under the lights.

And the guy...holy shit. He was good-looking with golden-brown skin, and younger. He had to be at least ten years younger than her.

Hector's hand tightened on the bar top and his shoulders became rigid. "Who the hell is he?"

Martin touched his arm. "Listen, man—"

Hector shrugged him off and stood. Adelaide was out on a date. A damn date! How could she? How could she when they'd had such great conversations this week? This was the 'plans' she'd told him about? The reason she couldn't spare a couple of hours with him tonight, because she had a date with another man?

And what the hell was going on with the makeover? She looked shiny and new and happier than he'd seen her in years.

Hector tossed some bills on the bar top. "If that doesn't cover my bill, pay the balance for me and I'll pay you back."

"What are you about to do?" Martin asked with a worried frown.

"I'm about to say hello to my ex-wife," Hector bit out. His gazed flew to the window, but they'd walked out of his line of sight. Shit.

"I don't think that's a good idea. I think you should—"

Hector didn't hear a word Martin said after that. He charged toward the door, pushing through what seemed like a mile-long obstacle course. He wound in between the tables, sliding past a waitress carrying a tray filled with drinks and then half-shoving his way through the crowd at the entrance.

He finally escaped and rushed outside along the waterfront. Under the night sky, couples strolled arm in arm and kids squealed as they ran ahead of their parents. He hurried in the direction he'd seen Adelaide go in, craning his neck for a glimpse of her and the pretty boy.

After minutes of brisk walking, twisting his head to and fro and almost having a heart attack every time he caught a glimpse of red, Hector finally admitted defeat. He stopped in the middle of the walkway and stared out at the dark water. He had no idea where they were or where they'd gone. They could have sauntered into one of the other restaurants or into one of the shops. Hell, they could have left already.

"No," he muttered, chest hurting at the thought of her leaving with that guy and possibly going back to his place. Or worse, back to her place. *Their* house. No, she wouldn't be so brazen. He had called her cell phone twice but she hadn't answered, and he already regretted the frantic message he left asking her to call him right away.

They were divorced, so it made sense that she'd moved on. That's what people did. But he was damn near panicking at the thought of her leaving him behind and starting a new chapter with someone new.

"Calm down, Hector. She wouldn't do that right now. Not while the two of you have been talking regularly."

Would she?

He didn't know for sure, but he knew how to find out.

JOSEPH PULLED his rental behind Hector's Jeep Cherokee. "Looks like you have company."

Adelaide frowned. "That's Hector's car."

Hector exited the vehicle and rested his hands on his hips, staring at them. She couldn't see his face well but knew from his intimidatingly rigid stance that he was displeased for some reason.

"Uh, need me to stick around?"

"No, it's fine. He and I are good, but I didn't expect to see him. Thanks for the night out. I had a great time."

"I did, too," Joseph said.

"Have a safe flight back." Adelaide squeezed his arm and climbed out of the car. As Joseph pulled out of the driveway, she waved. He honked twice and disappeared down the street.

When she turned to face Hector, his grim expression gave her pause. "Hi. Is something wrong?"

"I don't know, you tell me."

"What?"

"You were on a date at Seaside Village with the man who just left. I saw you tonight when I was there with Martin. It's now…" He made a big show of looking at his watch. "Almost twelve o'clock. I've been waiting here for three hours. What were you doing for three hours, Adelaide?"

He hadn't raised his voice, but tension vibrated in his tone.

"Excuse me?" She wasn't sure that she'd heard him correctly.

"I left a message on your phone, which you haven't responded to."

"I turned off my ringer because I wanted to have an uninterrupted night."

"You never turn off your ringer because we have kids. What if something had happened to one of them?"

"I didn't have these kids by myself. You're their father. If something happened to one of them, they could call you, too."

"That's not the point. You know as well as I do that they'll call you first."

"This isn't about the phone, is it?"

"No, it's not. I thought you and I were getting closer, but then you go and get all dressed up for some young buck. Is all this for him—the hair, the sexy dress, the makeup?"

Adelaide straightened her spine. "All of this is for me. I wanted to feel pretty."

"Pretty for him, but never me," Hector said bitterly.

"Not for him, and you're being ridiculous." Adelaide marched past him.

"I'm not done talking to you."

"I'm not going to argue with you in the driveway so the neighbors can hear," she said over her shoulder.

She let herself into the house and Hector followed close on her heels.

In the bedroom, she swung around and faced him. "Do you mind?"

"We're not done talking."

"We can talk when I get finished changing. You can wait in the den or the kitchen."

"Who is he?"

Adelaide released a long breath and tossed her purse onto the bed. Folding her arms over her chest, she replied, "Joseph. My cousin's son. The one who lives in Tucson."

"What?" He looked genuinely perplexed and she had a hard time not laughing.

"I've talked about him before. Joseph, and we all call him J.T. He's here on business and headed back to Tucson tomorrow. He offered to take me out, and I jumped at the chance to get dressed up and...do a mini-makeover with my hair."

She touched her hair and Hector's eyes followed the movement.

"Oh." Hector rubbed the back of his neck. "J.T. I thought..."

"You thought I had a hot date even though we've been talking the past few nights," Adelaide finished for him.

"And you let me think that. Why?"

"I kinda liked that you were jealous," she admitted with a shrug.

"I almost yanked open his door and beat his ass."

"You wouldn't have done that."

"Don't be so sure," Hector muttered, running a hand over his face.

"What would you have done if he really was a date and I brought him inside?"

"I don't know, broken down the door, thrown a brick through the window."

Adelaide laughed and then he let out a short laugh.

"You're as bad as Danny," Adelaide said.

"Worse. I'm too old to be doing stupid shit like that." His gaze roamed her face and then lowered to caress her body. He looked at her the way he used to. Long ago. "You're so beautiful, *mi amor*. It drove me crazy thinking that you were dressed like this for him."

"Thank you," Adelaide said softly. "I just wanted to go out."

"I could take you out."

She shook her head. "I don't need you to take me out, out of pity." She stepped out of her shoes and tossed them in the closet.

"It wouldn't be out of pity."

"Well, whatever. I'm fine. Do you mind? I want to change." She went to the dresser and removed her earrings. She met his eyes in the mirror.

"I told you I wanted to spend more time with you, and I meant that," Hector said.

Slowly, he came forward and stood so close the warmth from his body reached out to hers. "What happened to us?" he asked, voice a low rumble.

Adelaide's heart began to race. "I'm not sure, but I knew our marriage was truly over when we took Danny to school and didn't say a word to each other the entire ride back."

He ran his knuckles up the bared skin of her back. "Damn, you look beautiful, *mi amor*." Lust was thick and heavy on his tongue.

She lifted her gaze. His gaze was lowered, eyes focused his movements.

"But you've always been beautiful, without even trying."

When he brushed her hair out the way and tasted her neck, Adelaide shivered. He released the clasp at the top of her dress.

"What are you doing?" she whispered.

His eyes finally met hers. "You said you need to change. So I'm helping you undress."

10

———

The top of the dress fell around her waist and exposed her breasts to his hands.

"Don't you need help?" Hector whispered huskily.

Adelaide's eyes closed as her nipples pebbled against his palms. "I do."

She breathed with difficulty through her mouth, the noise at the back of her throat conveying need and a desperate longing that filled her nights and disturbed her days.

His tongue teased her earlobe, and Adelaide gripped the dresser, leaning back into the strength of his chest, warm desire pooling between her legs as he continued the relentless massaging of her breasts.

She turned in his arms, anxious for a kiss—anxious for the taste of his mouth again. He kissed her collarbone and then moved higher to her neck, sucking gently on the underside of her chin, and finally connected their lips.

His fingertips skimmed up her bare back before he pushed her against the wall with an impatient growl. Fingers sliding across his nape, Adelaide caressed the back of his head and let them climb into his hair. Her nails scraped his scalp the way he liked and he shuddered, forcing her mouth wide.

Hector knew how to kiss, and touch, and arouse her body to a fever pitch. Granting him deeper access, she allowed his tongue to slice into her mouth. He went deep, tongue tunneling in and sweeping from one end to the other—tasting and reclaiming what had been his for years.

His hands glided down her back to her bottom and squeezed. Adelaide shivered against him, nipples turning into tight pebbles against his hard chest.

She moaned and pressed closer, angling the lower part of her body toward his so that she could feel his rigid erection. She could never get enough of this man. He was her first love and her last love.

Hector broke free and showered amorous kisses along her upper chest and lower to one breast. He took the nipple in his mouth and sucked, tugging with his lips.

His hands were everywhere. On her breasts, squeezing and teasing. Then lower to her waist, caressing as if reacquainting himself with the concave curve. Then between her legs, where she was hot and aching for him.

"Hector," Adelaide whispered, her voice trembling. All this time she'd missed him and never dreamed she'd be held by him in such an intimate embrace again.

She raised onto her toes to make it easier for him to devour one breast and then the other, teasing with the edges of his teeth and the tip of his tongue while he held her tight against his body. A horrible ache possessed her, the need to be taken by the man she adored, the man she loved almost from the day they met.

Hector slid his hands up her thighs and under the dress, and the material bunched on his forearms as he grabbed her bare ass.

"You're wearing a thong?" He looked into her eyes, his eyebrows arrowing down. The question sounded like an accusation, a how-dare-you tone to his voice.

"I didn't want any panty lines," she whispered.

His hands slipped beneath the crotch, and he rubbed circles

around her clit with his thumb. He used her own wetness against her, sliding over the thickened bundle of nerves.

"Hector," she whispered with her lips trembling against his throat. She lifted her leg and grinded her hips against his like a cat in heat.

"*Dime*," he commanded.

"I want you inside me." She tugged down his zipper and freed his erection, and with a forceful push his pants fell around his ankles.

"*Impaciente*," he said shakily.

"I'm *very* impatient. I want you *now*."

Hector pressed her against the wall and trailed kisses down the side of her neck, his breath harsh against the sensitive skin. "I've missed you so much," he said hoarsely.

"I've missed you, too," she whispered.

He pulled the hem of her dress higher and shoved the thong down her legs. Adelaide knew what to do. She stepped out and wound her arms around his neck. He lifted her from the floor and she quickly wrapped her legs around his waist.

Hovering her lips next to his ear, she whispered, "Hector, baby, please."

He guided his erection between her open legs. The tip kissed the entrance in a gentle tease that curled her toes and fingers in anticipation before he pushed into the silken sheath of her sex with an energetic thrust. He laid claim to her body and they both released heavy groans as her softness stretched around his girth.

Keeping her propped against the wall, he continuously surged inside her. She was slippery and wet and absorbed every advance while cursing each retreat. Whimpering, she dug her fingers into his muscular shoulders, angry that he wasn't yet naked so she could feel his soft, warm skin. She ached for naked flesh against naked flesh, but this would have to do.

Aggressive kissing joined the powerful thrusting of his hips. She wanted to swallow him whole. She never wanted to lose the taste of his salty skin on her tongue again.

They groaned simultaneously, the reacquainting of their bodies sending an explosion of heat through her loins. Panting, Adelaide lifted up and down as he pumped his hips, both hands gripping her backside.

"Yes, yes," Adelaide moaned.

She kept her legs and arms tight around him and kissed his face and neck. She took deep lungfuls of air filled with his male scent, their breaths mingling together in yet another hungry kiss.

He was like an animal, his fingers digging into her flesh as he fucked her against the wall. Each solid thrust hard, relentless, and taking her higher as over and over he slid in and out. His teeth nipped at her neck and collarbone as his harsh breaths washed over her achy breasts. He'd surely leave marks on her skin, but she welcomed the branding, tightening her clamped legs around his hips and arching her throat to take more of the delicious bruising.

As pressure built in her abdomen, Adelaide buried her face against his throat. It wouldn't be long before she exploded. Her toes and fingers tightened in anticipation of the release. Hector's deep grunts matched her whimpers, his hips landing with more solid blows between her open thighs.

He knew what to do. He just knew what to do to satisfy her—to damn near bring her to tears. White-hot pleasure bolted through every cell, and her high-pitched cries filled the room. She bucked against him, panting and clawing his shoulders, digging in her nails as she lost all control.

She came with a keening cry, and her head falling backward as pleasure tore up her spine and lambasted her insides.

Hector pumped his hips faster, his hands gripping her bottom. His breaths came deeper and harder, the words he whispered in Spanish lost at the end of a groan that left him trembling when he climaxed too.

"Addie," he half-gasped—the sound of a tortured man finally getting what he most desired.

He let loose a series of F-bombs as he crushed her against the wall, his body frozen to absorb every drop of ecstasy.

Finally, at the end of a moment that seemed to last forever,

Adelaide lowered her feet to the floor and rested her forehead against his shoulder. Before she could utter a word, Hector kissed her nose and the corner of her mouth.

"Bed," he said, as if that was the only word he could manage.

THEY SLEPT SOUNDLY, but in the middle of the night, Adelaide awakened Hector by nudging her bottom against his hips. When he moved restlessly, she turned to face him and caressed his chest down to his abs. He was almost naked now, and she was able to take pleasure in the hairs that covered his chest and arrowed below the waistband of his boxer shorts.

In a haze of lust, she touched his hard body in all the places she'd longed to in the past year. His hips, his powerful thighs, and then higher to his swollen erection.

"Addie."

He came fully awake and slid his hands between her legs. His mouth wreaked havoc on her hard nipples, and her breathing stuttered as he guided his tongue over her curves and stroked her damp sex until his fingers were coated with her slick arousal.

She slipped out of her underwear, and he pushed the nightshirt high on her waist and entered her with one smooth stroke. Pleasure slashed through her abdomen. She gasped. The muscles in his back and legs flexed under her hands. Gripping his back and wrapping her legs tightly around his waist, the lower part of her body lifting frantically against his.

Adelaide came with a sharp cry, and he came with a loud groan, muscles quivering from the intensity of their lovemaking.

When he rolled off of her, they finally settled down to sleep again.

Spent but satisfied.

A delaide's fingers wandered through Hector's tousled dark hair as he slept, gently so she wouldn't wake him. She couldn't believe she could touch him again the way she wanted to.

She eased out of bed and picked up the discarded clothes from the night before. She went over to the walk-in closet and tossed them in the hamper. Then, slipping on her robe, she tightened the belt around her waist.

Before entering the bathroom, she took a good look at Hector, sprawled across the mattress, bare chest lifting up and down, one arm flung away from his body in abandon, his norm. He was a bed hog and had denied it for years until she took a picture one day and showed him the evidence.

Shaking her head but smiling, Adelaide walked quietly into the bathroom, splashed water on her face, and started brushing her teeth. She planned to make a nice breakfast and then relax on the sofa for a movie marathon with Hector, the way they used to. She wondered if he would be open to the idea or if he had to go home right away.

As she brushed her teeth, Hector shuffled naked into the bathroom, his hair a mess and his eyes half closed.

"Morning," he mumbled.

Her poor baby. Definitely not a morning person.

She watched his bare bottom as he moved over to the toilet, lifted the lid, and proceeded to pee with one arm propped against the wall for balance. When he finished, he flushed the toilet and then dragged over to the second sink beside her.

"What?" He squinted at her, half asleep as he washed his hands.

"Nothing." Adelaide hadn't realized she'd been staring, but he was acting so normal. She set down the brush and rinsed out her mouth. "You look tired," she said.

"I am." Hector turned off the water. He dried his hands and then kissed the side of her neck. "Come back to bed."

He hooked a finger in the belt of her robe and pulled her after him. He used to do that all the time—hook his fingers in the waistband of her jeans or slacks and pull her with him or toward him for a kiss.

Breakfast could wait as she indulged in renewed intimacy with her former husband.

They cuddled in the bed and soon fell asleep again.

ADELAIDE YAWNED as she and Hector entered the kitchen.

"I can eat a couple of horses," Hector said.

"Me, too."

After snuggling and falling asleep, they woke up later and made love and dozed off again until hunger drove them from the bed. Adelaide took out the pots and dishes they'd need to prepare brunch.

They worked together in perfect harmony as Hector prepared the one dish he'd perfected—French toast with cream cheese and thinly sliced strawberries. Adelaide worked on poached eggs and fresh fruit.

"Inside or outside?" he asked.

"Outside," she said. She hadn't enjoyed breakfast outside in a while, and doing so with him would be perfect.

"What do you have planned for the weekend?" Hector asked as he worked at the stove.

Adelaide cut up the fruit on the counter beside him. She could have gone to another spot in the kitchen but wanted to stay close and experience the occasional brush of his arm as they worked together.

"Selena invited me over to her house to hear Nicky's newest composition."

"And you're going?" Hector glanced at her.

She nodded.

"Why? You know you're not going to enjoy it. Selena paid for all those lessons, and Nicky still can't sing or play the piano."

"Be nice."

"It's the truth."

Adelaide laughed. He was absolutely right. Selena's daughter was an aspiring performer, and every now and again Selena invited friends over for food and drinks and to hear her daughter perform. Not very often, and some people only went because it was something to do and Selena—head chef at a popular restaurant—always provided plenty of delicious food.

"I couldn't think fast enough of a reason why I couldn't go."

"All you have to do... oh, never mind. You couldn't use me as an excuse."

"No, I couldn't."

Over the years it had become a running joke between them to use each other as an excuse when they wanted to get out of a particular activity.

My husband won't let me.

Adelaide won't let me.

Hector already has something planned.

Let me check with my wife.

Those excuses had worked perfectly for years, but Selena's unexpected question had thrown her off, and unaccustomed to coming up with excuses on short notice, Adelaide stumbled along. With only gentle pressure, Selena had worked a yes out of her.

"Have fun," Hector said dryly.

She shot daggers at him and he chuckled as he flipped the toast in the pan.

Adelaide placed the fruit in the refrigerator while she waited for the water to heat for the eggs.

She came up behind Hector and patted his butt. "You been working out?"

"Why?"

"Your ass is tighter." She squeezed his bottom.

"Hey, hey, I'm trying to work here. Behave," he said, holding the spatula aloft.

"You can't work with me touching you and kissing on you?" Adelaide placed her hands around his waist and kissed his shoulder blade through his shirt.

"So you're giving me a dose of my own medicine, is that it?"

Adelaide laughed. "Yes, this is how you've treated me before when I'm trying to cook. Learn to multitask." She slipped her hands beneath his shirt and rubbed his taut belly. His skin was firm and deliciously familiar with a sprinkling of hair along his lower torso.

"Keep that up and I'll turn off this stove and take you back to bed."

"Promises, promises." She rubbed his nipples.

"Goddammit, Addie—" Hector turned and she scuttled away with a laugh.

"Okay, I'll behave."

"Too late now." Hector set down the spatula and cornered her against the counter. He took a handful of her hair and wound it around his fist, pulling her head back so he could look down into her face with lust-filled eyes. "If you can't take the heat, stay out of the kitchen."

"Oh, I can take the heat, *señor*." Adelaide raised up on her toes and brought her lips close to his.

"Oh, yeah?"

"Mmm-hmm."

Hector flicked his tongue against her lips and then pressed his mouth to hers.

Adelaide moaned softly and smoothed her hands over his chest as she kissed him back. "Hector," she whispered.

"*Sí, mi esposa, mi rosa.*" My wife, my rose.

He hadn't said that in so long, she flung her arms around his neck and kissed him harder. She opened her mouth to give his tongue entry and pressed her aching nipples against his chest.

The door opened and closed.

"Mom!"

Hector let go of her hair and stepped back, shaking his head. "That damn boy," he grumbled.

Amused, Adelaide pushed at him.

"No."

"Hector." Her eyes widened.

"In here!" Hector called over his shoulder before bringing his gaze back to hers.

Adelaide held her breath. She wasn't so sure it was the right decision to let their son know they were on very good terms again.

She heard, rather than saw, when Daniel entered the kitchen and come to a halt. "Whoa."

Hector finally stepped back and turned to face their youngest. "Hi, Danny."

"Hey." His eyes darted between them, a frown creasing his brow. "What's going on?"

"Your mother and I just got up and are preparing breakfast—or rather brunch, at this time of the day. You hungry?"

Danny's eyes widened. "You just...you and Mom?"

Adelaide's cheeks burned.

"Yes," Hector answered.

"Nah, I'm good. Already ate. I'll leave you two alone." He sniffed and looked over at the stove. "Something's burning."

Hector cursed and dashed over to the pan while Daniel exited the room.

"You have to pay attention when you're in the kitchen, honey." Adelaide patted his butt again.

"Thanks," Hector said dryly.

They finished cooking and took the food out to the patio to eat.

"You're awfully quiet," Hector said after a few minutes.

"Why did you do that with Danny?" Adelaide asked.

"Because he needs to get used to seeing me here," he replied matter-of-factly.

"Were you planning for us to do this again?" She hadn't thought that far ahead. She'd simply wanted to bask in this moment and last night's lovemaking.

Hector set down his utensils and studied her from across the table. "Are you my ex-wife, or has someone else invaded her body? Someone completely fine with casual sex and no commitment?"

Adelaide smiled. "It's absolutely me. I'm just surprised. I really wasn't sure what happened. It's not as if we planned last night."

"Or this morning," Hector added, heat in his voice.

An answering throb bloomed between Adelaide's thighs. "Or this morning," she agreed.

"We can't pretend that we didn't make love, but I admit, in a weird way, this is all new—practically groundbreaking."

Adelaide nodded her agreement and rested her chin in her hand. Her heart hurt because this was the man she had married and raised children with and had expected to spend the rest of her life with in this house. Now he was here again, but not as her husband. Simply as a lover. She wanted to grab onto him and what she was feeling, but at the same time she was afraid and wanted to let go so she wouldn't be hurt again.

"Maybe this is a way for us to fix what was wrong between us," Hector said.

"Sex doesn't fix problems."

"I wasn't talking about using sex to fix our problems, although more sex would be perfectly fine by me." Hector's lascivious smile made her blush. He reached across the table and took her hand. "I want to continue making love to you, and I want to date you, too."

"Date me?"

"Yes. Are you open to that?"

"Yes," Adelaide said softly.

His lips expanded into a winsome smile. "Okay then." He sliced into a piece of French toast.

"When?" Adelaide asked.

"Let me worry about that," Hector said, and popped some of the tasty bread into his mouth.

The sun was setting as Adelaide and her best friends strolled onto the outdoor patio with beverages and snacks in hand. They sat at the rectangular glass table, Jackie and Adelaide at one end and Renee at the other.

"Who wants to go first?" Jackie asked.

"I have nothing to share, except Clive and I are still going strong," Renee said.

Jackie raised her hand. "I'll go next." She grinned, blushing a little. "I met someone, and he's younger than me."

Adelaide rested her chin on her hand. "Oh."

"How much younger?" Renee asked.

"Almost thirty years younger."

Adelaide and Renee gasped.

"You're fifty-five years old! You're practically robbing the cradle," Renee exclaimed.

Jackie rolled her eyes. "No, I'm not. Anyway, he's wonderful. Tall, dark, handsome, young, and malleable. How we met is absolutely hilarious." She proceeded to tell them how she ran over the young man on her bike while riding in the park.

When they finished laughing, Renee pretended to write a note. "Buy a bicycle and run over a hot man with it," she murmured.

Jackie cackled and shoved her friend. "Stop! We all know you're doing no such thing because you're happy with your quarterback."

"Tight end, and I am," Renee admitted, with a serene smile.

"Is your relationship with this young man serious?" Adelaide asked Jackie.

"Too soon to tell, but in all honesty, I doubt it will be. I just want to have fun. Whenever we get around to having sex, I'm sure it'll be fantastic and memorable."

Jackie talked like someone who had sex often, but she actually had a thirty-day rule that Adelaide could only remember her breaking once, and she'd regretted it because the relationship—if one could call it that—fizzled and died, leaving her broken-hearted and jaded for a long time.

"How about you? Dating anyone yet?" Jackie asked Adelaide.

A smile touched Adelaide's lips.

Renee turned her whole body in Adelaide's direction. "Spill. It."

Adelaide laughed. "You're not going to believe this, but Hector and I might be getting back together." She waited for her friends' reactions.

Jackie's eyes widened. "Hector Flores, your ex-husband?"

Adelaide nodded.

"The husband you divorced about six months ago?" Renee asked.

Adelaide nodded again.

"Care to explain how this happened?" Jackie asked.

Her friends already knew that her son was having a baby, so she explained the tie-in with the change in her and Hector's relationship. She told them about the kiss on the sofa, their nightly conversations, and finished with his reaction when he saw her with her cousin.

"Nothing like another man to make a man realize what he's lost," Jackie said, her eyebrow arched before taking a swig of lemonade.

"I believe it's more than that," Adelaide said. "More than jealousy or some crazy belief that he wants to hold on to me because he doesn't want anyone else to have me. Being with Hector this time feels...different. He's different and I'm different. We're much more aware of each other's needs and moods and we're laughing a lot—more than we did the last few years of our marriage. He's attentive and wants to spend time with me. For instance, one day last week, he came by after work and joined me in my afternoon walk around the neighborhood. He said that he'd like for the two of us to take a trip together when he wraps up the expansion of Solar Beams. Oh, by the way, he and Martin are opening a new location in Carlsbad." She beamed with pride.

"That's great! He's wanted to do that for a while, hasn't he?" Jackie asked.

Adelaide nodded. "Anyway, we have plans to go out this coming Friday night. He's taking me on a sunset boat ride."

"That's so romantic," Renee crooned with a sigh.

This was exactly what she'd longed for before their split—more time with her husband. Hector had become so busy with work, and when he came home, he simply ate dinner, maybe caught a little bit of TV, and then went to spend time in the home office before coming to bed. Some nights they barely said a full sentence to each other.

She'd felt neglected. When they did spend time together, he was always on his phone or seemed distracted—in the room but not present. The only time he paid her attention was to have sex, the frequency of which eventually dropped off and made her believe he no longer found her desirable. Now she knew that wasn't the case, but she'd been devastated before, insecure and hurt. Getting her hair done and putting on a new outfit had renewed her confidence, and she'd appreciated the admiring glances she received from other men.

"I'm excited for you. You look really happy," Jackie said.

"I'm cautiously happy but ready to jump headfirst into whatever this is. It's like being in a new relationship." And the excitement of a new relationship sent adrenaline coursing through her veins.

"It would be nice if you two get back together," Renee said.

"I don't see why that wouldn't be on the table. It's almost like we are back together again, before we started having problems."

"Don't get too attached to him right now," Jackie, the voice of reason, interjected. "And make sure he doesn't have another woman somewhere."

Adelaide hadn't considered that he'd moved on, and Jackie's practical comment burst her happy bubble a little bit. "I'm pretty sure he doesn't have anyone else, and I'm so excited! Maybe splitting up was exactly what we needed to appreciate each other. It certainly seems to have opened his eyes about me."

"What's going on with your cooking classes?" Jackie asked.

"I'm still going to take the classes, but I hope I'm mentally ready to meet the challenge of sitting in a classroom again."

"I have no doubt in my mind that you'll be able to handle the work. You love cooking, and you have time to pursue your catering dream now with the kids all grown."

"Are you still thinking about catering?" Renee asked.

Adelaide nodded. "I used to want to work in a restaurant, but that's exhausting work, and as I've gotten older, I've grown to appreciate my free time. I'd much rather set my own schedule and only work the events I'm interested in. Hector was so insistent that he would be able to take care of me and the kids, that I rarely envisioned going back to school. He did take such good care of us. Now I have to admit that a part of me regrets not taking classes and setting up my business earlier, but it's not too late. Is it?"

"Not at all. You'll succeed. There's no doubt in my mind," Renee said firmly.

"I'm definitely looking forward to it."

"Have you mentioned to Hector that you're going to get your diploma?" Jackie asked.

"I did." Adelaide broke off a piece of brownie, hesitant to divulge his lackluster response.

"What'd he say?" Renee asked.

"He congratulated me on my decision," Adelaide answered.

That was the truth, and they didn't need to know about her disappointment from his comments. She was moving forward with the decision regardless. She was doing this for her.

Adelaide looked at both of her friends. "I have a confession to make. I'm *extremely* worried about failing."

Jackie covered Adelaide's clenched fist on the table. "What did you tell me when I was worried about becoming a mom at my age? You said that I wouldn't be doing it on my own. You'd help me. Renee would help me. You think we're gonna have you out there on your own, struggling? No ma'am."

"That's right. We won't let that happen. Where's the brochure?"

"Now?" Adelaide asked.

"Yes, now. And bring your laptop," Renee said.

Adelaide hesitated, but the scolding look on her friends' faces made her stop delaying. She went inside and retrieved the brochure and her computer. When she came out, Renee had dragged her chair around to the same side as hers.

As Adelaide sat down, Jackie perused the brochure. "You can do everything online, including pay the application fee. Let's go. Chop-chop."

She knew better than to argue with them in this mood. At the school's website, she completed all the fields, and Renee helped her craft an impressive short essay. She plugged in her credit card information and hovered over the *Submit* button on the screen. Tears filled her eyes as she chewed on her bottom lip. Could she do this?

Renee took her hand and whispered, "You're going to be the best student they ever had. They'll be asking you teach the classes."

Jackie nodded in agreement.

Adelaide inhaled deeply. She'd dreamed of having a career, something separate from the family for a long time. Now was her chance, and she couldn't let fear keep her from achieving that goal. With a wince, she pressed the button.

And then the tears fell.

Jackie hugged her against her side and rested her head against hers. "You did it! Congratulations on this new chapter in your life. Soon you'll have your diploma and you'll start your catering business."

Renee squeezed her hand tighter. "And good luck to you and Hector. The two of you were always my ideal couple, so I would love to see you get back together, the way you used to be."

Adelaide grinned through her tears. "A new career and a second chance with the man I love. My life couldn't be better."

13

Wow.

Hector's eyes remained glued to Adelaide in the doorway. She wore a forest green wrap maxi dress that brought out the green in her hazel eyes and looked great against her dark gold skin. A skinny waist tie showed off her narrow waist while the gauzy fabric flowed down the length of her body to where tan, one-inch sandals peeked from beneath the hemline.

"Ready?" Adelaide asked.

"Ready." Hector offered his arm, and when she took it, he placed a kiss on her mouth.

Adelaide smiled up at him, her pretty eyes glowing. "I've been looking forward to this sunset cruise all day."

"Happy to hear that. It's supposed to be really nice," Hector said.

He opened the passenger door and Adelaide slid in. When both sides of the wrap dress fell apart and exposed a thigh, he bit back a groan and closed the door. He was a lucky man to have her back in his life, and he promised himself he wouldn't squander this second chance.

"You look nice. I like your outfit," Adelaide said when he slipped behind the wheel. She squeezed his thigh.

He appreciated her open affection. So often, a man was expected to be the one to pay compliments, but Adelaide was not shy about letting him know when she liked an outfit or that she was attracted to him.

Today's comment was particularly welcomed because the cream pullover and brown cargo pants were a calculated choice intended to snag her attention. She liked him in this shirt, stating in the past that it made his chest and back look particularly broad. She also liked the cargo pants, which she said made his thighs look bigger.

"These old clothes?" Hector said.

"Yes, those old clothes," she said with amusement.

They leaned toward each other and kissed again briefly before he backed out of the driveway.

Focusing on the business, he'd missed spending time with her. Putting in more time at work meant less time with his wife. The withdrawal had been gradual—so gradual he hadn't noticed, but now deeply regretted not prioritizing his marriage. But with the changes he had planned, lack of time would no longer be an issue.

"How is Danny doing at Solar Beams?" Adelaide asked.

"Excellent. The other day he submitted some ideas for the business."

"Danny? *Our* Danny?"

Hector nodded, taking a left at the end of the street. "I'm as surprised as you are. He typed up a nice report with recommendations for the website and the store. Some of the ideas are pretty good." Pride filled his voice.

"So it wasn't a mistake for him to come work for you?"

"I don't think so."

"What do you think about him not going to college?"

As he cruised to a stop at a traffic light, Hector remained silent for a while. "I've changed my position on my ideas about college. I'm glad Karen and Junior went and found their passion, but college isn't for everyone. I didn't finish college, and I turned out fine. Danny will, too."

"I think he will, honey. You know what else I think?"

"What?"

"He's more like you than you realize, or that you want to admit."

Hector laughed softly. "That's probably true. Hell, the trajectory of his life is looking awfully familiar. Screw up in school, get a woman pregnant, drop out of college, start selling renewable energy products. Damn, Danny is me."

Laughing, Adelaide said, "We should have named him Junior."

"We should have."

"So how long is this excursion?" she asked, crossing her legs.

"Two and a half hours," Hector replied.

Then he placed a hand on her thigh and sent a smile in her direction. His mood was happier and much lighter now.

Adelaide and this second chance had transformed him into a new man.

WHEN THEY ARRIVED at the Sunset Resort Marina, the skipper of the *Freedom* sailing yacht met them and introduced himself as John.

A Caucasian man with dark hair and a generous smile, he gripped Adelaide's hand and gave it a firm shake. "I'll be your host for the next couple of hours. My grandson, Decker, is my helper today. He's a great photographer and can take any pictures you like."

A young man with strikingly similar features, who looked about sixteen, said hello and smiled politely at them.

Adelaide glanced around. "Is anyone else coming?" she asked.

"Normally we have other guests, but Mr. Flores booked the entire boat for your leisure."

"He did?" Adelaide said, pleasantly surprised that Hector had gone through the additional expense.

"If we're going to do this, we have to do it right," Hector said.

She wanted to kiss him again but refrained, opting instead to show her appreciation by squeezing his arm.

Hector climbed into the boat and offered a steadying hand to help her on board.

"I have plenty of refreshments below. Beer, wine, and snacks. Just help yourself," John said.

Because of the cool air out on the water, Hector threw a spare jacket he'd brought along over Adelaide's shoulders and wrapped one arm around her. Within minutes, they pulled into San Diego Bay with John at the helm. The *Freedom* glided through the water, and Adelaide and Hector stood in the boat, the air drifting over them.

John pointed out sights of interest, such as the great view of downtown San Diego, with the sun hitting the buildings and casting a golden hue across their exteriors. They passed by landmarks such as the Maritime Museum, Coronado Bridge, and Old Point Loma Lighthouse.

At one point, John let Adelaide take the wheel and she guided the boat through the waters, all while receiving cheers from the three men aboard.

"Sea lions!" Decker suddenly yelled, pointing.

Sure enough, a few of them played in the waves.

"Hector, look!' Adelaide moved to the handrail and watched the animals, who seemed to put on a more elaborate show for them as they passed by.

When she turned to Hector, he snapped photos of her, and she decided to play to the camera. Removing the jacket, posing with puckered lips and bedroom eyes as the wind blew through her hair and whipped tendrils across her face.

"Tease," he said huskily.

The trip ended with them sitting on the cushioned bench, Adelaide backed up to Hector, whose arm stretched along the top of the seat. With one foot curled under her and a glass of wine in hand, Adelaide wound down as the water lapped against the hull and serenaded them in the darkening day.

Regretfully, they couldn't remain out on the water all night. When they docked at the marina, Adelaide blew out a heavy sigh.

"We have to go," Hector said quietly, nuzzling her neck.

Before they disembarked, she gave Decker and John a hug and

thanked them profusely for an enjoyable evening before Hector took her hand and they walked slowly back to the car.

The ride to the house took place mostly in silence with Adelaide flipping through the photos in Hector's camera and smiling at each one. Decker had also taken several candid shots of them and texted them over. She particularly liked the one with them seated close together at the end, quietly sipping wine with the water and buildings in the background. She might blow up the image and frame it.

Back at the house, they walked into the bedroom, where they took a leisurely shower together, kissing and touching with all the intimacy and affection of a couple who'd known each other for a very long time. Finally, they dressed for bed—Adelaide in a nightshirt and Hector in pajama bottoms—and climbed under the covers. Adelaide flung her arm across his broad chest and rested her head in the crook of his arm. Eyes closed, she savored this happy place, her spirit full and content the same way a hearty meal might fill her stomach.

"Addie?" Hector said in a low voice.

"Mmm?" She was already half asleep, and shifted more comfortably against him.

"I never wanted the divorce."

Her eyes opened and she stared into the near-darkness of the room. "I didn't, either," she admitted. "I wanted our situation to change, and when it didn't, I thought it was better for us to break up."

They both became quiet.

Hector broke the silence. "I still love you."

For a minute, she didn't know what to say or do. She'd never thought she'd hear those words from Hector again.

Carefully, Adelaide eased back so she could see him in the dim light. Damn, her man was beautiful. Even in the moonlight-kissed darkness, she saw how handsome he was. That solid jawline, his thick dark hair, and those eyes that seemed to see deep within her, searching for all her secrets.

Hector had never been a very expressive man. Every time he told her he loved her had been a gift, because for him, his actions more than his words indicated his feelings. The lack of communication had been hard for her to comprehend at first because she was prone to verbalizing her feelings—needed to hear those words after growing up in a household where hearing the words *I love you* occurred as often as rain in the desert.

She smiled, caressing his jaw and neck, and the solidness of his shoulder—reveling in the fact that she could touch him again.

"I love you, too, Hector. You make me so happy. You're still the man of my dreams."

He rolled over and flung an arm across her waist, bringing their faces close together so they were staring into each other's eyes.

"And you're still the woman of my dreams. *Mi rosa.*"

She kissed him softly, tenderly—but soon the kiss became more amorous as their heated bodies pressed against each other. One hand stroked her inner thighs and her sex, making her mewl and arch her back.

"I'm going down to the Carlsbad, to the new location in a few days. Come with me," Hector whispered huskily. His tongue traced the shell of her ear.

"Yes," Adelaide answered. With the way he touched and kissed her, she would give him anything he requested.

Hector removed her panties and she pushed his pajamas low enough that he could slide home.

They both groaned and she wound her arms around his neck, thrusting her hips against his.

They climaxed almost simultaneously—bodies shuddering, and their breaths sounding like loudly whispered secrets in the dark room.

14

Hector entered the kitchen and planted a kiss on the side of Adelaide's neck. His lips were soft and moist and left her skin tingling.

"What was that for?" Adelaide asked.

"Because I can. Because I love kissing you." His eyes crinkled at the corners as he smiled.

Adelaide giggled and wrapped her arms round his neck.

"How did the doctor's visit go today?" Hector asked, backing her into the counter.

While he was at work, she had accompanied Jamie and Daniel on a doctor's visit. "Great. Jamie's pregnancy is progressing well, and she's healthy and following doctor's orders."

"Good to hear. When is the next scheduled visit?"

"Next month."

"I'd like to come."

"That would be nice, honey. I'm sure Danny would love to have you there."

"Now for other matters. Ready to head to Carlsbad? We can have dinner there before we come back."

"Ready," Adelaide said.

They left the house, and as they pulled out of the driveway, they waved at a neighbor walking his dog. Once they hit the road, the short trip reminded Adelaide of when Hector and Martin had opened their first store. They had been so excited. She and Hector celebrated over an expensive dinner and way too much liquor with Martin and his wife. Having already made plans for a babysitter to stay all night, they took a cab to the hotel where they would be staying and fell into bed and made love. The next morning, hungover and drunk on happiness, they took care of each other and laughed at their behavior but realized they were on their way —an upwardly mobile couple with three kids, ready to take on the world.

In about thirty-five minutes, they arrived at the location. Adelaide stepped out of the Cherokee and looked at the almost-finished building.

"When does the sign get here?" she asked, resting her hands on her hips. There was no permanent sign on the building, but a banner displayed the name of the new business, Solar Beams III.

"I told Martin I wanted to wait, have the sign hung last."

"You want to make a big deal out of it." Adelaide understood the idea behind the ceremony of the permanent sign.

Hector draped an arm around her shoulders. "Exactly."

"You can be sentimental at times," she teased.

Hector shook his head. "Not me."

Adelaide chuckled and circled her arms around his waist, gazing up at him. "Yes, you."

He didn't seem to hear her, eyes focused on the building in front of them.

"Are you thinking about him?" she asked.

That was the thing about knowing someone for decades. You became attuned to their moods, their hesitations. Thoughts of his father weighed heavy on his mind, and without explicitly asking, he knew she was referring to Papi.

Hector's father had still been alive when they opened the first store, and no one had been happier or prouder than Papi Flores.

Adelaide was certain that everyone in the state of Michoacán knew about his son's success.

"I wish he were alive to see me achieve my dream. Three stores, just like I told him."

"I believe he sees you. And he's proud."

"Yeah," Hector said, but his voice sounded distant and filled with longing. He rubbed her back and then took her hand. "I have something else to tell you. As you know, Martin's mother-in-law is in a fragile mental state with onset Alzheimer's, and Paula's been spending a lot more time in Jamaica to take care of her and her younger brother."

Adelaide nodded. Paula's brother had Down's Syndrome, and her mother had been his primary caregiver all these years. Now that her mother's health was declining, she'd hired someone to live in the house with them, but also spent months at a time in her home country.

"Martin and Paula want to permanently move to Jamaica to help with Paula's mother and her brother, so he wants me to buy him out."

Adelaide stepped back. "Really?"

Hector nodded. "We started talking about the possibility a year ago, and two days ago my loan application was approved."

"Oh, my god, Hector!" Adelaide squealed. She flung her arms around his neck and he laughed, squeezing her tight against his body.

She stepped back. "So you're going to be the sole owner of the Solar Beams company? All three stores?"

"All three stores. All mine."

"Oh, baby. I'm so happy for you. You've worked so hard. Congratulations."

"Thanks." In typical Hector fashion, he remained calm and cool, except for the gleam of pride in his eyes.

"We're having champagne with our meal," Adelaide said.

"I like that plan. Let me show you inside and then we'll head to dinner."

The interior was still under construction, but already Adelaide saw this store boasted a sleek and modern design, a contrast to the first two stores and their warehouse feel.

For dinner, they settled on an Asian fusion restaurant that served Chinese, Thai, and Vietnamese dishes. Once seated at the table, Adelaide flipped open the expansive menu and perused the list of choices.

"How hungry are you?" she asked, glancing at the appetizers.

"Get what you want. You know I'll end up eating two-thirds of it anyway." Hector grinned across the table at her.

"Untrue. Okay, partially true." They both laughed.

Idly, Adelaide scanned the sushi choices, thinking maybe they could start there. She was about to suggest that to Hector when she had the feeling they were being watched. She searched the room, and her eyes landed on a woman seated two tables over. She sat with a man who had just accepted the bill from the waiter, but she didn't pay him or the waiter any mind, her entire focus directed at Hector.

Something about the way she looked at him made Adelaide uneasy. There was so much longing in her expression that she was certain this wasn't a simple case of a stranger finding her ex-husband attractive. Adelaide was certain they knew each other.

The woman's gaze locked with Adelaide's before quickly looking away.

"How about we start with sushi?" Hector said.

Adelaide swung her gaze back to him and he looked up from the menu. "Um, I was about to suggest the same thing."

"Let's get the assorted platter. Do you know what you want for dinner?"

"I'll have the hibachi shrimp."

"Mongolian beef for me." Hector closed his menu.

Should she say something about the woman? The decision was taken out of her hands when the woman and her date came over to the table.

"Hello, Hector, how are you?"

Adelaide kept her eyes trained on Hector, watching his reaction.

He didn't react much, except for a quick frown. "Hi Rita, how are you?"

"I'm doing fine, thanks. This is my brother, Bert."

"Nice to meet you," Bert said.

Hector stood and shook the other man's hand. "Hector. Nice to meet you. This is my...this is Adelaide."

"Adelaide?" Rita said her name in surprise. "The ex-wife?"

Interesting. He'd talked about her with this woman.

"Yes," Hector said shortly.

"Nice to meet you." Rita extended her hand.

Adelaide stood and shook hands with Rita. "Nice to meet you, too."

"Are the two of you back together?" Rita's voice sounded normal enough, but the smile on her face looked unnatural and stilted.

"I think we better go," Bert interjected, cheeks turning red.

Rita laughed self-consciously. "I'm sorry. I'll see you later, Hector. The two of you have a nice meal. The food here is delicious. Good night." Once more Rita glanced at Adelaide before they both disappeared.

Hector and Adelaide sat down and Adelaide sipped her water. She avoided Hector's eyes but could feel him looking across the table at her.

"Do you want to ask me anything?"

She could say No and ignore the weight of suspicion in her gut, but she couldn't.

She looked across the table at Hector, suddenly having difficulty with the idea that he was her ex-husband and not her husband.

"Have you slept with anyone since our divorce?" The question came out softer than she expected because she was afraid he'd give the answer she expected.

He answered gently, his eyes never leaving her face. "Once. Right after we divorced."

She let him take her hand while her heart broke a little. She didn't want to think of him making love to another woman.

"With Rita?" she asked dully.

"Yes. She's my next-door neighbor and I shouldn't have done it. I wasn't ready and it felt unnatural, like I was cheating on you."

"Why did you sleep with her in the first place?" Adelaide asked.

"I don't know...loneliness? I was at a low point, and she was kind and friendly. I regretted it afterward." Hector rubbed his thumb over her fingers. "No one in the world can replace you, Addie. I'm right where I want to be, with the woman I should have never left. I should have said no when you asked for a divorce. I hate like hell I gave up when I should have fought for us."

His sentiment went both ways. Maybe she gave up too easily. True enough their marriage hadn't felt happy for a few years, but what was a few years' rough patch in light of two decades of love, laughter, and happy times?

"Do you want to know about me?" she asked.

"No," Hector answered swiftly, his hand tightening over hers. The lines in his face became sharper.

"I didn't sleep with anyone else though I thought about it, as a way to exorcise the ghost of you in my head."

He closed his eyes briefly and squeezed her hand again. "It wouldn't have made a difference to me if you had, but I..."

"Didn't want to know," Adelaide finished for him.

"Right."

She wished she hadn't asked him about Rita. Knowing he'd been with someone else, even once, hurt. But knowing he loved her and regretted what he'd done, eased the pain.

"We should call the waiter. I'm starving." She sent a reassuring smile across the table.

"*Te amo, mi rosa*," he said, gaze intense.

"I know. I love you, too."

They loved each other, and that's all that mattered.

"My favorite couple has arrived! I don't care who else shows up."

While it was strange to be considered a couple again, Adelaide took the compliment in stride. She always enjoyed dinner at Matt and Eleanor's house for the adult conversations, good food, and plenty of laughs.

Eleanor flung her arms wide and embraced first Hector and then Adelaide. Decked out in a black dress, pearls, and heels, with her blonde hair pulled into a low ponytail, Eleanor was, as usual, over-dressed for her own dinner party.

Behind her, her husband Matt, dressed more comfortably in jeans and a short-sleeved button-down shirt, nudged his glasses higher on his nose and smiled. "Welcome."

Adelaide and Hector entered the open great room and were greeted by the other two couples present. A Caucasian couple named Jessica and Brad—both lanky with dark hair—and the couple she'd been looking forward to seeing—Martin and Paula.

"Eleanor acts as if we're not even here. I'm kinda hurt." Paula stood and greeted Adelaide with a warm hug. A statuesque woman with brown skin and thick natural hair, Paula wore her hair in a blonde Afro. They hadn't seen each other in a long time, since Paula was busy flying back and forth to Jamaica to look after her family.

"You know I love you, but I've never made a secret of my love for the Floreses, and of course I have a soft spot for Adelaide because she always brings the most delicious dishes." Eleanor removed the casserole dish from Adelaide's hands. "Please tell me this is mac and cheese."

"Mac and cheese, as you requested." Adelaide knew she couldn't walk into the house without the dish. Though Eleanor was hosting and provided the food, Adelaide was the only one she asked to bring side dish. "I also brought an apple crumb cake. I practically had to beat Hector to keep him from cutting a slice."

Holding the plastic cake dish in hand, Hector deadpanned, "I'll show you my bruises later. Just know that it wasn't easy to behave myself."

"But I'm so glad you did. I would hate to cancel our friendship over crumb cake." Eleanor shot him a teasing smile and then glided toward the kitchen. Matt took the cake from Hector and followed. "The roast is warming in the oven. Give us five minutes and we'll be ready," she added.

Little more than five minutes later, they were all seated around the dining room table with the food spread out family-style. Matt said a short prayer and then they started passing around the dishes.

"I have good news," Jessica said, spooning a hearty serving of macaroni and cheese on her plate. "I got the promotion!" Blushing and smiling, she accepted the round of congratulations that filled the room.

"I'm so glad to hear your hard work paid off. You've worked in HR for how long...twenty years now?" Eleanor asked.

"Almost, and when Lola retired, I knew this was my chance to become HR director, but I wasn't sure if they'd give me the position or hire someone from the outside."

"I retire next year and she starts bringing in the big bucks. Perfect timing," Brad said with glee.

They all laughed.

"I predict you're going to be very bored at home. Ask Matt how he feels about retirement." Eleanor looked pointedly at the other end of the table where her husband sat.

Matt grunted as he placed a portion of the delicious-smelling roast onto his plate.

Plates continued to be passed around before everyone settled down with their meals. Eleanor arched an eyebrow. "Can I be the one to mention the elephant in the room?"

"Eleanor..." Matt warned.

"What?" Eleanor widened her eyes innocently. "We're all thinking it, aren't we?" She looked around the table.

Hector put down his knife and fork and shook his head. "Go ahead and ask, Eleanor."

"Well, if you insist. Are the two of you getting back together, for good?"

The room fell quiet. Adelaide looked at Hector, and he took her hand.

"Yes. We've decided to give marriage another try."

"Hallelujah!" Eleanor threw up her hands. "You have no idea how invested I was in your marriage. Before Matt and I got married, I told him this is my second marriage and this time I want to do it right. I said I wanted a marriage like yours. Real and loving. I was devastated when you divorced, so I'm glad you're back together. We have to do drink to that."

There were big smiles around the table, as well as "Congratulations" and "We're so happy for you two," all of which brought a smile to Adelaide's lips. It was nice to be in the company of her friends again, and even nicer to know how happy they were that she and Hector were reconciling.

Eleanor held up her glass of red wine. "Cheers!"

They all clinked their glasses together.

"Lots of good news tonight," Martin said. "Might as well tell you all about the third store Hector and I are opening. This one is in Carlsbad."

"Wait a minute, aren't you supposed to be retiring to Jamaica, but you're opening another store?" Jessica asked.

"I still plan to retire if I can get this man right here to buy me out." He pointed his fork at Hector.

"I want to, believe me. It's definitely something I'm thinking about." He glanced at Adelaide beside him, sending a silent message that he hadn't yet told Martin he'd been approved for the loan. Knowing what a perfectionist he was, she figured he was still crunching numbers and ironing out the details.

"Do you need Adelaide's permission, is that it?" Eleanor asked mischievously.

"He does not," Adelaide said. "Don't start trouble, we just got back together. He'll make the decision on his own, when the time is right. You know Hector—he'll sit down with his calculations and turn the numbers over in his head, and then decide."

Hector slipped his arm along the back of her chair. "Until then, she's been very supportive. She's coming with me next week to watch them put the permanent sign on the store."

"Aww, how sweet. See, that's what I was talking about when I said I want a marriage like yours. You're supportive of each other."

"I'm supportive of you," Matt said, sounding a little hurt.

"Yes, you are, darling." Eleanor blew him a kiss. "Everyone is doing so well. Hector and Adelaide reconciled. Hector and Martin opening a new store. Jessica got a promotion, and Adelaide starts classes in the fall."

"Classes?" Paula said.

"Yes, I start culinary classes in September. I'm going for my diploma from the School of Culinary Arts."

Eleanor beamed at Adelaide. "She's going to start catering, and I can't wait to be her first customer!"

"That's wonderful!" Paula said.

"I thought you were putting that on hold." Beside her, Hector's voice didn't carry the same enthusiasm as their friends.

"I never said that."

He slowly removed his arm from the back of her chair, and silence filled the table as they stared at each other.

"Once we're remarried, when will you have time to cater events? Not to mention you're going to be helping Danny and Jamie with the baby, aren't you?"

Adelaide bristled. He was doing it again—squashing her dreams, and this time in front of others. "Actually, I'll have plenty of time because although I'll help Danny and Jamie with the baby, the baby is their responsibility, not mine."

He looked at her. She looked at him.

"More wine?" Eleanor asked cheerily, holding up the bottle.

"I'll have some," Paula said, overly bright.

Brad groaned. "This is really good macaroni and cheese. I can see why you want to start catering. The dishes you bring are always delicious."

Jessica kicked him under the table and he jumped.

"Ow! What did I say?" he asked, oblivious to the tension.

"Did I mention that Matt and I are thinking about getting a dog? We came up with this crazy idea after visiting my mother and seeing how her dogs..."

Adelaide tuned out Eleanor and watched Hector from the corner of her eye. He chewed slowly and like her, no longer participated in the conversation around them.

Three years ago, she allowed him to talk her out of her idea of starting a business, and he placated her by giving the kitchen a facelift and creating an outdoor living area that was great for entertaining. But her satisfaction had been temporary. She wanted to do more, but clearly he didn't think she could do more. In his mind, she was simply a mother, a wife, and a soon-to-be grandmother. He couldn't see her as a businesswoman.

His words hurt, and at some point they'd have to discuss why he had such a poor opinion of her and constantly tried to kill her dream.

Tonight was the night.

16

Hector slammed the door on her side. If slamming wasn't enough to convey he was upset, his rigid back as he walked around the front of the SUV certainly did.

Adelaide fastened her seatbelt and waited until he was settled behind the wheel before she spoke.

"I cannot believe how you embarrassed me front of our friends. I'm going to take the classes whether you want me to or not."

"Obviously. What I think doesn't matter."

"What exactly do you think? What's your problem with me taking the culinary classes?"

"It's not the classes," he said between gritted teeth.

"So it's as I thought—you just don't want me to start a business, am I right?"

"Could we not do this right now when I'm driving? Let's talk when we get home, all right?"

Adelaide folded her arms cross her chest and stared out the side window.

"All right?" Hector prompted again.

"Fine," she answered between gritted teeth.

They arrived at the house in record time. It seemed as if he'd pressed his foot all the way down on the accelerator, speeding through intersections and careening around corners like a madman. He completely ignored Adelaide's grunts and the times she grabbed onto the seat because of his reckless driving.

When he pulled into the garage, she glared at him. "Nice driving. Did you want to get us killed so we wouldn't have to talk?"

He ignored her and she exited the vehicle, following him into the house and into the master bedroom.

"Now are you ready to talk?" she asked.

He let out an exasperated sigh and turned to face her. "Yes, I'm ready to talk about why you feel the need to get a job when all your needs have been taken care of. When we've talked about getting back together. I don't understand why you're so adamant about starting a catering company when, for years, you told me that being a mother is the hardest and greatest, most satisfying job ever. What happened to all of that?"

"I used to feel that way."

"And now?"

"I want more, Hector. I want something else. The job is finished. Yes, I know we still have children and they'll always be my babies, but for all practical purposes, the job is finished. Junior is on another continent. Karen is in another city pursuing her dreams. Danny has a job and is about to start a family. They're all grown up. They don't need me anymore." Her voice quivered. "I need this, Hector. Why are you so against me starting a business?"

"Why am I so against you starting a business?" He laughed bitterly.

She had no idea why he was behaving this way. "It's not enough that I worked hard all these years, taking care of the kids, making sure you have a hot meal twice a day during the week and three times on the weekend? I did my part, so why can't you be happy for me? Why won't you support my dream?"

"I *have* supported you and done everything humanly possible to make you happy. You wanted this house." He gestured widely in the general vicinity of the walls. "I bought it for you. You wanted that kitchen with top-of-the-line appliances, and we did the renovation. You wanted three kids and a patio so you could socialize with your girlfriends. Everything you wanted, I gave to you."

"You gave me this and gave me that. That makes you feel like a big man when you say that, doesn't it? Look at what I've done for my wife, fellas. Maybe I want something that I earned on my own, that you didn't give me. And frankly, while I admit you're very generous, you didn't give me everything I wanted, as you so glibly put it."

"Tell me what you wanted that I never gave you. Tell me!"

Because he was yelling, she yelled, too. "Your time!"

His eyebrows snapped together. "Did you tell me that? Because I don't recall having that conversation. You clearly articulated your need for a state-of-the-art kitchen, but when did you tell me you wanted to spend more time with me? I'll tell you when. Never. Not once."

"Because I didn't want to beg. Why didn't you want to spend time with me, the way you used to? I never had to tell you that before. I was your wife."

She'd been embarrassed about her need to be with him, especially when it was so obvious he didn't feel the need to be with her. Coupled with the fact that the kids were all independent, she'd felt like a useless appendage.

"I didn't have time because I was busy giving you the life that you wanted."

"No, don't you dare blame this on me." Adelaide marched over to him and jabbed a finger in his face. "You wanted the three stores and the SUV and the family vacations. You're the one who sends money to your family back in Mexico and helped support your aunt when she got sick and couldn't work. That was all you. Choices you made that meant you had to work harder and longer hours."

"That's what a man does."

"You know what, I'm sick of your macho bullshit."

"Oh, now it's bullshit. Now you're sick of it." Bitterness filled Hector's abrupt laugh.

"A man isn't supposed to only provide financial security.

Emotional security, caring, that's all part of marriage." Adelaide trembled with finally unleashed rage. She didn't have to hide her feelings and comments anymore.

Hector narrowed his eyes. "You know what else is part of marriage? Getting the support you need from your wife. Hearing a goddamn 'thank-you' every now and again for providing a roof over your head and taking you and the kids on those expensive vacations once a year. But that's too much to ask because this marriage should only center around you."

"That is not true."

"You, you, you. Our entire marriage has always been about you, Addie. You and the kids. You know why we're divorced? Because you were unhappy. And me, I keep trying to fix every goddamn thing to make you happy. You didn't want to be with me, so I left, even though I was gutted by the thought that you'd stopped loving me. That I'd somehow fucked up and some other man was going to take my place in your life.

"The only thing that made me feel even remotely good was that I'd done my best all these years. I made sure we had shelter, food, the kids could go to the colleges they wanted and had everything they ever needed, but all you can do is tell me what I'm doing wrong. Did I do anything right? You want to spend time with me, and I'm giving you that now. I'm meeting your needs. But what about my needs?" He slammed his fist against his chest. "Do they matter? Can I get a damn thank-you, just once? Good job, Hector. No, that would be too much to ask, wouldn't it? Because it wouldn't be about you." He huffed and shook his head. "You want your own job, then fine, have at it. Show the world how little you need me. Show the world that I can't take care of my own wife."

"That's not what—" He pushed past her out the door. "Hector!"

He kept moving.

"Where are you going?"

"Out."

"We need to finish this conversation." She followed him to the garage.

"We're done talking. We've said everything we need to say to each other."

"Where are you going?" she asked again.

"Home."

That single word pained her. He hadn't referred to the apartment as *home* in weeks.

"Fine! Go! Maybe Rita can keep you company tonight." She gasped, wishing she could take back the words. She didn't mean them because she didn't want that woman anywhere near her him.

Hector glared at her and then pulled out of the garage.

Adelaide didn't move, staring after him as the door slowly lowered. When he was gone, she went back into the house.

She stood in her pristine kitchen, the one he'd rightly accused her of asking for. It had been a consolation prize when she'd given up the idea of starting her catering business, something she'd only recently admitted to herself.

Hector's angry words forced her to see him with new eyes. The gruff, macho head of the family had been quietly resentful, just like her.

Had she been that dismissive of his feelings? She had let him know that she appreciated the kitchen remodel, but he was right—the words "thank you" hadn't left her lips frequently. And he'd given her a life that many women didn't have. Perhaps she'd taken his hard work for granted.

A man took care of his family.

Those were Papi Flores's words and words that Hector not only lived by, they were the source of his pride. She did complain about his job—a job that he saw as an extension of himself. A job that he took very seriously.

"Oh, Hector." Adelaide's heart ached.

He'd been gone less than ten minutes, and she already missed him.

17

"Hey, Mom."

"Hi, honey. Don't you look nice." Adelaide paused in the middle of wiping down the kitchen counter.

"Thanks." Daniel adjusted his tie and straightened his jacket.

He'd cut his hair, wearing a fade with longer curls on top. Her baby was definitely growing up. He looked so mature.

"Did Dad tell you the good news?" Daniel asked.

"What good news?"

"He said if I keep up the good work, in another year I might be ready to take over the Carlsbad store."

"That's wonderful!" Adelaide pulled her son into a tight hug. "When did he tell you that?"

"Yesterday, when he and I went to lunch together. He also plans to hire this guy away from one of our competitors—a real go-getter, he called him. Funny thing is, even with all this good news, Dad doesn't seem as happy as I thought he'd be." Daniel frowned thoughtfully. "Are the two of you okay?"

Adelaide and Hector had always agreed not to involve their kids in their fights, and she intended to keep it that way. However, she did want to let him know a little bit of what was going on. "Your dad and I are good, but we need to talk."

"You guys aren't splitting up again, are you?"

"No," Adelaide answered, though that statement might be premature. Hector had been very angry, and they hadn't spoken in the past couple of days. "Listen, your dad may not say it much, but he's very proud of you. He wanted one of you to go into business with him, but the twins weren't interested. From what he's told me, he's really enjoyed having you work with him, and the fact that he's already thinking ahead to having you manage the Carlsbad store says a lot."

"I like working at Solar Beams, and I've learned a lot from him, Martin, and the other guys." Daniel cleared his throat. "Dad and I had a long talk about me and Jamie and the baby, and Jamie and I have decided we don't want to get married. I mean, if later on down the road we think we love each other, we'll do it. But right now, we just want to be good parents, and that doesn't include being husband and wife."

"I understand. We'll support you, whatever you decide." She squeezed his hand and picked up her shoulder bag. "I have somewhere to be."

"Where are you going?"

If she hurried, she could catch Hector. "To Carlsbad."

ADELAIDE PULLED into the vacant parking lot and watched her ex-husband from a distance. He stood leaning against the front of his SUV, legs crossed at the ankles, his eyes locked on the Solar Beams III building. He was all alone, and she hated that he'd come here by himself when they were supposed to make this trip together. She was supposed to celebrate this momentous occasion with him.

She walked toward him, and before she arrived by his side, he turned his head in her direction. He frowned briefly in confusion, but then his expression cleared and he simply watched her approach.

Adelaide stood beside him and took his hand. His fingers curled around hers. "What time are they putting up the sign?"

"In about ten minutes."

Adelaide stood very close to him, so close that their thighs touched. They watched the workers, neither breaking the silence, hand in hand the way they'd been together for over twenty years.

After about ten minutes, the men hoisted the blue and white sign onto the front of the building and secured it in place. Hector let out a breath, and a faint smile crossed his lips.

Adelaide clasped his hand in both of hers and kissed his shoulder. "You did it," she said, tilting back her head to gaze up at him.

He glanced down at her. "Yeah." His smile broadened.

"Danny told me that you want him to take over this location."

"Not right now—maybe in another year or so when he has more experience."

"He also told me that you're hiring away a competitor to work with the company."

"He's the best in the business."

"Better than you?"

"Nobody's better than me," he said mildly.

Still holding Hector's hand, Adelaide stood in front of him. "There's so much I want to say to you and I don't know where to begin. But I guess the best place to begin is at the apology. I'm sorry that you felt unappreciated, too. You're right, I never thought about what you might need from me or your feelings regarding the work you do, and I'm very sorry."

"I didn't mean to come down on you and complain."

"You meant what you said, and you're right. I've never said thank you for taking care of me. For our beautiful home and making sure the kids and I have everything we need. Thank you for going out there every day and facing traffic and angry customers and dealing with the stress of regulations and employees and financial statements and everything you've had to put up with to give us a comfortable life. Thank you for being such a good husband, because God knows there are some terrible ones out there." She let out a short laugh and stepped between his legs. She kissed his chin, then his mouth. "Thank you," she whispered. "I will always need you, and I want you to know that my decision to go back to school doesn't mean that you're lacking in any way. I want to continue celebrating your accomplishments, but I want accomplishments of my own. I want to have a celebration for the project that *I* complete. The work that *I* do."

"And that makes sense. And I want to celebrate with you instead of acting like a jealous fool."

"You're not a fool, and neither am I. It's just that somewhere along the way, you and I changed. We became slightly different people."

"Which is to be expected after twenty-five years of marriage."

"Exactly. Growing doesn't mean we have to grow apart. We can grow together."

He nodded and sighed. Then his arms enveloped her and squeezed her against his chest.

"Why didn't you call me to make sure I was coming today?"

"I felt like an ass, and I wasn't sure if you'd still want to come."

"Hector, of course I wanted to come."

"Even after that comment about Rita?" He arched an eyebrow.

Heat filled her cheeks. "It was a stupid thing to say. I was angry."

"She doesn't mean anything to me, Addie."

"I know."

"Do you really?"

She nodded. "I felt a little insecure, that's all. Only for a minute."

"You have nothing to be insecure about. What happened between me and her was a mistake and it ended as soon as it started."

"She has feelings for you."

"But they're not reciprocated," Hector said in a firm voice.

"Okay." She played with a button on his shirt.

Hector kissed her temple. "I was going to call you after I got through here. Martin told me about this book, *The Five Love Languages.* Ever heard of it?"

"Yes, but I've never read it."

"Maybe we can read it together, but anyway, I thought the five love languages was foolishness at first and never bought a copy. Since our fight, I downloaded the audiobook and listened to it to and from the store and while I worked out at the gym. It actually makes sense. I believe your love language is quality time and mine is words of affirmation."

"Interesting." She tossed around what he said for a bit. "Which means we weren't expressing our love in each other's love language."

"Exactly. And over time, that created a rift."

"Twenty-five years and we still have a lot to learn." Adelaide sighed.

Hector rubbed her back and she snuggled closer against him. She'd missed his warm hugs and being held against his solid body.

"When do you start classes?" he asked.

"September. I'm nervous about going back to school after all this time."

He looked into her eyes. "You'll be fine. You'll be making As and Bs and kicking everybody else's ass in those culinary classes. I'm glad you decided to go back to school, and I know your catering business is going to be a success. I'm really looking forward to all those home-work assignments and the different recipes you'll be making."

"You're willing to be my guinea pig?" she teased.

"I was happily your guinea pig for years. Why not?"

Adelaide raised up on her toes. "Thank you."

"For what?"

"For being you."

Hector cupped her face and gazed into her eyes. "Will you marry me again?"

Adelaide grinned. "Of course. I thought you'd never ask."

JACKIE & TYSON

1

"Jackie, your guest has arrived and I'm heading out."

Jackie Bryant looked up from taking inventory of a shipment of bedroom slippers in the back room of her store. One of her salesclerks, Cindy, stood in the doorway, her flaming red Afro sitting on her head in a huge puff.

"See you later, hon. Let him know I'll be out in a few minutes, and lock us in on your way out."

Cindy stepped farther into the room and dropped her voice. "Okay, but just know, I'm jealous of that tall chocolate god you managed to snag." She arched a brow and a small smile appeared on her face.

Jackie laughed. Of course Cindy would find him attractive. They shared the same taste in men. "Have a safe trip with your *husband*."

She let Cindy leave at the end of her shift instead of staying behind to close down the store. She and her husband were taking a trip to celebrate their anniversary tomorrow, and Cindy wanted to go home early to pack and get ready for their morning drive.

"I will. I'll see you next week, and have fun this weekend." She winked and left.

Jackie definitely intended to have fun. She had a hot date tonight with a younger man, not one of those stuffy older men who thought life ended in their thirties. As a woman in her mid-fifties, she had lots of life to live and no intention of slowing down anytime soon. Since it seemed men her age couldn't keep up, she'd been quite pleased when she ran into a younger one who not only appreciated a more seasoned woman, but a full-figured one to boot.

She finished up in the back and stepped onto the brightly lit floor space of Bodacious, the flagship location of three stores she owned that exclusively sold lingerie and sleepwear for women with big, bodacious curves. Owning this store wasn't just a business for her, it was a cause. Her greatest challenge wasn't finding the right size for her customers, but getting a fair number of them to reject the media's perception of their body type and accept that they were sexy in their own right.

She placed a few of the shoes on the display hooks and walked onto the sales floor to greet Kendrick Pafford. Twenty-seven, gorgeous dark skin, and a big curly Afro.

At six feet eight, she'd initially assumed he played basketball or some other sport, but according to him he'd never been the athletic type and had hoped to become a model but gave up a while back. His height was one of her favorite attributes, considering she easily reached six feet in heels. Lord, how she loved a tall man. As a plus, the man knew how to dress and tonight looked scrumptious in a long-sleeved black shirt and black pants.

Jackie's face broke into a smile. "Hey, you."

Kendrick strolled over. "Hey there." He gave her a quick kiss on the lips. His lips were warm and soft and made her body tingle.

She wrapped her arms around his waist. "I'm famished and looking forward to that excellent meal you promised me." After dinner at the restaurant, she planned to have his tight, muscular body for dessert. She'd already picked out the perfect lingerie set—a sheer lace teddy with a plunging neckline.

"Um...about that."

Jackie pulled back and gazed up at him. "What's wrong?"

"There's been a slight change of plans. We're still going out, but instead of us spending the evening together alone, we're going to have company. Remember I mentioned my father was coming to town?"

Jackie nodded.

"Well, he came early and wants us to do something tonight."

Well, damn.

Jackie resolved not to let the disappointment show on her face. This was, after all, the father he'd had a difficult relationship with for years, but Kendrick had recently confided that he very much wanted a reconciliation.

"We can cancel tonight," she offered. Their relationship was still young, and meeting his father made her uncomfortable. No telling how this man, whom Kendrick wanted to impress, would react when he saw his son with a woman old enough to be his mother.

"No, it's fine. I told him about you and he wants to meet you. But if you'd rather not..."

The words dangled in the air, and though she wanted to cancel, she could tell he'd prefer if she agreed to come with him. "No, let's all go to dinner and have a great night. I'm sure you've picked a wonderful place for us to eat."

"You're sure you don't mind?"

"Positive."

"Thanks, baby. He's meeting us here and should arrive any minute." Kendrick glanced at his watch.

"In that case, let me hurry up and get my bag."

Jackie left him alone, still uneasy but figuring she'd go with the flow. Besides, Kendrick might welcome the buffer between him and his father.

While in the back, the door chimed, indicating Kendrick had opened it. His father must have arrived.

She fluffed her wig, dotted her forehead with a tissue to get rid of the shine, and touched up her purple lipstick. Taking a deep breath, she strutted toward the front with her large purse slung over her shoulder. The voices of both men wafted to the back, but she couldn't clearly hear what they were saying.

As she approached, Kendrick's father said something about having a taste for steak.

Jackie raised an eyebrow. Nice voice, though a bit muffled by the distance. Deep and very sexy. She couldn't wait to see the man attached to that sound.

She passed by the register and stopped.

Oh, damn. She knew this man.

Bald-headed and dressed in a dark blue pinstriped suit, he had a mustache and well-groomed beard with gray sprinkled throughout. Normally, she didn't go for men with full beards—and ten years ago, it had been more of a goatee—but with his looks and body, exceptions could be made.

His skin looked like he'd been dipped in the deepest, darkest chocolate, without a hint of cream. His lips were full and luscious, and those eyes—when he lifted them to observe her approach—were the color of the blackest garnet stone. The man was absolutely breathtaking, and the way he wore his suit let her know that he still had the same hard body she'd licked all over during the hottest week of her life.

Kendrick flashed a welcoming grin to Jackie, and she gulped and walked slowly over to them.

"Jackie Bryant. Well, I'll be damned." Tyson's eyes sparkled with interest.

"Hello, Tyson."

Tyson Small. But there was nothing *small* about him. At least six feet five and well-*endowed*...which was an understatement.

Kendrick appeared startled, his brow furrowing. "Wait, the two of you know each other?"

"It's been a while," Tyson said, boldly looking her over from top to bottom. He hadn't changed a bit. He looked at her the way he did all women—as if she'd been placed on the earth for him alone to sample. "At least ten years, I would say."

Kendrick's frown deepened. "Oh, wow. Small world. How do you know each other?"

"We're business associates from when I went to Atlanta for work ten years ago," Jackie answered hastily. "I met your father at a bridal trade show."

"That's when I was trying to make a go of my retail business, one of the many businesses that I started but failed," Tyson said ruefully.

"Oh. Well, this is my date, Jaclyn."

Tyson stiffened, and it was his turn to look startled. His gaze swung from his son to Jackie and back again. "Th-this is Jaclyn? The woman you wanted me to meet?"

"Yeah. She owns this store, and like I told you, she has a great selection here. She could probably help you find something for your girlfriend...what's her name? Carrie?"

"Er..." Tyson seemed to lose his train of thought as his eyes locked with Jackie's. "She's just a friend, actually."

Jackie's lips flattened. Yep, he probably hadn't changed a bit. Same old Tyson, sleeping around with multiple "friends."

"Whatever you need, Jaclyn can help you. She has three stores." Kendrick placed his arm around her shoulders and pulled her closer. "You guys ready to head out? He's craving a steak. He's been limiting his consumption of red meat, so today is sort of a cheat day for him."

Jackie put on her brightest smile. "Steak sounds like a great idea to me."

She avoided Tyson's probing gaze, suddenly feeling like a dirty old woman. Now she wasn't so sure she should sleep with Kendrick. Actually, it was completely off the table. Though overdue for a night of wild sex, after finding out his father was Tyson—a former lover—the thought of sleeping with his son made her feel icky. At least for now. She had some serious soul-searching to do.

"Ready?" Tyson asked.

"Ready." Kendrick took her hand—something she hadn't minded in the past, but now seemed extremely awkward in light of Tyson standing right in front of them.

They all exited the store together, and she locked up on the way out. In the parking lot, Tyson got into his own car, a flashy gold two-seater, and she climbed into Kendrick's gray Toyota Highlander.

As they pulled out of the parking lot, Jackie knew at some point she'd have to tell Kendrick the extent of her relationship with his father. Tyson had been more than a business associate. She adjusted the vents so that the air blew full force onto her face.

Much more than a business associate.

Glancing out the window at the passing scenery, she recalled being consumed by him, high on his lovemaking and the excitement of being the center of his attention. He'd done an excellent job of making her feel unique, special. So good, in fact, that she'd been foolish enough to think she'd fallen in love with him.

2

_____

His son had great taste.

Kendrick and Jackie sat next to each other across the table from Tyson. The three of them were halfway through the meal at a steak restaurant overlooking the bay. The meal was delicious, the ambiance right, and the conversation flowed easily between them. Yet the entire time Tyson had difficulty keeping his eyes off *her*.

He was surprised his son was dating an older woman, but he understood the attraction to Jackie. Her skin was a pretty russet-brown and she had eyes that were a darker shade of brown. They sparkled when she laughed and kept him ensnared when she looked his way. Her lips were a thing of beauty and popped with a bold purple color that matched the purple shade in her purple and gold dress.

Courtesy of a dark wig, wavy hair cascaded down the middle of her back. From that week in Atlanta, he knew she liked to switch up her look with different wigs. One night she'd been a blonde with a French bob. Another night a cherry-red wig fell in straight lines to her ass. Still another night, she amped up the sexy and mystery in a black wig with bold eye makeup and sultry red lips. He never knew what to expect when he arrived at her door, and that had been part of the thrill.

Jackie was a tall woman—taller than anyone he had ever dated before, but he loved her body. Large breasts, hips for days, and thick thighs he could lose himself between.

Yes, his son had great taste, and with a guilty conscience, Tyson acknowledged being jealous of him.

"You haven't told me how the two of you met." Tyson lifted a piece of rib eye to his mouth.

They both looked at each other and laughed, and another bout of jealousy tightened his chest at their inside joke.

"Do you want to tell him or should I?" Kendrick asked.

"It's a bit of a funny story. So good, too good," Jackie said.

Damn, her voice. He'd forgotten how sexy it was, especially when it trembled as she whimpered his name because he was *so good, too good*. He'd all but forgotten the days and nights they'd spent together, but seeing her again brought back snippets of memory—little details that made him hunger for a taste of her again.

"I'd love to hear the story," Tyson said.

"You want to tell it?" Kendrick asked Jackie.

"No, you go ahead." She sipped her wine, eyes locked on Kendrick. She'd barely looked at Tyson all night and that irritated the hell out of him.

His son set down his fork. "Okay, so, I went for a walk in the park —needed to think about a few things and make some decisions, and I thought a walk would do me good. There I was, minding my own business, when all of a sudden I hear, 'Get out the way! Get out the way!' I turn, and this woman comes barreling toward me on a bicycle."

Jackie covered her face in embarrassment. "I hadn't ridden since I was a kid. Everyone says this or that is like riding a bike. It's easy and you'll remember. Well, not so much."

"Why were you on a bike if you couldn't ride?" Tyson asked.

She finally looked at him, and he was mesmerized, sucked into the dark depths of her eyes.

"I often go walking in the park to get a little exercise, but I thought riding a bicycle was a way to switch up my routine. I rented a bike and was doing fine, until the incline."

Kendrick laughed and took over the story again. "So there I was, walking down the incline, and I turn and see her. She's screeching at the top of her lungs, eyes wide. People are darting out of the way. I was so deep in thought I didn't hear her until the last minute. She panicked and didn't know how to brake and ran right into me." He slapped his hands together.

"Knocked him clean off his feet," Jackie said, giggling.

"We tumbled into the grass, arms and legs locked together. After I got over my shock, I made sure she was okay. A few people checked on us but I waved them off."

"He had such a good attitude about it." Jackie rubbed Kendrick's arm and Tyson gritted his teeth. Goddamn, the universe really had it in for him. No grace for being a shitty parent.

He caught the waiter's eye and held up his empty glass. "Another old-fashioned." He should have ordered two because he intended to down the next one with a quickness.

"You were apologetic, but I wasn't hurt." Kendrick shrugged.

"That didn't change how awful I felt. I'd knocked over a complete stranger. Haven't been on a bike since." Jackie shook her head, as if she couldn't believe she'd done something so wacky.

"We ended up walking to the deli, and she bought me lunch to make up for the accident. And that's how we met."

Kendrick smiled at her, and Tyson's stomach turned. Where the hell was that drink? Watching them together, laughing and talking, taking turns as they told the story, made the ugly green monster in the pit of his stomach snarl and rear its ugly head higher.

"That's interesting," he muttered.

"That's how we met, but getting her to go out with me wasn't easy. She thought I was too young, but I managed to convince her otherwise." His son draped an arm across the back of Jackie's chair.

"That's nice," Tyson said, relieved when he saw the waiter

approaching. No sooner had the young man set down the glass, he picked it up and swallowed a mouthful. "So it's serious then?"

Jackie's gaze met his. "We're getting to know each other. It's early yet."

Early yet. What did that mean? Had they slept together? Had she rocked Kendrick's world the way she'd rocked his?

Tyson shoved down the disturbing thought of her entwined in bed with his son. Smoothing a hand down his beard, he cleared his throat. "How long have you been together?"

"Officially a month, and this is our third date." Tyson resumed eating his grilled fish.

"Well, I'm glad my son met a nice woman. I was worried about him, but I see now I don't have to worry. So, are you planning to have a long-distance relationship?"

"Long-distance relationship? Why would we?" Jackie's brow furrowed.

"Your relationship will be long-distance when he moves to New York."

Jackie's frown deepened and his son shifted away from her and focused on his meal. Too late, Tyson realized he'd said too much.

"We haven't had a chance to talk about that yet," Kendrick said, speaking to the plate.

"You're moving to New York?" Jackie asked.

"It's something that I've been thinking about." Kendrick shrugged.

"I thought you had given up any thoughts of becoming a model."

He shrugged one shoulder. "Not completely, but this isn't about modeling. I might have a shot at acting. I wanted to share my good news with you a little later." He glared at Tyson. "I shared my decision with my father, but since he brought it up, I'll share it with you, too. I landed a small role in an indie movie and have been thinking about moving to New York permanently."

Jackie set down her fork. "This is quite a surprise. I had no idea."

"I didn't think it was that big of a deal. We can make it work. I was going to tell you."

"I heard you," Jackie said tightly. She sipped her wine.

Tyson interjected into the tense back and forth. "Listen, I'm sorry I said anything. I assumed that you'd shared the news with her, but I'm sure this won't change your relationship."

"We'll see," he thought he heard Jackie say.

Initially, Tyson had regretted mentioning Kendrick's move, but now he couldn't help feeling a little pleased that he'd prematurely relayed information his son hadn't shared. That probably made him a piece of shit, but he couldn't help himself.

He'd met Jackie during a period in his life when he was still enjoying his freedom and sowing his wild oats. Married young, he and his ex realized they weren't right for each other early in the marriage. When they divorced, she remarried, and he spent a lot of time partying, getting laid, and figuring out what he wanted to do with his life.

He hadn't been much of a father then. Basically, he'd sent money and visited his kids—three girls and Tyson—on occasion. Despite not being around much, his daughters loved him and he had a good relationship with them. Tyson, however, had grown into a sullen, resentful young man. The two only recently repaired their relationship.

So this situation with Jackie put him into a little bit of a dilemma. Jackie had left a deep impression on him, and seeing her again awakened ideas of what could have been. If she hadn't left Atlanta after a week. If she didn't live on the west coast. If he had been willing to pursue a meaningful relationship with her instead of chasing ass and dreams throughout the southeast. So many ifs.

He still ached for her. Still recalled in vivid detail the silky texture of her sex on his tongue. The only problem, the competition.

His son.

3

"Bye, have a good night." Jackie waved at her employees leaving for the night. The Fourth of July sale had been a smash hit. The store was closing early and she had plans to spend the rest of the day over at Adelaide's house.

As she turned the lock in the door, a familiar face approached and stopped on the other side. Her heart leaped in her chest and she froze.

She hadn't seen Tyson or Kendrick since the three of them had dinner four days ago. An inexplicable tugging sensation in her chest left her with an uncomfortable feeling. And when he flashed his brilliant smile, that tugging manifested between her legs. She was intensely attracted to Tyson and had to tread carefully.

He was once again dressed in a three-piece pinstriped suit, this time black, one hand casually placed in his pants pocket. The other hand hung by his side and he wore a gold pinky ring. From the other night, she recalled he wore his nails cut short and manicured. A neat freak, his Atlanta apartment had been spotless, and he took care of his body the way he did his possessions. Good grooming and dressing well were all important to him.

"Can I come in?"

She stared at him through the glass, happy for the barrier between them. "Why?"

"I'd like to talk to you for a few minutes."

Letting him in was a bad idea, but she felt foolish for forcing him to have a conversation with her through a glass wall. Jackie opened the door, and Tyson strolled in. She relatched the door before turning to face him.

"What are you doing here, Tyson?"

"I came to buy a piece of lingerie. This is a lingerie store, isn't it?"

"We're closed."

"But you let me in, so..." He shrugged.

She rolled her eyes, knowing his explanation was simply an excuse to talk to her. One trait she remembered from back in Atlanta —Tyson was persistent.

"Yes, this is a lingerie and sleepwear store."

"Good, let's see, the woman I'm shopping for likes bold colors. Red, purple, even orange..."

He rubbed his hands together and walked over to one of the racks. He flipped through the hangers, stopping every few seconds to examine one of the lacy garments more closely. Jackie stood nearby, arms crossed over her chest.

"What size is your friend?"

He turned to look at her, and his gaze devoured her in an indecently slow slide down her body. Her skin awoke with a blistering heat. She couldn't believe the effect this man still had on her. A crazy week in Atlanta should not be enough to make her weak-kneed ten years later.

"About your size. Your shape. Maybe you could try on one of these so I could get a better idea."

She glared at him.

"What?" he asked innocently.

"Why are you really here? I'm dating your son."

He flinched, as if the words wounded him. "*Were* dating my son."

"Let me guess, you think because you're back in my life, I should drop everything and everyone to be with you. Do I have that correct?"

"You did that before."

Her cheeks burned with the truth of his words. She had cleared her schedule to spend every free moment with him. "Your arrogance is unbelievable."

"That week we spent together was unbelievable."

"For who?"

"Both of us. I'm speaking facts and you know it."

"On the contrary, I came back to San Diego and continued with my life. Don't get me wrong, I had a great time, but it was one week, and quite frankly, I barely remember it." She lifted her right shoulder in a careless shrug.

"Huh. That's strange, because as soon as I saw you, those days and nights we spent together all came rushing back. I remembered that little black number you wore—the sheer one that showed off your breasts."

He groaned and held up his hands as if holding her breasts, reliving the experience and forcing her to relive it, too. Her nipples tightened, and she grabbed onto one of the sales racks instead of giving in to her body's unauthorized sway toward him.

"My favorite outfit of the weekend, as you can tell. I'm not too proud to admit you turned me out, and I regret not following up with you afterward."

"You had my name, you had my number," Jackie said in the same frigid voice.

"And you had mine."

She sent a tight smile in his direction. "You said you were sowing your wild oats, remember? Oats that you hadn't had the opportunity to sow because you married young and had kids. If anyone should have called, it should have been you."

"True. And again, I regret that I didn't."

Jackie examined her fingernails. "It's too late now. I'm seeing someone." She brought her gaze back to his and looked him steadily in the eyes.

"Yeah, about that. I'm gonna have to pull rank."

"What are you talking about?"

"I'm going to have a talk with Kendrick, and I figure in a few days he'll call and let you know the relationship is over."

"You're kidding me, right?"

"You and I both know your relationship won't work long-distance anyway."

"If both people want—"

"Both people don't want it. He'll be busy with his modeling and acting career, and you'll be busy with me."

"There's that arrogance again," Jackie said, wagging her finger.

"You damn right." Tyson flashed a grin, one that made her heart accelerate and reminded her of his prowess in bed. She truly hated he could still have such an effect on her.

His face suddenly became serious. "Let me lay my cards on the table. I want you, Jackie. I've made a ton of mistakes in my life, but over the past few years, I've been working hard to rectify them. One of those mistakes was not being a better father. I've healed the relationship with my daughters, but the relationship with my son is still a work in progress."

"I don't think hitting on his girlfriend is going to help the situation," she said dryly.

"You're not his girlfriend, and I know for a fact you haven't slept with him already, so I still have a chance."

"A chance at what?"

"A chance to win you over. Letting you go was one of the mistakes I made in the past, and I need to talk to Kendrick so he'll step aside and you and I can focus on each other."

Momentarily speechless, Jackie stared at him. "Wow. You're unbelievable. You had your chance."

"Now Fate has seen fit to give me another one. Kendrick has plans with friends tonight, but I'm going to see him tomorrow. I'll call you later this week. Is your number still the same?"

Jackie gave him a blank look and didn't answer.

"Never mind, I know where to find you."

"I'm not interested, Tyson."

"I don't believe you." His voice dropped lower and his eyes bored into hers. "Not after what we shared. It's my fault we didn't stay together, so let me fix it."

"What's the point? You're going back to Atlanta after this visit."

"Not right now. I finally made a success of myself—found what I was good at. Programming, if you could believe it. I created a piece of software that not only automates the process of creating a business plan, but lets the user know the probability for success based on finances, personality, and market factors. I sold it to a tech company, made a fortune off the initial sales, and was able to negotiate residual payments until I'm sixty-five. I'm *extremely* well off. Which means although I came here to see Kendrick, I can stay as long as I need to."

"I can't." Jackie shook her head vigorously. She couldn't fall for his tempting words.

He took her hand, and while she should have pulled away, she didn't, taking comfort in his warm touch. Fire sparked under her skin, and she almost swooned from his touch.

"Let me talk to Kendrick. If I can convince him to back off, would you give me a chance? Give me three dates. That's all I'm asking."

"What if I want to continue seeing Kendrick?"

"You don't," Tyson said softly, confidently.

"This is crazy," Jackie said.

"Crazy would be walking away from each other when there's still so much chemistry between us. I know you feel it, too. What do you say, Jackie? Give me a shot to correct my mistake?"

Jackie laughed. "You haven't changed a bit, have you? Whatever you want, you go after with a vengeance. I guess that's how I knew you didn't want me." Saying the words aloud crushed her heart all over again.

"You're wrong. I almost always go after what I want, but I messed up and didn't pursue you after that week. One of the biggest regrets of my life."

He knew all the right words to say, but was he being honest?

Jackie swallowed hard. "Three dates, that's it?"

"Three dates."

"All right, you talk a good game. Let's see what you're made of."

A wide grin spread across his luscious lips, and she almost pulled back the words because she wondered what exactly she'd just agreed to.

He stepped closer and planted an unexpected kiss to her cheek.

Startled, Jackie yanked away her hand and stepped back. "You shouldn't have done that."

"Sorry," he said, looking completely unrepentant. "Your skin is still so soft and you smell so good. Can I tell you something?"

"No."

He bit his bottom lip. "Okay. I'll keep my nasty thoughts to myself, for now."

He covered the short distance to the door and let himself out. As he strolled past the glass window, he flashed her a sideways smile. Then he tucked one hand into his pants pocket and continued his leisurely stroll, whistling.

Jackie remained pinned to the floor, dumbfounded for several seconds. Finally, she locked the door and went back to the register to close up.

The man was a heartbreaker, and certainly lacked boundaries. He behaved as if he was in competition with his son, which was a turnoff.

Okay, maybe not a turnoff. Maybe a bit thrilling. Flattering. Exciting, to think that he planned to somehow throw up a roadblock to her relationship with Kendrick because he wanted her for himself. A tiny part of her liked the idea of him pining after her ten years later, regretting that he'd let her go.

After she placed the money, checks, and corresponding receipts in the safe, Jackie picked up her large purse and left the store. On the way to the car, her phone chimed. Not breaking stride, she dug it out from the bottom of the purse and stood beside the car door in the almost empty parking lot, staring at the screen.

Tyson had sent a photo of the two of them hugged up in the jacuzzi, her planting a kiss on his cheek. He was bare-chested and she wore a gold one-piece with a halter-top neckline. She'd taken that photo of them with her phone and texted him a copy.

She looked so happy in the picture, not knowing that a few days later they'd go their separate ways—never to speak again. The message accompanying the photo was simple, and Jackie stared at the words with a lump in her throat.

I never forgot you.

4

"How's it going?" Tyson asked as he entered Kendrick's apartment.

Over twenty-four hours had passed and he still had Jackie on the mind—her soft hand, her soft cheek. He couldn't stop thinking about her. Every time he thought of her, his body hummed with the restraint he'd needed to resist gathering her in his arms and whisking her away to his short-term rental. But he couldn't do that, not only because of her alleged disinterest, but because first he needed to handle the situation with his son.

"All right," Kendrick answered, motioning toward his blue and red sofa.

Tyson sat down and crossed his legs. "How was your Fourth?"

"Ate too much. Want anything to drink?" Kendrick called from the kitchen.

"No, I'm good."

Kendrick's apartment was simply furnished. There was the sofa Tyson sat on, and across from that a blue armchair with a red pillow and a heavy coffee table between them. The dining area contained a dark wood, polished table and four chairs with a bouquet of artificial yellow flowers in a vase sitting in the middle of it.

A few abstract paintings hung on the walls, but what drew Tyson's eye was a black and white photo of his four kids—three girls and Kendrick—in a silver frame. Just their faces, all of them looking into the camera. He and his ex had made some pretty-ass kids, but shame filled him. He'd been less than a good father.

He wanted to provide for Tyson, but his son wouldn't accept any money from him, which was ridiculous.

After selling the software company, Tyson was in a position to provide for all his kids. His daughters had not been as prideful as his son, who proclaimed he wanted to make it on his own, though he regularly accepted money from his mother because he hadn't worked full-time in months.

Kendrick entered the living room and set a glass of water on the table without a coaster, which irritated Tyson. It wasn't his house or furniture, so he kept his mouth shut.

Tyson set his ankle on his knee. "I spent the weekend thinking about what I wanted to do while I was here. Tomorrow I plan to go on one of those tours where you hop on and off on the bus. Then I could meet you later for dinner. The next day I could hit the beach. What's the best beach around here?"

"Ocean Beach is nice. It's pretty laid-back and they have a lot of restaurants where you could grab a bite to eat. La Jolla is another nice spot with great views, but parking can be a pain in the ass."

"How about I do my tour tomorrow so I can learn the place, and then you and I go to the beach on Friday? What's your work schedule like?"

"I'll have to check and let you know."

Tyson's eyes didn't leave his son's face. His thick Afro had been pulled back into a huge puff at the back of his head with a rubber band. He only wore black jeans and a white T-shirt, but with his perfectly symmetrical face and smooth ebony skin, he appeared stylish and like the model he aspired to be.

He hadn't been surprised when Kendrick expressed interest in acting and modeling because people had always remarked on his good looks—friends and strangers alike. In fact, he'd won a pretty toddler contest and acted in a few local commercials as a teen.

"I was thinking about extending my stay so we could spend time together and do some guy stuff, you know? I want to hear about your acting and modeling plans and see if there's anything I can do to help."

"You don't have to do anything. Patrick and Mom are already helping me out."

Patrick was his stepfather, the man who took over raising him and his sisters when Tyson and his mother divorced.

"I want to do my part."

"No need. I'm good." His voice was deadpan. Emotionless.

Tyson sighed internally and changed tactic. "Got any plans this week, other than us going to the beach?"

"I'm going out with Jaclyn this weekend again."

Tyson rubbed a hand over his bald head. "You really like her a lot?"

"I like her enough. Why?" Kendrick's eyes narrowed.

Tyson shrugged. "She's quite a bit older than you, and I'm wondering where you think this relationship is going, especially once you move to New York."

"So you're worried about my relationship?" his son asked with quite a bit of skepticism.

"That might be hard to believe, but I am."

"Just say you want to fuck her, Tyson."

The accusation exploded in the room, taking him by surprise. The use of his first name no longer fazed him. Kendrick did it just to aggravate him, to make it clear that he didn't think of him as a father. As if taking his mother's maiden name at eighteen didn't make the point enough. The shit hurt like hell.

Tyson dropped his foot to the floor, readying for the tough conversation to come. "What makes you think I want to do that?"

"Because I saw the way you looked at her, and now you're dancing around the issue. I like her. She likes me. Apparently, you missed your chance ten years ago."

"Jackie is a professional woman, and you expect her to wait around while you work for peanuts in New York, trying to make it big? Plus, this is a young relationship. You're not being realistic."

"Jaclyn and I are gonna talk and figure everything out."

"You know as well as I do this relationship isn't going anywhere."

"Says who? You?" Kendrick lifted his head at a haughty angle. "I'm right, aren't I? You probably had a thing for her and she never gave you the time of day. How ironic that she's now *my* woman."

Kendrick couldn't be more wrong. Tyson's tongue knew every inch of her skin. He'd tasted the sweet nectar of her mouth, inhaled the musky perfume between her thighs, and buried himself between those same thighs as he pumped himself into heaven.

"Have you slept with her?" Tyson asked.

"Planning on it." He was almost gloating at this point.

Tyson released the tension in his shoulders. "Listen to me, son. I have a proposition for you. We both know you're not in love with her, so let me help you out in New York. I'll set you up in an apartment if you walk away from her now."

Kendrick stared him. "Bribing me. Huh. You really want her bad, don't you? You..." His eyes widened and he shot to his feet. "Hold up! Did something happen between you and Jaclyn? Did you...?"

Tyson rose slowly to his feet. This was not the way he'd wanted to divulge that he'd had a prior relationship with her. In fact, he'd hoped he could keep that a secret while at the same time helping Kendrick.

"Listen—"

"You slept with my girlfriend?" Kendrick demanded, his entire body tense and his face darkening with jealous anger.

"She wasn't your girlfriend back then."

"Were either of you going to tell me?" Kendrick asked.

"At some point I would have mentioned it, but I was hoping I didn't have to right now because of...well, because of our fragile relationship."

"This is unreal," Kendrick muttered, walking toward the sliding glass doors and staring out at the night.

Tyson knew how he felt because he had experienced the same disbelief when he saw them together.

Kendrick swung around. "Why'd you come here tonight? To gloat?"

"Like you just did? Hell, no. I do want to spend time with you, but I can't deny that I'm interested in getting back together with Jackie. I figured—well, I figured we could kill two birds with one stone."

"Get me out of the way and off to New York and then get her back."

"Something like that," Tyson admitted.

"I can't believe you just admitted that!" Kendrick exclaimed.

"I don't see any reason to lie. What would be the point, especially since I'm trying to re-establish a relationship with you. You're my son, and although I've repaired my relationship with your sisters, I can't get through to you. You won't let me get close. Coming out here to see you was me taking a chance. I know you think I'm not shit because I wasn't there when you were growing up. I've told you a million times that I'm sorry. Let me show you that I'm a different man than I used to be."

"I have a father. The man who raised me."

Those words jabbed his heart like a dagger, but he refused to give up. "I'm not trying to replace the man who's been a father to you. I'm trying to carve out a little space in your life for me."

Kendrick shoved his hands into his pockets and studied his father for a while. Tyson didn't speak, allowing him the opportunity to work out whatever he needed to work out in his head.

"This thing with Jaclyn is hella awkward," he said.

Tyson nodded his agreement. "I think we can work through that."

"You'll really pay for me to go to New York?" Kendrick asked.

"As soon as you're ready."

"I'll be ready as soon as you confirm you'll pay to transport my car to New York and cover my rent for a year, too."

"Done."

His eyebrows shot higher. "You really like her."

"I do." In fact, she was the one who got away, and he meant that with his whole heart. He'd have work to do convincing Jackie he'd wanted her when they first met and wanted her even more now.

"Okay. You have a deal," Kendrick said, though he sounded suspicious.

Relief washed over Tyson. "Wonderful. Now what about you and me? Our relationship."

"I don't know, man," Kendrick said with a shake of his head.

Tyson stepped closer. "Give me a week, that's all I'm asking. Let's spend time together before you leave for New York—time that we haven't been able to spend together because of me. I'm only asking for an hour or two here and there, and if you still believe that I'm not worthy of being in your life..." He swallowed. The pain of losing his kid when he was so close to having a real relationship with him was almost too much to imagine. "I'll leave you alone, and I won't try any more. If we do have a relationship in the future, I'll leave it up to you to reach out."

Kendrick's lips tightened. "You'll put in the time? You promise?"

The faint tremble in his voice, the vulnerable way he asked the question, tightened Tyson's chest with remorse. He'd done serious damage, but he was determined to change his son's mind. "I promise."

5

Tyson climbed into the gold two-seater rental and started the engine. Thankfully, he'd made progress with Kendrick. His son hadn't completely forgiven him, but spending time together would hopefully lead to a new, healthy relationship.

As he pulled out of the apartment parking lot, he dialed his ex-wife's number.

"Hey, stranger. Haven't heard from you in a while," Yvonne said by way of greeting.

"It hasn't been that long."

"You were supposed to call me in Texas."

On the way to San Diego, he had stopped in Texas for a few days to spend time with an old friend. His flight here had arrived in the afternoon, at which point he checked into a hotel and called Kendrick.

"I forgot. You know I have shit for brains. Anyway, how are you doing?"

Post-divorce, they'd become best friends. During the course of their marriage, they both realized that they shouldn't have gotten married in the first place. But even after that realization, it had been hard to walk away from the security blanket their life together had become. Financially, they had needed each other as well. But they were both seeing other people without actually coming right out and saying they were, and they finally divorced when Yvonne admitted she had fallen in love with Patrick, the man she was married to now.

Yvonne yawned. "Doing fine. Long day, but I have my mandatory glass of wine before I go to bed."

"Uh-oh, you'll be sleeping real good in a little bit."

Yvonne giggled. "I sure will."

"Where's Patrick?"

"Already asleep. The early morning shift is kicking his butt. I'll be glad when he goes back to his regular schedule so he can keep me company at night."

"They still got him going in at the crack of dawn?"

"Yes, unfortunately. He's the only warehouse supervisor they can depend on, so they're going to keep him on that schedule until they get that shift straightened out."

"I won't keep you since you got your sleeping-pill-in-a-glass already. I just wanted to let you know that I left Kendrick's a few minutes ago, and we had a good talk. I feel like we finally turned the corner. You were right, I needed to come out here and see him in person."

"When am I ever wrong?"

He laughed, slowing to a stop at a traffic light. "Never."

"Thank you."

"One more thing, I'm paying for his trip to New York and setting him up in an apartment."

"Whoa, you two had a *great* talk."

"Depends on how you view it."

Tyson launched into an explanation about Jackie and the agreement he made with Kendrick.

When finished, Yvonne asked, "Is Kendrick okay? Because maybe he's pretending to be okay about Jackie, but he's really not."

"He's fine, trust me, but I'll pay attention and make sure he's not harboring ill feelings or hurt about her."

"I'll check on him tomorrow anyway to be sure. Tell me something—is Jackie the woman you told me about years ago, the one you met at the bridal show here?"

"That's the one."

"Oh, Ty, that's wonderful! I mean, the whole thing with Kendrick is a little weird, but I always suspected you still carried a torch, even though you only spoke about her a few times. Don't screw this up, please."

Tyson laughed and pulled away from the light. "I won't. At least I hope not. I've got three dates to win her over, and I plan to work harder than I ever have to get her."

"Good luck. About Kendrick, you're going to continue to give him the same allowance while he's in New York?"

"I'm going to increase his support by a couple hundred dollars."

Although Kendrick wouldn't accept money from him, Tyson contributed to his lifestyle without his knowledge. Yvonne had agreed to pretend that she and Patrick were the ones who actually subsidized his living expenses.

"You still don't want me to tell him?" she asked with disapproval in her voice.

"Not yet. Maybe later, but I want him to feel more comfortable with me first, and we're not there yet."

"Okay, I won't say anything."

"All right, I'll catch up with you later and keep you up-to-date on the progress I make with Kendrick."

"Hang in there. And good luck."

"Thanks, sweetheart."

~

"I CAN HANDLE TYSON," Jackie insisted.

She trailed behind Adelaide and Renee as they took the steps down to the beach at La Jolla Cove. Late in the afternoon, many of the families that had crowded the area earlier in the day were gone. During the descent, she spotted a little girl waving at—and dangerously close to—a couple of sea lions on the rocks before her mother rushed over and scooped her up.

"Sure you can," Renee said over her shoulder.

Jackie ignored her friend, removed her sandals, and stepped carefully onto the sand.

"How about here?" Adelaide pointed to a spot well back from the water.

"Perfect," Renee replied.

They spread out Renee's blanket and Adelaide placed the picnic basket she'd brought in the middle.

Once they were all seated, Jackie popped the cork on the white wine she'd brought and poured them each a glass while Adelaide handed out the contents of the basket.

"What do you have for us today?" Renee asked, reaching across Jackie to take one of the sandwiches wrapped in wax paper.

"Grilled chicken sandwiches with smoked gouda, sliced avocados, and basil mayonnaise. There's also individual fruit cups with nectarines, cubed watermelons, and my very own honey-lime dressing."

Jackie sniffed her sandwich and moaned. "You're too good to us."

Adelaide, seated on the opposite side of the basket from Jackie, laughed and bit into her sandwich.

Renee nudged Jackie with her right elbow. "Back to the topic we were discussing. When you came back from Atlanta, you were a mess. You talked about Tyson for months nonstop."

"Not nonstop," Jackie said.

"*Non*stop. When you finally accepted he wouldn't call, you buried yourself in work. Not long after that, you opened your second store, remember?"

"That had nothing to do with him," Jackie muttered unconvincingly.

Adelaide pointed her wine glass at Jackie. "We weren't friends back then, but even *I* know how dangerous this man is to your heart. The few times you've mentioned him, you made it very clear that you still carry a torch."

"A torch of anger, not a torch of lust."

"You don't think you'll be tempted to sleep with him?" Adelaide asked.

Jackie shook her head vigorously. "No way. No how."

"The lady doth protest too much, methinks. That's Shakespeare," Renee said.

"I know what the hell that is, Renee, but it doesn't apply here," Jackie said.

A look passed between her friends.

"You know what, we're here to watch a sunset because that's what Adelaide wanted to do, not talk about my inability to resist Tyson Small."

"Renee, behave yourself," Adelaide said.

"*Me*?" Renee said with an exaggerated gasp. "You're just as bad."

"You're both terrible," Jackie said.

"Okay, we'll behave, but you promised to tell us what Kendrick said when he called," Adelaide reminded her.

"Oh, yeah. Well, that was a strange conversation. He called a couple of days after Tyson came by. We were supposed to go out this weekend, and I assumed he was calling to confirm our date."

"I can't believe you were still going to date him," Renee muttered.

"I wasn't sure I wanted to, to be honest. After my conversation with Tyson, I was feeling so…"

"Confused?" Adelaide supplied.

"Maybe," Jackie said in a low voice, loath to admit that Tyson could upset the equilibrium of her life the way he obviously had.

"Then what happened?" Renee asked.

Curling her toes into the cool sand, Jackie continued. "He said he didn't think it was a good idea for us to be seeing each other anymore. He's leaving for New York soon, and he said he wasn't comfortable dating someone his father had slept with."

Adelaide gasped. "So Tyson told him everything?"

"Maybe not everything, but enough that he knows Tyson and I had been lovers."

Renee groaned. "Well, at least you don't have to have the awkward conversation where you tell him yourself, but does he know his father is trying to get back together with you?"

"I'm pretty sure he does," Jackie replied.

"Interesting. Which means he stepped aside so Tyson could make a move." Adelaide sipped her wine, watching Jackie closely.

"That's what it sounds like, but Tyson's only here for a short time, which means he's looking for a fling."

"He said letting you go was a mistake. That's not fling talk to me."

"You agreed to three dates and said earlier you can handle him, but..." Renee's words trailed off with the arch of an eyebrow.

"I'm going to have fun. That's what I'm going to do. You're with your handyman, and you"—she turned to Adelaide—"are back together with Hector. I don't know where this is going, but I know what's not going to happen. I'm not going to get my feelings tangled up in Tyson. This time, I'm in control. I have no expectations of a future with him so he can't disappoint me again. Besides, you know my philosophy about relationships has kept me sane all these years. Rule number one..."

"Never need a man," Renee said.

Jackie turned to Adelaide. "Rule number two..."

"Always have your own."

"Exactly, ladies. The only thing I would really need a man for is to have a baby, and I don't even need one for that." She laughed.

Adelaide's face softened. "The adoption," she said.

Jackie nodded, a smile of pure joy breaking out on her face. The state was conducting a review of her background, to include criminal, medical, and employment history, among other factors. According to the caseworker, the assessment should be over soon. Once she was approved, she'd be able to pick a child, and the empty hole in her life would finally be filled.

"Very soon I'm going to be a mother, and I won't have time to worry about Tyson and whether or not he really cares about me. I'll be too busy with my little girl."

She'd spent years concentrating on building a business and neglected having a family. She had four godchildren, ten nieces and nephews, thanks to her sister and two brothers, and three grand-nieces. Loving on them used to be enough, but over time she longed for more.

Renee placed an arm around Jackie. "You're going to be a great mom. I can already see your little girl now, buying snack packs at the grocery store and selling the individual bags of chips for a profit at school."

"I actually did that as a kid," Jackie said with a sideways twist of her lips.

The other two laughed.

"Why am I not surprised?" Adelaide said.

"We need to toast to motherhood." Renee held up her glass.

"To motherhood!" Adelaide and Jackie screamed, so loud a five-member family lounging nearby turned in their direction.

Smiling and laughing, the three of them clinked their glasses together and hooted and hollered some more.

Finally, they calmed down, sipping wine as the sun went down behind the horizon and splashed its red and orange rays across the blue sea.

6

Their first date was at his apartment. How convenient. The short-term rental offered a great view of the city from three wide windows that overlooked the water.

He'd even put out a bottle of Cabernet Sauvignon, her favorite red, which she sipped as she watched him work in the kitchen. He wore a long-sleeved forest-green shirt and black trousers under a white apron with the words *You know you want some* embroidered in red on the front.

And boy, did Jackie want some. Tyson was a triple threat. Good-looking, good-smelling, and on top of all of that, he cooked. But she'd already made up her mind that she would *not* sleep with him and would stick to her decision, no matter what Renee said.

That didn't mean she couldn't look her best, though. She wore a paisley purple and green wrap dress and three-inch strappy heels. She'd gotten her teeny-weeny Afro colored red to hide the grays that had taken over a third of her hair, and for her biweekly mani-pedi at the spa, she'd had them paint her toenails and fingernails lavender.

The rib eyes Tyson picked up from the butcher sizzled on the indoor grill when he turned them over with tongs, and their scent filtered into the living room where she stood.

Jackie sauntered over to the bar, rested on her elbows, and watched him work. "Those smell heavenly."

"I'm not going to brag like a lot of men do and say this is my own special recipe, but you're going to love them, believe me." He turned away from the grill long enough to flash one of his megawatt smiles before going back to work.

Jackie's gaze made its way down his back to his firm behind. Lord, that man had a beautiful ass—so beautiful she was tempted to grab it.

"You want to listen to some music?" Tyson asked.

"That would be nice."

"Old or new?"

"What do you think?"

He chuckled and wiped his hand on a towel and picked up a remote from the counter and pressed a button. The lights in the room lowered. She looked at him but he only smiled and then pointed the remote at the system in the living room. "Never Too Much" by Luther Vandross came through the speakers.

Jackie swayed to the music.

"That's his greatest hits album. The only artist I enjoy more is Charlie Wilson," Tyson said.

"I like him, too, but Luther does something to me. We're going to have to listen to the whole album."

Tyson watched her dancing solo in his living room. "You have some great moves," he said.

"So I've been told." *Stop flirting. Stop flirting.*

His lips parted as he was about to speak, then he shook his head as if he'd changed tactics, and said, "I'll get the salads together."

Jackie would've offered to help, except he'd already refused her first two offers. Clearly, he wanted to be responsible for making tonight special all on his own. He set a big salad in a wooden bowl on the table in the alcove off from the kitchen. Soon, twice-baked potatoes, the rib eyes, and the bottle of red wine joined the bowl.

"Dinner is served," Tyson said. He neatly folded the apron and placed it on the counter. Then he pulled out one of the chairs at the table.

Jackie sat down with a flourish and glanced over her shoulder at him. "This all looks delicious. I feel rather special."

He bent to her ear. "You *are* rather special."

His breath brushed her skin and she froze, aware of the heat and warmth his body exuded. Only when Tyson was seated opposite her did she breathe easy.

"*Bon appétit*," he said.

Jackie ate several bites of food before she looked across the table at him. "Delicious. How did you learn to cook like this?"

"It was a matter of survival. After my wife and I split, I realized how spoiled I'd been. Growing up, I never learned to cook because that was the responsibility of the women in my family. Then I got married, and Yvonne took care of the house and the kids and made sure I had a hot meal waiting for me every day after I came home from work, even though she worked, too."

"She was a saint," Jackie said, taking a sip of wine.

"Yeah, she was. Married to a great guy now."

"You're still friends?"

"We are, but that's because she and I admitted we'd made a mistake getting married because she'd been pregnant with our first daughter."

"An amicable divorce. That's rare, but not surprising with a man like you. I swear you could sell ice in a snowstorm."

Tyson laughed out loud and dabbed his mouth with the napkin. "Thanks, I think."

"So you divorced the woman you married and then decided to play the field and never get married again?" Jackie asked.

"Not as bad as all that. Before Yvonne and I divorced, we had an unspoken... understanding."

Jackie lifted her eyebrows in a silent request for him to expound.

"We were married but seeing other people," he explained.

"*Oh.*"

"Unconventional, but like I said, we recognized we didn't belong together. When she and Patrick decided to get married, it forced me to move out and work in earnest on my business ideas. I never had much money, and man, did I want to succeed. But I wanted to have a good time, too, because she and I had married so young. We had both just graduated high school when she got pregnant and we got married, thinking it was the right thing to do. Eventually, I felt like I'd missed out and decided that I'd experience everything I hadn't experienced."

Jackie cut into the tender rib eye. "I'm going to assume that means women?"

Tyson laughed and shrugged. "Of course. But not only women. I partied hard, drank a lot, and, in general, acted like a fool."

Because she was learning more about him in one night than she had during their week in Atlanta, Jackie couldn't stop asking questions. "What finally got you straightened out?"

"A pregnancy scare."

Her mouth fell open. "One of your girlfriends?"

"More like a hookup. We scratched each other's itch from time to time. I wish I could tell you the scare happened when I was younger, but it happened when I was old enough to know better, a couple of years after you and I met. I was forty-nine years old. When she told me she was pregnant, I was devastated. My girls were grown and Kendrick was already in his late teens, I was making good money at the financial services firm where I worked—not great—but okay, so the last thing on my mind was having a child. That stage in my life was over." He shook his head.

An uncomfortable heaviness weighed in Jackie's chest. Staring down into her glass of wine, she thought about how she still wanted to be a parent. And here he was, talking about not wanting to go back down that path.

Across the table, he watched her with a frown creasing his brow. "I know what you're thinking. He ain't shit. Believe me, I know that. At least, I wasn't. I'm a different man now."

"I wasn't thinking that," Jackie said.

"Then I misunderstood the look on your face."

"You did. What happened with the baby?" she asked, curious despite herself.

"After she had the baby, we did a DNA test and learned that it wasn't mine. I had already known there was the possibility that the child could be another man's, so it's not like she tried to trap me or anything. But I'd never been so relieved to get a negative test in my life. That's what turned me on the straight and narrow. No more running around for me. I continued consulting, and after hours and on weekends I worked hard on the software idea that had been at the back of my mind for a while. Five years ago I sold it and my life has been good ever since."

"Congratulations," Jackie said sincerely. When they met years ago, he'd expressed a desire to run his own business because he'd grown up poor and didn't want that life for himself or his family. To see him finally achieve a lifelong goal gave her an immense sense of satisfaction.

At the end of the meal, they walked out to the balcony—Jackie with remnants of wine in a glass—and stood overlooking the water. In the distance, the lights of a few boats twinkled in the dark.

"We've been talking about me the entire time. What have you been up to? Still traveling?"

"Not as much as I'd like to, but I plan to change that in the future. More traveling is definitely in my plans."

"You own two more stores now, right? Congratulations."

"Thank you. It's lots of work, but I love it. That's about all I have to say on the business front. On the personal side, my parents are settled in Florida now. I helped them buy a condo on the beach, which was a longtime dream of theirs."

"What about your sister—the one who was in your hotel room that one time I stopped by? She was crying about something, and I left so the two of you could talk."

"Oh, Fiona. She was going through a messy divorce. She finally got rid of her cheating husband and went back to school. She became an anesthesiologist and still lives in Atlanta."

"Have you visited her in the intervening years?"

Jackie opened her mouth and quickly shut it. An awkward silence overwhelmed the small balcony.

"You have been back. And you never called," he said in a heavy voice.

"You never called me, Tyson," she reminded him, her voice thick with unwanted sorrow. If he'd called just once, she would have hopped on a plane and met him anywhere he asked.

"I know." The burden of regret pressed his shoulders into a downward slope.

Jackie drained her glass and set it on the metal table nearby. "It's late. I should go."

He took her hand, and once again she was overwhelmed by his touch. Her fingers trembled and her body awakened with a need that defied reason.

"I wasn't ready. I'm not making excuses, I'm explaining."

"I don't think I can do this." Her voice shook.

The night had been going so well, but the emotional turmoil he inflicted threatened to sully the minutes that remained. She wanted to escape. Needed to be free from him and the fantasy life she conjured every time she considered what could have been if they'd stayed in touch.

Jackie tugged her hand, but Tyson's grip tightened. "Three dates. That's what you agreed to."

She swallowed hard and cast her gaze to the concrete floor at their feet.

Tyson lifted her hand to his lips and slowly placed three kisses —*one, two, three*—across her knuckles. By the time the last kiss landed, her fingers had curled tight around his and a flare of yearning so deep consumed her that she almost begged him to screw her.

He stepped closer, forcing her to look up into his dark eyes. His mouth temptingly near. His gray-speckled beard close enough for her to rub her cheek against. How was it possible to want him so much after all this time? Yet she couldn't take the final step and reach out—

pull him close and end the misery that had plagued her since he showed up at Bodacious that first night.

"How long do you plan to stay here, Tyson?"

"As long as it takes to win you over."

Jackie shook her head. "That's not what we agreed to."

His lips flattened with disappointment, and then he said, "All right then. Two more dates, like we agreed. That's all I'm asking."

"Two more," Jackie agreed, wishing she were strong enough to say no...and simply walk away.

7

Today's date was a bit unorthodox, and Jackie had not known what to expect when Tyson called and told her to dress casually, they were going to do some exercising. With only her keys and a small change purse attached to the keychain containing her I.D., credit cards, and a little cash, she rounded the corner of her house and met Tyson in front of the driveway's three-car garage. To her surprise, he had a new vehicle—a black Cadillac SUV with two bikes hitched to the back.

"You changed cars," she commented, walking slowly toward him.

Of course he looked scrumptious in a set of blue joggers and a navy T-shirt. She wore red joggers and a white T-shirt.

"The two-seater wasn't practical in general, and definitely not for what I have planned today."

"And what do you have planned today?" She eyed the bicycles with dread.

"You and I are going on a bike ride."

"Oh no, we're not. Been there, done that. I learned my lesson. Remembering how to ride a bike is not as easy as everyone says."

"Come on, you can't give up that easily. You're telling me you can take all the lumps that come with opening and running a business, but you give up on something you want to do because you have one accident in the park? And by the way, I'm not even mad about you running over my son, otherwise you and I would not have reconnected."

"Be that as it may, I am in no way prepared to ride a bike in the park. What if I fall again?"

"I'll be right there with you. I'll make sure you don't fall."

He opened the passenger side door and gestured for her to get in.

Jackie folded her arms over her chest. "You're serious? You're going to force me to get back on a bike?"

"You fall down, you get up."

"I did get up and accepted that bicycle riding is not for me. I'm not getting back on a bike!"

"I may not have been the best father, but I did teach two of my girls how to ride their bikes, and I'm pretty sure I can do the same for you. You have to trust me."

He waited with the door open, and Jackie hesitated. If she busted her ass in front of Tyson, she would be mortified.

"I won't let you fall," he said again.

He seemed so certain, she finally let out a dramatic sigh. "Fine. But if I do have another accident, you're going to be sorry."

"Fair enough. Hop in."

They went to the park, the same park where she had knocked down Kendrick, and immediately her anxiety spiked. Nonetheless, she climbed out of the Cadillac and waited for Tyson to unlock the bikes from the back.

She took one and glanced at its pristine condition. "Where did you get these?"

The bikes were in good shape, the tires fully inflated, and the frames looked almost brand-new.

"Rented them from a bike shop. You ready?"

Her belly fluttered with unease. "No."

"You got this," he said reassuringly, and gave her arm a squeeze of encouragement. Against her better judgment, Jackie took one of the helmets he handed her and followed behind him. They walked in silence to a section of the park that ended near some trees and was away from the general foot traffic.

"We're going to practice here," Tyson announced, pushing down the kickstand on his bike.

"I'm so nervous," Jackie said, looking at him for reassurance.

"I got you. Put on your helmet and hop on."

She did as he instructed and within seconds, was riding on the bike. Riding on a level surface was the easy part. The problem had arisen when there was an incline, but she followed Tyson's instructions, riding around their little area, practicing how to brake slowly and suddenly, as she became more comfortable on this new bike.

Tyson walked along beside her and made sure she remained steady and balanced. When she was completely comfortable, they both hopped on and went for a slow ride along the paved pathways. They eased past joggers and speed walkers, and Tyson rode behind her, keeping an eye on her progress.

"Take it easy," he coached, when she wobbled a little bit.

Her fingers tightened around the handlebars and she tensed.

"Relax," he advised, pulling up beside her. "Take a couple of deep breaths."

She followed his instructions and finally relaxed, the two of them cruising along beside each other. She became so comfortable that when she saw people walking in front of her, she no longer semi-panicked. She simply rang the warning bell and most people scooted out of the way. For those who didn't, she carefully went around them.

"Want to try going a little faster?" Tyson asked.

"Okay."

They increased their speed, and after a few minutes of tension, Jackie relaxed again. She was doing this. She was *really* doing this!

"I can't believe I'm riding this bike!" She let out a loud laugh and her gaze connected with Tyson. His grin said *I told you so*, and she couldn't fault him.

"You're a good coach," she said.

"Could you say that a little louder? I might need to record that so I can hear you repeat it over and over again later."

"You're a good coach. Satisfied?"

"Very."

When they approached the area where she had knocked into Kendrick, her stomach tightened a bit and her fingers clenched around the handle bars.

"Remember what I told you. Relax, guard your brakes, and go as slow as you need to. I'm right behind you."

Jackie nodded her understanding, and they started down the incline. Her fingers closed on the lever, slowing the bike down. It wasn't the smoothest slowdown, but at least she didn't scream and careen into anyone like she did the first time. When they ended up on level ground again, she let out a squeal of victory.

"I did it!"

Tyson pulled up beside her, his grin as broad as her own. "Yeah, you did. I knew you could."

TYSON PULLED into the driveway of Jackie's house and parked in front of the three-car garage. The exterior of the two-story Spanish-style home was a sunny golden color, bright like the woman who lived within its walls. One day he hoped to see the inside, but he knew better than to suggest any such thing right now.

The day had gone better than expected. After riding for a bit, they went for lunch and then walked off the food on the beach. Jackie was a great conversationalist, and once she relaxed, he learned a lot about her. She'd opened up more than she had the other night at his house.

She'd never been married, but had one failed engagement under her belt. Though he'd known she opened her first Bodacious store in her thirties, he had no idea her parents had tried to talk her out of the venture. But she'd seen a need in the market, believed in herself, and opened the store anyway. Very impressive.

They walked slowly around the side of the house to her front door.

"How did I do today?" Tyson asked.

"Not bad," she replied.

Not exactly enthusiastic.

They stopped outside her red door and Jackie twirled on the heel of one foot to face him. "Thank you for a lovely day. I enjoyed myself."

"Was that so hard?"

"I can't let you get a big head," she said.

"Me, a big head? Noooo." He wrinkled his nose, and she cracked up.

Having her laugh at his jokes all day, no matter how minor, had given his ego a major boost. There was no doubt in his mind that they would make a great couple, and no doubt the attraction he felt for her was reciprocated. But he was no fool. Jackie might be bold and daring in business, but she was definitely cautious, downright hesitant with him. He'd have to move slowly, though all day he'd been imagining her naked—or semi-naked in one of the sheer lace teddies he'd drooled over on her website—and contemplated all the things he would do to her once he got the chance.

Tyson eased closer. "I know it's only our second date, but I was hoping I could squeeze in a kiss this time. I've been wanting to kiss you all day. That's a lie. I've been wanting to kiss you since I saw you at Bodacious that first night."

"I was with your son then."

"And I never wanted to fight that kid more in my life."

She smiled, her eye softening. "Still selling me something, Tyson?"

"Myself, if you'll have me."

She tilted her head to the side, eyes assessing him for the moment. "No, I don't mind if you kiss me," she whispered.

Tyson reined in the fierce urge to grab her into his arms and attack her mouth. Instead, he cupped her cheek in his hand and lowered his lips to hers. He'd intended for it to be a soft peck, but the moment their mouths connected, his brain short-circuited. He heard Jackie's sharp inhale, reflecting his own surprise at the charge of excitement that zipped through him.

Slipping his arms around her body, he pulled her close—her soft breasts, belly, and thighs smashing against his harder frame. A throbbing ache manifested in his pelvis, and he groaned in frustration because he'd give anything to have this woman horizontal right this moment.

The kiss continued, his mouth pressing harder into hers, the smacking sound filling the night air as they tasted each other. One of her arms slipped around his waist and ran up his back while the other caressed his neck and stroked his bald head. That simple touch spiked heat in his blood, and he prolonged the kiss, nipping at the corner of her mouth and licking the moist insides.

When he finally released her and stepped back, they were both short of breath. Tyson licked his lips, reliving the flavor that he knew he would not forget for a very long time.

"Well...ahem." Jackie straightened her T-shirt, which his roving hands had pushed up and twisted in the heat of the moment.

Tyson bit his bottom lip. Shaking his head, he said, "I think you better go inside before I forget I'm supposed to be patient."

She stood there for a few seconds longer, looking like she was about to say something to him—lips parted, eyes wide. Then she abruptly turned to the door and let herself inside. "Thanks again for a lovely day and for making sure I can now comfortably ride a bike."

"Glad I could help."

Jackie closed the door and he remained there for a while, chest constricted like a tight fist. Turning, he strolled around the house and climbed into the SUV. Regret was beating at him.

More than ever, he believed she was his future. She was sexy, driven, and their chemistry was still off the charts.

He had to convince her they belonged together.

8

_____

"I'm going to sleep with him."

Jackie's announcement was met with an eye roll from Renee.

"We already knew that, sweetie," Adelaide said. She stood in front of the stove and held out her hand. "Give me that plate, would you?"

Jackie handed over the dish, perturbed by the lack of confidence her friends had in her. It was Sunday afternoon and Adelaide was making omelets for their brunch meal. Jackie had brought large cinnamon rolls smothered in icing, and Renee had shown up with a fruit salad.

"Don't judge me."

"I'm not gonna say I told you so, but that didn't take long." Renee looked at her wrist, though she wasn't wearing a watch, and if she was, it wouldn't tell her how long Jackie had taken before she weakened.

"I don't want to give in, but he was so nice and so damn sexy during our daytime date. Grr." Jackie covered her face.

Renee patted her shoulder. "Happens to the best of us. Have you figured out which piece of lingerie you're going to wear?"

"I'm down to two options," she answered. If these weren't her best friends, she'd be embarrassed, but they already knew she had planned out her wardrobe of seduction. It was good to have people in her life who understood her. She had to decide between a black teddy or a red bustier. "Am I crazy?"

Adelaide slid a mushroom, onion, and green pepper omelet onto the plate and handed it to Jackie. "Crazy, no. But I do hope you're being careful, the same way you told me to be careful about Hector, remember? Do you know for sure that Tyson doesn't have a woman back in Atlanta?" She led the way to the back patio.

Jackie could only imagine what her friend went through after being married to someone for twenty-five years, having your life intertwined with that person, having children with them, living with them for all that time, and then having all of that severed with the stroke of a pen. She'd missed Tyson terribly and been a wreck after *one* week.

"No, I don't know for sure."

They sat at the table with their meals.

"Tell us everything. How did the two dates go?" Adelaide asked.

"Both times were wonderful."

She gave a quick synopsis of their activities and ended with the passionate kiss at the front door. She actually blushed from the memory of that encounter. Tyson had her all discombobulated.

"Having him cook dinner for me was nice, and I learned a lot about him, but our second date was my favorite. We had fun, and now I feel comfortable on my bike." She paused, and leaned toward her friends in earnest. "You know how some men find it hard to have a good conversation? Not him. He's open and shares his thoughts and feelings. He let me know all about his past, how he married young after his girlfriend at the time got pregnant, because he thought it was the right thing to do. And his screwups. He admits he wasn't the best father because he wasn't present in the lives of his children once he and his wife divorced."

"You really like him. You're glowing," Adelaide said.

"Am I?" Jackie touched her cheeks with both hands and laughed. "I haven't felt like this about a man in a long time. Being with Tyson is exciting, but a little bit scary."

"Because you're afraid of getting hurt again?" Renee asked.

"Yes." Admitting that out loud put a damper on her excitement. "I guess I'll just have to see how things go. He says he wants to be with me, but who knows what will happen down the line. Right now all we've shared is a couple of meals and a very hot kiss. I'll see what happens on our third date."

"Which tie?"

Tyson held up a navy tie and a red and navy tie against the powder-blue shirt he planned to wear on his date tonight with Jackie. Seated at the kitchen counter, Yvonne bent her head toward the screen to get a closer look. Her mahogany-brown skin was makeup free, and her short hair tucked neatly behind her ears.

"The red and navy one. The color from the red is a nice touch." She sat back.

Her husband, Patrick, sauntered into the frame and placed a hand on her lower back. "Hey, baby," he said.

"Back so soon?" Tyson asked.

"Yeah, I didn't plan to stay long. I just wanted to see the riding lawnmower up close, and now I'm pretty sure that I'll get it. What are you two talking about?"

"Yvonne said I should go with this tie. What do you think?" One after the other, he held up the options again.

Patrick shrugged. "I'm more inclined to go with the solid blue one, but maybe you should do what she says."

"He should absolutely do what I say, because I'm right."

Patrick chuckled. "And there you have it."

He disappeared from the screen, and Tyson heard him open the refrigerator.

"Okay, I'll go with the red and blue. I have a feeling she's going to like this one better, like you said." Tyson tossed aside the other tie and placed the other on the bed beside his jacket and matching pants and vest.

"What's the plan for tonight?" Yvonne rested her chin on her hand.

"Dinner at a restaurant in Little Italy, and if she's up to it, a walk along the beach later."

"Sounds nice. Make sure you have a towel to clean your feet after you go down to the beach," Yvonne said.

"Yes, ma'am. Anything else?"

"I think you got it." Yvonne tilted her head to the side. "Nervous?"

"A little. I really like her, Yvonne. She's the one, and if she's interested, I'm going to stay in San Diego."

Yvonne gasped. "You're serious?"

"Yeah. I might as well. Hell, I'm not getting any younger. I want to spend the rest of my days with someone whose company I enjoy and who I have things in common with. I want what you and Patrick have."

Her features softened. "I'm definitely lucky."

Patrick came back onto the screen with a can of Coke in hand and dropped a kiss on the top of her head. "I'm the lucky one. I'm going upstairs. Good luck tonight."

"Thanks, man." Tyson waited until Patrick was gone before he continued. "He's right, you know. You're a good woman. If anyone is lucky, it's him."

"Thank you, and I hope Jackie knows what a catch you are. You've changed a lot, for the better. You're not the same man I divorced over twenty years ago."

"The selfish, immature man who only cared about having a good time?"

"Don't beat yourself up. I, for one, am proud to call you my friend."

"Thanks, sweetheart." Tyson inhaled a deep breath. "Okay, so the striped tie, right?"

"Definitely."

"This is date number three. My last opportunity to convince her to give me a chance."

"I'll keep my fingers crossed for you. Good luck."

"Thanks."

9

W as it possible to swallow your tongue?

Based on his inability to speak when he saw Jackie, Tyson was certain it was possible. She came to the door wearing a long wig with wavy dark hair that lay over the tops of her breasts. Her makeup was minimal and natural looking, cheeks highlighted with bronzer and her thick, luscious lips painted the same brown color, which made them look moist and enticing.

As if that wasn't enough, her dress was unspeakably sexy. Black, with loose long sleeves and a neckline that dipped to the wide black belt around her waist. The material lay on her more-than-a-handful-sized breasts in an eye-catching way, but that wasn't the best part. Two slits, one on either side, stopped almost to her pelvis, leaving him to wonder if she was wearing any panties. And if she was, what color were they? What do they look like—a thong, a cheeky, lacy or cotton? He had so many questions.

"Are you just going to stand there and stare?" Jackie asked with an amused expression on her face, a hand on the doorframe.

Tyson shook his head. "Forgive me, but you need to warn a man before you appear looking like his every fantasy."

"I'll keep that in mind," she said softly. Her voice had taken on a huskier tone, and the skin on the back of his neck prickled, sending a signal that he'd only just picked up.

The Jackie standing before him was different from the woman who'd gone on the previous two dates with him. This Jackie, he was almost certain, would sleep with him tonight if he played his cards right. That sultry look in her eyes, and the way she eyed him like he was a cool drink of water after a run in the park, indicated that his chances of getting laid tonight were definitely good.

With a faster heartbeat, he took her hand and kissed the middle knuckle. *Don't screw this up*, he warned himself.

Jackie retrieved her hand and locked the door. "Where are we going tonight?"

"Ever been to The Glass Door?" Tyson asked, mesmerized by the sway of her ample bottom as they made their way to the Cadillac.

"Yes, but it's been a few years. Great food and even better views, especially at sunset."

Tyson opened the passenger door. "I heard about the sunset, and that's why I picked the restaurant. Then after dinner, if you're up to it, we could go for a walk on the beach."

Jackie settled into the seat. "I'm always up for a walk on the beach."

She looked him directly in the eyes, and his stomach contracted. If he wasn't careful, he'd come in his pants before the night was over.

"Good."

Walking to the driver side, Tyson breathed in and out very slowly to calm his raging libido. He climbed in and they were soon on their way to the restaurant. They arrived at the perfect time to get seated and have a good view. The Glass Door was located atop the Porto Vista Hotel on a hill in Little Italy, with views of the rooftops of homes and businesses and San Diego Bay only a few blocks away.

The dining room contained approximately forty tables, but they opted to sit in one of the high-back chairs in front of the long counter that looked out at the scenery. A barrage of vintage lamps hung from the ceiling and cast a faint glow of light over the guests.

"How is your drink?" Tyson asked, breaking the silence between them. Her predinner drink contained orange and red, reflecting the orange and red colors splashed across the late afternoon sky as the sun set.

Jackie took another sip and set it on the bar. "Delicious. Better than delicious."

"With a name like foreplay, it better be darn near orgasmic," Tyson said, sliding an arm across the back of her chair.

"That's not why I chose it." I mean, how could you go wrong with peach schnapps, grenadine, and pineapple? Want to taste?"

She positioned the glass between them and Tyson took a sip. He nodded his agreement. "Definitely good." He licked his lips.

Jackie laughed and shot him a glance through her lashes. "Told you."

Yep, she was definitely feeling him, definitely flirting.

Boldly, he rubbed his thumb along the nape of her neck under her hair. She didn't move or slide away, a good sign.

"How did you find this place?" she asked.

"I did my research. Unlike the last time."

She frowned in confusion.

"Ten years ago, Thursday night, we were both starving and turned up at the restaurant—I can't even remember the name now—but it was one of those trendy, popular places that gets written up in the magazines and makes all the lists. All I knew was that the food was good, they had violinists playing in the dining room, and I wanted to impress you."

Jackie laughed, nodding her head as the memory came back. "That's right. We showed up, and the place was closed. Looked like they'd been closed for months."

"At least. And I was completely humiliated because I talked it up so much."

"Don't worry, I didn't hold it against you."

"I was worried."

She laid her right hand on his thigh, and his quadriceps muscles tensed. Leaning on her left elbow, she turned her entire body toward him. She opened her mouth to speak, but right then the waitress arrived to take their order.

The moment was lost, and Jackie straightened in the chair. She chose the grilled pork chop with truffled pasta, and he ordered the pan seared beef tenderloin with vegetables. They both chose red wine for dinner.

"So what made you decide to come to San Diego?" Jackie asked.

"I wanted to establish a better relationship with Kendrick. I have a good relationship with my daughters, but for some reason he and I have never gotten along. I suppose it's because he's the youngest and didn't have as much time with me as the girls did. He still resents me for leaving and for not spending as much time with him as I should have." Frowning, he twisted the gold ring on his little finger. "My ex-wife is actually the one who suggested I come here and spend time with him and see if I could repair our relationship since nothing else had worked. He and I talked, but our conversations were always short and stilted. I take full responsibility for that, though."

"You have an interesting relationship with your ex-wife."

He nodded. "Some people find it strange, but the truth is, she and I used to be friends. We grew up next door to each other, our parents knew each other, we went to the same school. She was one of my best friends."

"How did you end up hooking up?" Jackie asked. She took a sip of her drink.

"I made a pass at her and she caught it. My fault again."

"If she accepted the pass, then it's not exactly your fault. She was at the very least a willing participant."

"True. But had I not made a pass at her, we would have continued being friends, and she wouldn't have gotten pregnant. Don't get me wrong, I always thought that she was attractive. She thought the same about me, too, but we never acted on our feelings because we were friends."

"Until you made that pass," Jackie interjected.

"Yes, until I made that pass. It was prom night and neither of us had a date, so we went together. We ended up hanging out in a hotel room with a bunch of other kids playing spin the bottle, and the bottle landed on her and I had to kiss her. Frankly, it wasn't bad, it was... great, actually. And, instead of taking her home like I should have, like her parents trusted me to, we parked somewhere and had sex."

Jackie's eyebrows shot higher. "And then what happened?"

"And then we continued hooking up. Next thing I know, she's my girlfriend, and we were with each other all the time because it was summertime. Everything kind of snowballed. A few months later, she told me she was pregnant, and a few months after that we were standing in the courthouse getting married."

"Wow." Jackie's chin rested on her hand, eyes never leaving his face as she listened intently to him recount the story.

"The marriage worked for a while, but after some years we had to admit that being married to each other was not what either of us wanted."

"And eventually you started seeing other people."

"Yes. We stayed together to save money on the bills, but when she fell in love with Patrick—and he knew about our unique situation—it was time for me to get lost."

He didn't talk much about his marriage and his failure as a father with other people, but he felt comfortable telling her and didn't see judgment in her eyes. "OK, your turn."

"Me?" Her eyes widened.

"Yeah, you. Who's the guy that broke off the engagement?"

"He was my banker." She grimaced.

"You dated your banker?"

"He was a great guy!" she said defensively. "But it was completely inappropriate for him to ask me out in the middle of processing my loan application. At first I thought he was using the loan as some kind of leverage, but then I realized he was too nice of a guy for that. His timing was just off. We dated for about a year, and then he asked me to marry him. I said yes. But then..."

"But then what?"

Jackie shrugged. "But then I broke off the engagement because I realized that he wasn't what I was looking for. Sure, he was stable and good to me, but there was no passion. No excitement. I wanted what my parents had. I wanted what my best friend Adelaide had with her husband, and I didn't want to settle for less. I didn't need him for security because I could take care of myself. But what I really needed, he wasn't offering, and I eventually had to tell him so."

"Bet that was a tough conversation to have," Tyson mused.

She nodded emphatically. "It was. Painful, but necessary. There was no way I could marry him, because I knew that in another five years or so, I would be asking for divorce. I took the advice of another girlfriend, one who's been married three times."

"What was her advice?"

"Never settle for good enough. Because it's never actually...good enough."

10

H and in hand, Jackie and Tyson strolled the sand at La Jolla Cove. The sea lions had converged on the beach, barking and grunting as if to get the attention of the smattering of people leisurely walking along the shore.

"This is the perfect end to the evening," Jackie remarked.

"I agree." Tyson squeezed her hand. He carried her shoes in his right hand.

Great food and great conversation meant a memorable night. No doubt she'd fallen for Tyson ten years ago, but the man she'd come to know over the past three dates was intriguing in a different way. She not only enjoyed his company and the sexy undertones of attraction, they were connecting on a deeper level, opening up and sharing more about their lives.

"When do you go back?" Jackie asked, thinking about how much harder the separation would be this time.

They stopped and Tyson stood with his back to the water. "I told you before I can stay as long as I want." His eyes searched her face. *Is that what you want*? he seemed to ask.

Jackie glanced away at the dark water. She couldn't answer the unspoken question yet because as much as she enjoyed her time with Tyson, she was still overwhelmed.

"What were you about to say back at the restaurant, before the waitress arrived to take our order?"

She had to think for a minute because the incident had occurred a couple of hours before. "I was going to tell you that not only did I not hold the mistake of the restaurant against you in Atlanta, I always had a good time whenever we were together." Her cheeks heated.

"That means a lot to me, and I can't tell you again how much I regret not following up. I should have, but I didn't."

She shrugged. "We all make mistakes."

"We shouldn't make life-altering mistakes like that." He tugged her closer and placed his lips against her cheek. It wasn't a kiss. More like a snuggle or simple show of affection. Nonetheless, being held so close awakened her desire for him. She played with the button on his shirt, glad for the cool ocean breeze blowing on her heated skin.

"I have a surprise for you," Tyson whispered.

"You do, do you?" Jackie arched an eyebrow.

Tilting back her head, she rose up on her toes. She had a surprise for him, too, and it included the two of them going back to her place and—

The sounds of violins pierced the night air. Startled, she turned and her mouth fell open at the sight of three tuxedo-clad men coming toward them on the sand.

"Tyson..." she whispered, her throat clogging with emotion.

He hooked an arm around her waist and pulled her back into his body. "Surprise," he whispered.

People gathered around as the three men serenaded them on the beach. Tyson kept his arm closed around Jackie as if he couldn't let her go. She enjoyed the close contact, being held by him, in the warm circle of his arm. The surprise was over-the-top, romantic, and she loved it.

When the violinists finished playing, they and the small crowd that had gathered clapped profusely and whistled their appreciation.

The men bowed, smiled, and then began their retreat. The crowd dispersed, and Jackie and Tyson were alone once again.

"You are really knocking it out of the park tonight," she said, taking hold of one of the buttons on his vest.

"Go hard or go home. That's my philosophy."

Jackie gazed up at him. The cool wind coming in from the water gently blew her dress and the slits exposed her thighs.

"I want you to stay, as long as you can. I want this. I want you." She was laying her soul bare to him, and it was terrifying. If he wasn't the same man he was ten years ago, she was in for a treat. If he was, she would be devastated all over again. But she hadn't gotten where she was in business without taking risks, and maybe it was time for her to take a risk in her personal life—one that would pay great dividends.

"I want you, too. More than I've ever wanted any woman." He touched his forehead to hers and wrapped his arms around her. "You're it for me. You're what's been missing from my life."

Tears came to her eyes, and she lowered her lids to keep them from falling. Tightening her fingers into the material of his vest, she ached to tell him about what had been missing from her life. The fact that she wanted her own family and was so close to getting that now. Would he understand? Would he want to be a part of her plans? If they seriously talked about a future together, was he willing to become a parent again?

Those questions needed to be answered, but not tonight. Tonight, she wanted to make hot, fiery love to him, forget all the doubts, and just enjoy being with this man who she'd never forgotten.

"There's no woman waiting for you in Atlanta or anywhere else, is there?"

"Absolutely not. I can't believe you asked."

"I had to ask. I had to be sure. When you first arrived, Kendrick mentioned your *friend*, Carrie." She arched a brow.

He nodded with a wry twist of his lips. "Ancient history, and I promise you, there's no one else."

"In that case," Jackie said quietly, leaning in close, "how about you take me back to my place, and I'll show you how much I missed you."

Eyes gleaming with desire, Tyson cupped her face in one hand and planted a hard, wet kiss on her mouth. "Your wish is my command," he whispered, his warm breath brushing her lips.

They took their time walking across the sand and climbed the stairs hand in hand to the top where Tyson had parked the SUV. Strolling along with the other pedestrians, they passed restaurants where guests dined al fresco as they gazed out at the dark ocean.

Tyson opened the rear door of the vehicle. "Have a seat," he said.

When Jackie sat down, he pulled a towel from the back and crouched in front of her. He proceeded to clean the sand from her feet.

Flexing her toes, she said, "I feel like a princess."

"Does that make me your prince?"

"Do you want to be?"

Their gazes idled on each other.

"You should already know the answer, but if there's any doubt, the answer is yes, unequivocally yes."

With a full heart, Jackie watched as Tyson slipped the shoes back onto her feet and then kissed each of her ankles. The gentle press of his mouth sparked fire on her skin and inflamed her lust even more.

They left the beach, and on the way back to her house, chatted about mundane topics, their gazes lingering, and the occasional touch on the thigh or arm amping up the tension between them. By the time he pulled in front of her garage and helped her from the vehicle, her panties were wet and her sex was throbbing with need for him.

Jackie opened the front door but Tyson held back.

"What's wrong?" she asked. He stood outside the door, their hands still entwined, but she was on the inside.

"Jackie, you know I want this more than anything. But are *you* sure? I don't want you to have any regrets, baby. I don't want you to have any doubts about me, either."

Tilting her head at him, she smiled. "You really have changed,

Tyson. Ten years ago, I don't think you would have cared one way or the other about my feelings as long as you got what you wanted, and you would have expected—or at least hoped—that I wanted the same thing, too. But I don't have any doubts about you, or about us. Let me tell you a secret. I have a thirty-day rule. I broke it for you ten years ago, and even though we didn't end up together, I don't regret it. So get in here before I change my mind."

Tyson flashed his megawatt smile. "You don't have to tell me twice."

He pushed his way inside and, laughing, they ran up the stairs. At the door to her master suite, Jackie threw open the door with great ceremony and flourish.

"So this is where the magic happens," Tyson said, walking slowly across the rich beige carpet.

"This is where the magic happens," she confirmed.

She tilted up her lips, bringing them ever so close to his without touching, allowing her breath to feather across his mouth in a whisper of good things to come. She palmed the front of his pants and felt his dick come to life.

He backed her up to the bed and planted a kiss on her lips, his arms wrapping her in a tight embrace. She held him close, too, moving her mouth over his and enjoying the pressure of his lips. They transformed into a frenzy of kisses that consisted of mouths and hands and pelvic grinds.

When he finally let her up for air, she stepped back and pressed a hand to her chest. "Excuse me for a moment. I'm going into the bathroom to slip into something more comfortable."

"Don't take too long." He bit his bottom lip, his gaze crawling down her body in slow motion.

"I won't." Jackie slowly backed toward the bathroom. "Don't go anywhere."

With one last saucy smile, she slipped into the room and closed the door.

11

Jackie went into the bathroom, where she had already set aside her lingerie choice before leaving the house. She came out and stood in the doorway. The long hair of the wig hung over her right shoulder, and she bent her left knee in a sexy pose, extending a hand up the length of the doorframe.

Tyson sat at the foot of the bed in his boxers, and when he saw her, his lips fell partially open. He looked like a man ready for action, his chest on display, all his smooth dark skin exposed to her hungry eyes.

"Damn," he said, sitting up straighter.

"Like what you see?" Jackie knew she looked sexy in the red bustier and red panties, breaking up the color with black fishnet stockings and black heels.

"Sure do."

She sashayed across the carpet with an exaggerated swing in her hips. His eyes remained glued to her body, his breathing coming in shorter spurts by the rapid rise and drop of his chest. She stopped in front of him, hands on her hips, and he licked his lips.

Jackie turned in a slow semicircle and stopped to show him the back, giving an up-close view of her bare ass.

Tyson groaned. "Baby, you look so good. Better than I remember."

Her skin warmed at the compliment. This man was so good for her ego.

With a smirk, she tossed a look at him over her shoulder just as he rose to his full height of six five.

"I'm not letting you tease me all night," he said.

"I never tease," she returned with a lofty arch to her eyebrow.

"This is a tease." Tyson slid his hands down her waist and onto her exposed bottom. When he squeezed her fleshy behind, her brain shut down.

He ran his nose along the curve of her neck and sucked her earlobe. "Gimme a kiss," he commanded, and cupping her chin, tilted back her head against his shoulder and covered her mouth with his.

The upside down kiss was hot and nasty. He swiped his tongue along her teeth and pushed until it touched hers, deepening their connection into moist, dirty movements. His free hand slid between her thighs, and when his fingers discovered the crotchless panties, he groaned and slipped two fingers into her wet cleft.

Jackie inhaled sharply, shoving her hips against his probing hand to appease her dripping sex. His clever fingers teased the folds, alternating between massaging her plump lower lips and slipping inside to torture her to the very edge of climax.

Needy and greedy, she let out a frustrated whine and twisted in Tyson's arms. Face to face, she planned to take control, but he grabbed the back of her neck and kissed her harder—continuing to violate her mouth with the rough swipe of his tongue. She could almost come from his kisses alone. Guiding her fingers over the shape of his bald head, she smoothed them down to his nape and over his shoulders to explore the firmness of his skin.

Tyson brushed his mouth along her exposed shoulder, and the barely-there kiss made her insides tremble with anticipation. She wanted him so much but vacillated between a desire to continue this delectable foreplay or give in to the yearning and have him spread her legs and take her right away.

"Let's get you out of these clothes," Tyson said against her ear.

"To think, I spent all that time deciding what to wear, only for you to remove my clothes within minutes."

He compelled her backward until the back of her legs hit the bed. "I appreciate the effort, but you could have been wearing a shower curtain and I would have the same response."

He unhooked the stocking straps, then standing close so his hard chest touched her breasts, reached behind her and took his time opening the closures at the back of the bustier—one by one until he dropped the red covering to the carpet. His possessive gaze traveled over the fullness of her large breasts, and she trembled a little, anxious for his touch and to experience the full measure of his lovemaking.

"Sit, let me take off these stockings."

Jackie sat on the bed and lifted her left leg, and Tyson removed the high heel then took his time rolling the stocking down her leg, his fingers igniting sparks of electricity down to her ankles. After he flung it aside, he placed a kiss on the fleshy part of her calf, one on her knee, and the last on her inner thigh. He did the same to the other leg, taking his time and making her skin sing before he pushed her backward onto the bed and removed the lacy G-string.

He kissed her sex and flicked her clit, and her skin cried out for more as she widened her legs. Tyson swirled his tongue around her clit and skimmed her bare lower lips, sending a surge of pleasure arching up her spine. He teased her inner thighs, taking his time to go down to her ankles and moved back up, nipping the tender skin with the edges of his teeth and nibbling on the crease of her hips. Stroking his bald head, she urged him to continue with encouraging moans and by arching her back.

He obliged, tormenting the tips of her breasts with his tongue and running his hand all over her naked body. He had complete control, turning her into nothing more than a quivering, needy mess of heightened nerves and aching loins.

One hand trailed over her breasts, sliding down the rounded

curve of her belly to the flare of her hips and settled on her sex, which dripped with lust and desire.

"Tyson," she moaned.

"Right here with you, baby."

His lips brushed her belly and his tongue slipped into her navel. Moving restlessly, she savored every touch, each caress that he sprinkled all over her skin making her dizzy with pleasure.

His teasing fingers crept up around her throat and tilted back her head, and she sighed with abandon. It felt so good to be free and uninhibited with a man who knew what he was doing. And everything Tyson did felt good. Every touch. Every kiss. Every movement made her crave more.

She ran her hands up his torso over skin that was firm yet soft, and she spread her fingers to engage as much of his flesh as possible. "You're next," she said, pushing at his boxers.

He slipped off the bed and shoved them completely down his thick thighs and exposed the fullness of his arousal. Her eyes went wide. Thick, dark, and long, his hardened flesh stood up against his hard abs in a lusty salute.

"See something you like?" he asked with a cocky grin.

"I do," Jackie replied, sounding breathless. "I remembered you were big, but I forgot you were this big."

"Don't tell me you're afraid. You handled it last time. "

"Oh, I can handle it this time, too."

"That's what I want to hear."

He grabbed the condoms from his pants and tossed them onto the bedside table. Capturing her mouth again, he plied her lips with deep, languid kisses while they moved backward toward the pillows. Jackie gripped his ass and sank in her fingernails. She rubbed her aching sex against his erection, and when he released her mouth, she whimpered as his teeth played with her erect nipples.

"Tyson, I..." Need beat like a hammer in her blood. She couldn't get the sentence out, but they were so in tune he still understood.

"I hear you, baby." He breathed the words in a rough whisper against her shoulder.

With fluid movements, he took one of the packets from the table and sheathed his immense length. Gazing down at her, he shook his head as if he couldn't believe his eyes. "Look at you. So damn beautiful."

Nostrils flaring, he took possession of her—hard into soft, firm into wet. She cried out, the sound torn from her lungs as excruciating pleasure sank its claws into her body. Tyson buried himself deep, his hard, penetrating thrusts making her blurt incoherent words like a worshiper speaking in tongues. Pumping her hips, she clung to him and clawed his back, the throbbing deep inside of her reaching a crescendo and creating an explosion so intense she screamed as her entire body quaked through the climax.

With labored breathing, Jackie closed her eyes and felt the tension ooze from her satisfied body. That was the best orgasm she'd had in a long time. Maybe ten years. If she could freeze this moment in time, this feeling, she would, and keep it close to her heart for good.

Tyson eased away and fell onto his back.

"You didn't come." Jackie rolled onto her side. He was still fully erect.

"I will in a minute, when you get on top of me. You know I like to watch you."

"You'll have to wait. I don't have the energy I had ten years ago."

"I'll wait."

"Well...I don't want you to wait too long." She smoothed a hand down his chest and clasped his dick in her hand.

He flinched as if she'd hurt him. "How long is not too long?" he squeaked.

"Right this minute."

Jackie took the top position and guided Tyson between her legs and sank onto his silken length.

"Like this?" she asked coyly, moving her hips.

"You know damn well—"

His words broke off when she moved in a circle. She took her fill the way she wanted—slow, sliding repeatedly up and down and alternating by rolling her hips over his pelvis.

Holding onto her waist, he cursed softly as he watched her, eyes mere slits, nostrils widening with each deep breath as he fought for control. Watching him struggle made her want to drive him crazy even more. Hands on his sternum, she let herself go, biting her bottom lip as she indulged. His hip movements intensified and the raw power of each thrust filled her body. The way he moved underneath her was both heaven and hell—a tortuous blending of sensations that left her dizzy with agonizing desire.

Her hair fell forward and shrouded her face, and Tyson caressed her breasts. He squeezed her nipples, each tweak of his thumb and finger sending a pulse of heat right between her legs.

His movements increased with speed and force and she struggled to keep the pace. "Tyson..."

He flipped her onto her back and took control—pumping his hips, bringing them both closer to climax.

"How the hell did I let you go before?" he growled in a ferocious whisper.

Those were the last words he uttered before she came, another loud cry tearing from her throat as she soared to unimaginable heights. Tyson didn't let up until he came, too, and with a loud shout careened off the edge right along with her.

12

———

Tyson woke up slowly. Rubbing a hand over his bald head, he blinked against the light coming through the windows before registering that Jackie stood in the doorway.

His breath caught. Like the night before, she looked incredible, but in a different way. The wig was gone, and her short curls were on display, red and vivid against her brown skin. A short-sleeved, button-down sleep shirt with vertical lines showed off her legs, and in her hand was a cup of coffee, its caramelized scent enticing him from across the room.

"Good morning," she greeted him.

"Morning. How long have you been standing there?" Yawning, he sat up.

"Not long." Jackie walked over and handed him the cup.

"Thank you." Steam filtered into the air, and Tyson carefully took a sip, his gaze traveling over her voluptuous figure as the memories from the night before came back with a vengeance. She had been uninhibited in their lovemaking, and her cries of passion still echoed in his head.

"What are your plans for the day?" she asked.

"Whatever you're doing, I'm doing." Tyson set the cup on the table nearby. He swung his legs off the side of the bed and, resting his hands on her hips, pulled her between his legs.

Placing both hands on his shoulders, she said, "I have to work. Around noon I'm going to one of my smaller stores. You want to come with me and help stock merchandise and change out the displays?" A teasing glint filled her eyes.

"No, ma'am. I'll make myself scarce for a bit and head home. I have to call my granddaughter later and wish her a happy birthday."

"You have a granddaughter?"

"And a grandson. My oldest, Carina, is their mother. Hold on, I got a ton of pictures."

As he hopped off the bed, Jackie sat down. He pulled on his boxers and pulled his phone from the jacket he'd worn on last night's date. Taking a seat beside Jackie, he opened the album with photos of his grandchildren and handed her the phone.

"That's Bethany, named after her paternal great-grandmother, who raised Carina's husband. Jackson was named after my father. We call him Jack for short."

"They're adorable," Jackie murmured, swiping through the photos. She laughed at a picture of the kids taking a sudsy bubble bath together when they were toddlers, and *ahhed* at Bethany's kindergarten graduation photo.

He smiled at a photo he took with the kids, one on each knee, sitting on a balcony. "Took that one last year when I took Carina and her family to Hawaii. We rented a villa on the beach for two weeks. My youngest daughter, Niecy, flew in for a week to hang out with us. We all had a great time. Several times during the trip, I watched the kids so Carina and her husband could spend time alone sightseeing. We went to the beach, ate ice cream, watched the movies they wanted to watch. I swear I know every animated Disney movie now. Those kids know how to work me over. They're spoiled rotten, let me tell you."

"That's the way it should be."

"Yeah. I'm just glad I'm able to spoil them in a way I couldn't spoil my kids. And, at least my girls don't hate me."

"Are you saying that Kendrick does?"

"'Hate' might be a strong word, and he's definitely changed his attitude toward me since I've been here. The other day we went to the beach, and he taught me how to surf. I fell off the board so many times, I'm surprised he didn't give up. He stuck with me, though." Tyson chuckled, shaking his head at the memories.

Jackie's eyes widened. "Are you crazy? I can't believe you got on a surfboard!"

"Sure did. Hell, I liked it, too. It really wasn't that bad once I got over the fear of falling. I'm thinking about taking a class so I'll get better. I figure it'll be a nice hobby to take up once I move here." He kept his eyes on her to see her reaction.

Jackie blinked. "Oh. You're thinking of moving here?"

"I am." Tyson looked into her eyes so she understood the gravity of his words. "*You* are here."

"Tyson..."

"Jackie, you know how I feel about you. I'm pretty sure I fell in love with you ten years ago, but instead of following my heart, I chased success and wanted to experience everything I'd missed out on as a young husband and father. The older, wiser Tyson knows that he can't let you go. I told you, I'm taking a chance and fixing my mistakes."

"We've only been on a few dates."

He took her hand and leaned closer. "Tell me something, did you really forget about me like you said you did? Or did I make a deep impression on you the way you did me?"

Jackie paused, then nodded her head, admitting in a low voice, "You made a deep impression on me. It took a long time for me to get over our time together."

He breathed easier. "You don't have to make me any promises. I just want to be nearer to you so I can woo you." He smiled.

"I don't want to talk you out of moving here, but I don't want to make any promises, either." Jackie seemed to choose the next words carefully. "There's a lot going on in my life, plans I'm making, and if you move here, I'm not sure how...how you'll fit into my life once those plans are implemented."

"Business plans?"

"No."

The cryptic answer intrigued him. "Can you tell me what those plans are?" Tyson asked, ready to convince her that he was willing to do whatever was necessary so she would allow him space in her life.

"Not yet, but it's definitely something we should talk about. At some point," she added hastily.

He pondered her words, wondering what she could possibly be planning that would have her hesitant to share with him right now. "You can tell me anything, but I'll let you tell me about these mystery plans when you're comfortable. Until then, know that I'm in this for the long haul. No games. No running away this time."

"Good to know."

Her lovely brown eyes met his, and she squeezed his hand, squashing the surge of anxiety he felt when she initially mentioned plans. If she still had doubts about him, he needed to continue putting in the work to convince her to trust him completely, and he was up for the task. He needed to make some phone calls and get the ball rolling on his transition to the west coast. He'd need to sell or rent his condo and ship more of his clothing and belongings to San Diego since he'd be here longer than expected. For now, he'd keep *his* plans under wraps.

"How about breakfast? My housekeeper will be here soon, and you can put in a special order for whatever you'd like."

"How soon will she be here?" Tyson asked.

Jackie glanced at the bedside table. "In about thirty-five minutes."

"Hmm, that gives us thirty minutes to fool around, with five minutes to spare." His lips found the side of her neck and she moaned, turning her head and kissing the corner of his mouth.

She smelled earthy and sweet like the goddess she was. He sucked gently on her fragrant skin and flicked the tip of his tongue against her clavicle.

"I like the way you think," she whispered.

TYSON RUBBED a hand over his face and smothered a yawn. "Why are you up so early? It's Sunday," he grumbled.

The past week passed in a blur of dates, snuggling on the couch, and rushing from the house early in the morning to get to work since more often than not, they dallied over coffee because she didn't want to say goodbye and leave for the day—having to wait until nighttime before she saw him again. Jackie had gotten accustomed to the mad dash out the door, then making a quick stop at the Starbucks drive-thru for an egg sandwich and more coffee before she headed to work.

"I've always been an early riser, never needed an alarm clock. And since I always go into work early, I keep the same schedule even on the weekend." Jackie shrugged.

He watched her slip on a pair of red boy shorts with lace edging and a white stretchy top with a big red heart on the front.

"I'm going to have to break you from this habit. Maybe give you a reason to stay in bed longer." His narrowed eyes and his softly smirking mouth promised more pleasurable moments like last night.

"Look at you. We've only been together a short while and already you're trying to change me."

"Usually it's the woman in a relationship who tries to make the changes, isn't it? We're doing this all wrong." He yawned again.

Jackie gave him an indulgent smile. "How about some breakfast?"

"Breakfast would be nice." He folded both arms behind his head.

"Coming right up, but don't get too used to this. I'm only cooking because my housekeeper has the day off. I don't make breakfast often —or cook in general. Too much work."

"You just need someone to make it worth your while, that's all."

"Just appreciate what I'm doing, okay?" she said tartly.

"I promise to appreciate everything you offer me," Tyson said, licking his lips.

"Your mind stays in the gutter." She shook her head, tossing over her shoulder on the way out the door, "When I get back I have something for you."

"I can't wait!"

Laughing softly to herself, Jackie went downstairs and prepared a quick meal of scrambled eggs, ham, toast, and coffee. She took the tickets she'd printed the day before off the printer and set them on the tray with the food.

Back in the bedroom, she found Tyson strolling out of the bathroom in a pair of navy boxer shorts. He was a beautiful man who took time to exercise regularly, and it showed. He had long, toned legs, a smooth firm chest, plus a high-wattage smile that never failed to make her heart thud faster.

He rubbed his hands together. "Right on time."

"Follow me."

She led the way out to the balcony, afforded privacy by the cluster of trees that bordered the edge of her property.

"This looks good. Thanks, baby." Tyson gave her a quick kiss, and she tasted the peppermint from the toothpaste.

"You're welcome." Jackie sat down and waited for him to notice the tickets.

He sat across from her. "What's this?" He picked up the printed pages and his eyes widened. "You got Charlie Wilson tickets?"

"Surprise!"

"Hot damn! I haven't seen him perform in years, but he always puts on a good show." He kept staring at the printout.

"My sister planned to go, but she had to cancel so I bought her tickets and thought you and I could go instead. I figured since you're such a big fan, you wouldn't mind. They're great seats, near the front row. Do you have plans on Saturday?"

"Let's see..." He frowned, thinking. "Actually, Kendrick and I were going out, but we can move that to another night. Charlie Wilson, baby. I can't wait!" He hopped up, clutched her face, and gave her another loud smack on the lips. "I love my surprise." He whispered the words against her mouth and then sat down.

With warm cheeks and fullness in her chest, Jackie bit into a piece of buttered toast. His enthusiasm was addictive, and being with him was so easy. Their relationship was loving, fun, and she looked forward to his calls and every moment they spent together.

Tyson reached across the small table and took her hand. He brought her fingers to his lips and looked in her eyes. "This sounds corny as hell, but I was thinking about our relationship this time around, how much deeper it is than when we first met. Even though I was crazy about you ten years ago, what I feel for you now is different. I literally can't imagine my life without you. When we met before, the timing was wrong. This time, everything feels right, you know? I want to move here and spend the rest of my life with you, like this. Having breakfast, traveling together, going to concerts, making love until my eyes roll back in my head." He grinned, but his eyes remained serious as they searched hers. "Do you feel even a little bit of what I feel?"

Jackie nodded. She hadn't expected the second iteration of their togetherness to be so enjoyable. She'd expected something temporary, fleeting. Yet every time she saw him, all she thought about was...forever.

"I do. I want to be with you, Tyson."

"Then we're on the same page."

Except for one detail. Her adoption plans. She thought about telling him, but if she wasn't approved, it wouldn't matter. So she set aside the conversation for now, one they could have at a later date.

"We're definitely on the same page," she agreed.

13

That smile made her day. The smile of a woman who found a clothing item that fit.

"I love it," the customer said, flipping her dark hair over one shoulder and turning to the left to get a better look at the side view in a hot pink corset.

"You look amazing. Pink is definitely your color," Jackie said. She stepped back to survey the fit with the black leather pants the woman had brought in. The ensemble screamed sexy night-on-the-town.

The woman continued to study her image in the mirror. "Do you have any babydoll nighties in the same color?"

"Not in the store, but we can order one for you. Let me show you our selection."

She took the woman over to one of the racks, and they spent a few minutes discussing the different styles. Eventually, she settled on a see-through mesh design with the matching underwear that could arrive in the store in a week. Jackie took the order, rang up both purchases, and sent her out the door with a smile.

Cindy came behind the counter, wearing a sea-green pantsuit and her red Afro in two big puffs today. "You headed to lunch now?"

"Yes. I might be a little late coming back. I have to stop by the bank for a bit. I'll see you later."

"I've got it. Take your time."

As Jackie left the store, she pulled out her phone and saw a missed call from her adoption case worker, and he'd left a voice message. Her heart sped up. What could this be about? Surely it was good news, right? Yet she was afraid to call and find out.

"Just check the message, Jackie," she said out loud, smiling at a man who gave her an odd look as she walked by.

She was about to do just that when she spotted Kendrick walking toward her. He was dressed casually in a navy-blue Biggie Smalls T-shirt and jeans, his thick hair picked out into an almost perfect circle of curls around his head.

"Kendrick. Hi," she said cautiously.

"Hey beautiful, how are you?" he replied.

Interesting word choice.

Jackie stopped but maintained what she considered a safe distance because something about him was off. "I'm well. How about you?" She watched him closely. His eyes were red, as if he hadn't been getting enough sleep.

He shrugged and started walking again, so she followed suit.

"I'm living. I was on my way to your store to see if you wanted to have lunch with me."

"Lunch?"

He laughed. "Yeah, lunch. You know, the meal people eat around this time of day. The one in between breakfast and dinner."

"Sorry about that. I'm just surprised to see you. We haven't talked in a long time, and..."

"And you're dating my father."

Jackie cringed. She couldn't help feeling a little embarrassed.

"How are things going with you two?" Kendrick asked.

"Fine." Her footsteps slowed to a stop at her silver BMW.

"Your relationship should be better than fine, and that answer makes me think that I was right to come here today. I've been thinking a lot about us, and I believe I gave up too easily."

Whoa. Jackie's eyes widened. "Kendrick, before you—"

He grasped her arms and stepped into her personal space. Eyes earnest and intense, he said, "I still have feelings for you, and I'm willing to do whatever it takes to win you over."

Caught off guard by the scent of liquor that infused his breath, Jackie leaned away from him. Coupled with his red eyes, it was obvious he'd been drinking quite a bit even though his words didn't slur as he spoke.

She eased out of the grip of his long fingers. "Kendrick, I'm very flattered, but our time has passed. Your father and I are together now, so your being here is a bit awkward." Her shoulders tensed as she braced for his response.

"So what, he just swooped in and won you over, just like that?" He snapped his fingers.

"I knew him before," Jackie said gently. She didn't want to hurt him, but he needed to understand that the feelings she had for Tyson started long before this summer.

"So that's it? I get nothing?"

"Honey, I don't know what you mean. Aren't you and your father working on your relationship?"

"Yeah, sure. We're working on our relationship," he said, the bite of sarcasm deep in his words.

"I thought you were getting along."

"He and I had plans tonight, but he canceled. And he told me he canceled because he made plans with you. Am I right?" He challenged her with his eyes.

Jackie pressed a hand to her chest. "I'm sorry. That's my fault. I surprised him with tickets to a concert, not thinking much about the fact that he would have other plans. I should have—"

"No. *He* should have told you he couldn't make it and had other plans. Of course he'd choose you over me. Everybody comes before me." He laughed bitterly, the hand at his right side clenching into a fist. "You know what, forget it. Forget you. Forget him, especially. I'm out of here."

Jackie grabbed his wrist before he could turn away. "Don't leave.

Let me take you home. You've obviously been drinking and are in no condition to drive."

He glared at her. "Don't treat me like a child. I'm a *man*."

"A man who I cannot let drive," Jackie shot back in a hard voice.

Her fingers tightened on his wrist. She didn't know how, but she would keep him from getting into his vehicle in his condition.

The fire in Kendrick's eyes died, and with a defeated sigh, he slumped against the door of her BMW. All the fight had drained out of him. "Fine," he muttered.

Relieved, Jackie unlocked the doors and they both climbed into the car. He closed his eyes and rested the back of his head against the seat.

Before she pulled out of the parking lot, she shot Tyson a text, letting him know she was with Kendrick and taking him home because he'd obviously been drinking. He responded quickly that he would meet them at the apartment, and she started the car.

When she pulled into the parking lot of Kendrick's apartment, Tyson was already waiting and jumped out of the Cadillac SUV. He looked good in a pale rose-colored shirt with the top buttons undone and a gold rope necklace glinting against his dark brown skin. Concern marred his forehead as he watched her and Kendrick climb out of the car.

"Thank you," he said, keeping his eyes on his son.

Kendrick slowly walked past him, hands hooked in the belt loops of his jeans. He didn't even acknowledge his father.

Jackie touched Tyson's arm and captured his attention. She quickly told him what Kendrick had said to her about their plans and that he felt everyone else came before he did in Tyson's life.

With a grim nod, Tyson said, "Thanks." He leaned toward her, as if to give her a quick kiss, and then thinking better of it, shook his head. "I gotta talk to him. I'm sorry about tonight, but I'll call you later or tomorrow—as soon as I can."

"Take your time. I'm not going anywhere." Jackie climbed in her car and drove away.

TYSON JOGGED to the building and caught up to Kendrick at the elevator. They rode to his floor in silence and entered his apartment in silence.

"Say what you have to say and then go." Kendrick tossed his keys onto a side table and plopped onto the sofa. Not once did he look at his father.

Tyson sauntered over. "I don't have anything to say, but I'm sure you do."

His son snorted. "I went after your woman. I know you have *something* to say."

"Okay, I'll talk."

He sat on the coffee table, directly in front of Kendrick. Kendrick finally looked at him, but his eyes remained expressionless. Tyson shoved down his dismay at the emotional distance between them. If anyone had to fix this rift, it was him, and he couldn't do that focused on self-pity.

"You weren't going after my woman. You were trying to get my attention, and now you have it. Tell me what you're feeling."

"I don't have shit to say to you."

"You don't want to tell me how disappointed you are in me? Tell me that the shit I do is not what a real father does?"

"You've heard all of that before," Kendrick said, with a bitter twist to his upper lip.

"Yes, I have," Tyson said, pain piling up from the bottom of his stomach. "I thought we were getting closer. I thought..." His teeth clenched in frustration. He didn't know what else to do. He couldn't be wasting his time, could he? "I'm sorry about tonight. I do want to spend time with you. I love you."

Kendrick's gaze flew to his. "You don't."

"I do. Whether you believe it or not. I didn't do a good job of showing you when you were growing up, but I do love you. I didn't cancel our plans tonight because I don't care. I wasn't thinking, but I promise to do better."

"It's not just tonight's plans. I'm surprised you came to San Diego because you never seemed to want to spend time with me before. You took Carina and her family on vacation last year, but you didn't ask if I wanted to come."

"I didn't think you would. I figured—"

"You got all this money now and you don't do anything for me. Three years ago you bought Niecy a car for her birthday, but Patrick and Mom pay for everything for me. You gave up all your responsibility to me, and I'm your only son."

"You said you didn't want my help."

"You're supposed to still try!" Kendrick bellowed. "I don't get emotional or financial support from you." He slammed his fist into his palm.

The silence in the room sounded extra quiet after his outburst.

Maybe Yvonne was right again. He should have told Kendrick how he contributed to his lifestyle, because clearly his son had secretly been holding what he considered Tyson's lack of financial support against him.

With a boulder of dread in his stomach, Tyson said the words he'd been afraid to say before, for fear of further alienating his son. "I covered your car payment three times since you've been out here, and the down payment for the car that you thought came from your mom came from me."

Kendrick's frown deepened and surprise lit his eyes.

"When you went part-time, I started subsidizing your rent."

"Mom and Patrick—"

"Your mom and Patrick promised to keep quiet about what I was doing. I asked them not to say anything and told them I would take care of whatever you needed."

"Why would you do that when you know I barely wanted to talk to you?"

"You're my son, Kendrick."

He swallowed and surveyed the room. "You really been helping me with my rent and...and the other stuff?"

Tyson nodded. "I had to do something—even if you didn't know

—to make up for all the times I screwed up. For missing your basket-ball tryouts, for instance."

"You didn't miss anything. I sucked," he mumbled.

"That's not the point. I should've been here," Tyson said, resting his elbows on his knees. "I should've been there when you auditioned for the commercials and shouldn't have been late those two times your mother asked me to pick you up from your friend's house."

"Three times," Kendrick quietly correctly.

Only three times and he still managed to fuck it up.

Tyson placed a hand on his son's knee. "I want to come with you when you go to New York next week."

"Nah, you don't have to do that. I've already made contact with a few people, and the talent agency said they'd helped me find a roommate."

"I want to. Come on, Kendrick. I want to spend as much time with you as you'll let me, and I don't want you to have to make that move on your own. This is a major decision, and you should have support, and not from someone who wants to make money off of you, but someone who cares about you as a person."

Silence filled the room, and Tyson waited, worry eating a hole in his chest while his son kept his eyes trained on the floor.

"You would do that for me?" His voice cracked.

"Yes," Tyson said quietly, hating that his son doubted his love and support, his willingness to move mountains and rid his path of any obstacles.

"What about Jackie? You gonna leave her for weeks to hang out with me?"

"She'll understand that I can't let my kid go off to New York to start a new life without being there with him if I'm able. I missed so many other milestones, I don't want to miss this one, too. So what do you say? Me and you in New York for a couple of weeks, while you get settled?"

Kendrick sniffed and rubbed a thumb under his nose. "I guess. I mean, if you have time." He kept his eyes trained on the floor.

Tyson squeezed his knee. "I got plenty of time. Let me do this, okay?"

A few seconds passed before Kendrick nodded and lifted his watery gaze. "Okay."

Tyson grabbed him by the back of his head and kissed his forehead. "I love you. I'ma do better, I promise. Just give me a chance?" His own voice was shaking.

"A'ight."

Tyson patted his shoulder, and Kendrick stood, swiping at his eyes. "I need to use the bathroom."

"When you come out, let's go get some dinner."

Kendrick paused, studying him, as if making sure he hadn't imagined the entire exchange. "Okay." He disappeared into the bathroom.

Progress. Finally.

14

"Hey." Jackie opened her arms and hugged Tyson.

He squeezed her tight and nuzzled her neck. "Mmm, you smell good."

"Thank you. Come on in." She stepped back and allowed him into the house.

"Sorry to come by so late, but I had to see you. It's been too long."

"I've missed you, too, but I know you've been busy with Kendrick and your plans to travel to New York. How is he?" They hadn't seen each other since their brief meeting outside Kendrick's apartment, but they'd exchanged a few texts and talked on the phone briefly once.

Tyson followed her into the living room where she'd been sitting on the tan sectional sofa. Her open laptop rested on the seat, and he dropped down beside it.

"Canceling my plans with him turned out to be a good thing because it forced us to talk. We've never been closer."

He looked relaxed and happy, like a man who'd cracked the code to a million-dollar riddle and awaited his prize.

"That's fantastic news. I want to get all the details, but first, I was warming up some chicken for a late night meal. I made some oven fries, too. Want some?"

"You have enough?"

"I do. I kind of overdid it, so you'll save me from eating too much so late."

"Then yes." Tyson stretched his arm along the back of the sofa.

"Anything to drink?" Jackie asked as she went toward the kitchen.

"Whatever you're having is fine," he called out.

She removed the fries from the oven and placed an even amount on two paper plates and then added chicken to each plate. Using a tray, she carried the plates and two canned sodas back out to the living room. "All right, here we go."

"What's this?" His eyes were focused on her laptop.

Jackie peered at the screen. *Damn.*

She'd forgotten she'd been on that site. She'd become distracted by a phone call and then went to the kitchen to prepare her meal. Might as well have the conversation with Tyson that she knew she needed to have ever since she found out she'd been approved for the adoption.

"Those are the kids available for adoption in the county." She set the food and drinks on the coffee table.

"Oh." He frowned and looked at her. "Why are you looking at them? Somebody you know adopting?"

Now or never.

"I am. The day Kendrick came by my store, I talked to my caseworker and he told me the good news—that I've been approved to adopt a child, and I immediately started looking at potential children."

"Wait a minute, you want to adopt? We've entered the grandparent stage of life, baby. Are you serious?"

"Yes, I am."

The half-smile died on his face. "I had no idea you wanted kids. *Now?*" Perplexed, his brows knitted together.

She understood his reaction. She'd received a similar reaction from almost everyone she told about her desire. They couldn't understand why a fifty-five-year-old woman wanted to become a single mother.

"I don't have a lot of regrets in my life, but not having children is one of them. I want to be a mother."

Tyson glanced at the screen again, the frown deepening on his brow. "So you're looking for a baby?"

Jackie shook her head. "Initially, I thought a toddler, but after learning that so many older kids remained in the system because most people want babies or toddlers, I decided to adopt a slightly older child. A girl."

Tyson stood and smoothed a hand over the back of his bald head. Confusion continued to overshadow his face. "This is a lot to take in, Jackie, because I didn't have an inkling you wanted to be a mother. I mean, I know you love kids, but...do you have any idea what you're getting yourself into? Children are a huge responsibility."

"Believe me, I know. I have friends who have children, I have godchildren and nieces and nephews who have children. Not to mention part of the screening process for adoption includes an evaluation to make sure I'm able to care for a child both financially and emotionally, *and* I took an eight-week class on child-rearing for adoptive parents. This is not a decision I entered into lightly. I thought about it for years before filling out the application and going through a process that took months before I finally got approved."

"I don't know what to say."

"You don't have to say anything. This is my decision."

"Last week we were talking about being together. I put up my condo for sale. I'm moving here, to be with you."

"I had no idea you'd done that. I never asked you to do that."

"It was a surprise. I told you I want to move here and want a future with you—marriage, traveling—like you said you wanted. Children have never come up in our conversations and were never... in the plans. "

"Two months ago, *you* weren't in my plans. But I want to have a child, and that's not going to change because you say you want to be with me now."

His jaw flexed. "This is crazy."

"Why is it crazy? Why can't I have a child now?" Jackie demanded.

"I've already had my kids, and I fucked up being a parent. I definitely wouldn't want to put another child through that. And at my age, I don't see myself being a daddy again. Grandpa for sure, but daddy?" He shook his head, shoulders dropping a fraction.

"This isn't about you, Tyson!"

"How is it not about me? Haven't we been talking about a future together?" He glared at her.

Jackie calmed her voice. "Yes, we have. But now you know, that future includes a child. This is what I want, what I crave. Can you understand that?"

"No, I can't."

His voice sounded tired and his eyes filled with sadness. Her heart broke. She had suspected they'd have difficulty navigating this part of their relationship, but he didn't seem likely to budge. Reflecting on his comments the night of their first date, she'd known to expect this type of reaction from him, yet she'd hoped for a different result.

When she told me she was pregnant, I was devastated.

"Baby, I love you. You know I do, but my parenting days are behind me."

"We can figure this out."

"You want a child, but I don't. There's nothing to figure out."

"So our timing is off again?" Jackie whispered, finding it difficult to speak over the hurt of rejection. Was she really losing him for a second time?

"Seems that way."

They stood in silence, neither looking at the other. She didn't know what to say, because she wasn't changing her mind. She'd come too far—and she really, really wanted to be a parent.

For as long as she could remember, she'd concentrated on accruing accolades and piling up money in the bank. Voted most likely to succeed by her senior class. Graduating with honors from high school and college. She'd been SGA president, French club treasurer, and when she worked in retail—employee of the year. As a businesswoman she'd been profiled in magazines and interviewed on talk shows.

She spent so much time on her career and smashing goals that she missed out on marriage and having children. At her age, having a biological child was out of the question, but adoption was an option. She couldn't walk away now. Not when she was so close.

"So there's no real future for us."

She dared to look at him and wished she hadn't. The same emptiness that filled her heart was reflected in his eyes. There was no compromise with this type of difference. Someone had to give, and she knew he wouldn't.

Tyson rubbed his palm up and down the back of his head. "I hate the sound of that. As far as I'm concerned, you are my future."

"Except for one glaring issue—the fact that I want to adopt."

He swallowed. "I don't suppose there's any chance..." He let the words trail off into the air, perhaps knowing that even as he formulated the sentence, his request would be unreasonable. "Kendrick and I are leaving for New York in a few days. That's the other reason I wanted to stop by to see you, because I'll be gone with him for a few weeks."

"Adelaide's daughter lives in New York. If you like, I could ask for her number and that's someone you could touch base with when you get there, and Kendrick could have a friend in the city." She sounded as devoid of emotion and lifeless as she felt.

"Thanks, I'd appreciate that, and I'm sure he will, too."

Tyson remained still, and she didn't move, either. After a while, she huffed a deep breath and said, "You should probably go now, and I need to get back to sorting through the photos of available children."

He glanced at the food and the computer, but didn't comment.

"Tyson."

He nodded. "I heard you. It's just...this feels so final. I don't want to lose you from my life just because...I want us to stay in touch. At least until I get back, so we can talk some more."

"About what?"

"I don't know. I...never mind." He pulled her into a hug, and she melted against his solid frame. "I love you."

"I know. I love you, too." Jackie wrapped her arms around his torso and squeezed him tight. Nuzzling his neck, she breathed in his cologne and savored the moment in his arms.

His lips found hers, and he kissed her gently, softly, before releasing her with great reluctance. "I'll call you when we get to New York." His voice sounded thick with sadness.

Unable to speak, Jackie merely nodded.

She followed him to the door and waved goodbye as he exited. Then she shut the door and stood frozen on the threshold, her heart feeling as if it had been ripped in two and glued back together with all the rough, jagged edges exposed.

She squeezed her eyes shut, a futile attempt to contain the tears that nonetheless ran in rivulets onto her cheeks.

15

"Hi, Hector, I'm sorry to bother you guys at this hour, but is Adelaide here?" Jackie stood on the doorstep of her best friend's house, light shining down on her like a beacon in the darkness.

"She is. Come on in."

"Thanks," she said gratefully.

She followed Hector into the den.

"She was just getting out of the shower. I'll let her know you're here. Can I get you anything to drink?"

"I'm good, thanks."

After he left, Jackie heaved a sigh of exhaustion and paced the room. She'd been driving around for almost an hour, trying to clear her head but couldn't. She was miserable and heartsick. No doubt about it, she was in love with Tyson, and the thought of being married to him someday had at one time filled her with joy.

But the adoption—something she'd looked forward to for years, had become a roadblock on the way to happiness and proved difficult to get around. In fact, she saw no way to get around it, and she had to face the unimaginable thought of losing him again.

She only had two choices—Tyson or the child she always wanted. What kind of choice was that?

"Hey." Adelaide came toward her, dressed casually in shorts and a loose-fitting tee, concern for Jackie creased into her brow.

"I'm sorry to come here so late."

As she sank down on the chair, Adelaide dismissed the apology with a wave of her hand. "It's only nine o'clock, so it's not late, and even if you came by at two o'clock in the morning, you know I'd still talk to you. What's going on?"

"I'm torn about Tyson. I'm in love with him, Adelaide, and I don't know how in the world I'm going to get over him. Did I make the right decision in sending him away?"

"I can't answer that. Only you can," her friend said.

Jackie groaned and sat down beside her. "That's not what I wanted to hear."

"I know," Adelaide said with sympathy in her eyes. "Look, ever since I've known you, you've talked about your desire to be a mother, and I know you regret not turning to adoption sooner. You have to think about what you want, in your heart of hearts. What would make you happiest?"

"Raising a child with Tyson."

"But that's not an option."

Jackie played with the long dark strands of her black wig. "He wants to stay friends. He's been texting me every day, keeping me up-to-date on progress with Kendrick. I'm happy for him, for them both, because I know Kendrick wanted to have a better relationship with his father. But as I'm reading the texts, I keep thinking about how much I want that, too —the opportunity to love a child and help them and expose them to new ideas and experiences. There's more to life than work and spreadsheets and going home to an empty house. I want a family, and I want to give and receive unconditional love. But if I'm going to be with Tyson, that type of future is lost to me because he doesn't want another child. And I can't really blame him, because we're not exactly spring chickens."

Adelaide nodded slowly. "Then maybe you have your answer."

Jackie closed her eyes for a moment. "You're right, I do. I'm not going to be one of those people who gets married and has to forgo having children because her partner doesn't want any. Those relationships are often fraught with problems."

"You know about the trouble Renee had in her second marriage because her husband wanted kids and she didn't. I know of two other couples who were at odds about children, and they both ended up divorced, too. One couple divorced because the wife got pregnant when her husband had specifically told her he didn't want children. He was very upset because she stopped taking her pills. You'd be taking a huge risk being with a man who's made it clear he's not interested in rearing kids at his age."

"You're right, which brings me to another decision—a tough one that I didn't want to make. I can't keep seeing him, Adelaide. It's too hard."

"Are you sure you want to cut him off completely?"

On the drive over she'd thought long and hard about the decision and knew it was the right one. "I want him too much. I want the life I had hoped to have. I...I have to separate myself from him."

Adelaide's eyes filled with sympathy. "I understand. You know I'll be right here if you need me, for support. And you're not going into motherhood alone."

"I know."

Adelaide grabbed both her hands and squeezed. "You're going to be a mommy!"

Jackie smiled for the first time since she arrived. "I'm going to be a mommy!"

Beaming with happiness, they both hugged.

PLEASE DON'T TEXT me anymore. I don't think it's a good idea for us to keep in touch. I'm sorry. It's just too hard.

When Tyson read those words, his senses dulled to everything in Times Square. He didn't see the swarm of people crowding the sidewalk. He didn't hear the noise of conversation or smell the exhaust from the honking cars.

For the past two weeks he had kept in touch with Jackie because... He didn't know why. She'd been clear about her decision to adopt, and he'd been honest about not wanting to raise kids again. Neither had minced words or been willing to compromise, but he couldn't let go. Now she was telling him he had to.

Erasing Jackie from his life wasn't an option. They wouldn't get married, but he'd hoped to continue seeing her, at least.

"Check this out." Kendrick walked over and presented a colorful flyer promoting an eating tour of the city, from an insider's point of view. "We could do this tomorrow after my morning appointment, and that way I'll get in the know about all the cool places where the locals eat, instead of the usual advertised restaurants tourists go to."

Tyson took the flyer but couldn't focus on the details. All he saw were the words from Jackie's text, emblazoned in his mind. *I don't think it's a good idea for us to keep in touch.*

"Hey, something wrong?"

He met his son's worried gaze.

"I could pay if you want, since you've been treating the whole time," Kendrick added.

"No, I don't care about the money."

"What's wrong? You looked...strange for a minute, like you were upset."

"I'm not upset, and believe me, a seventy-five-dollar tour is not going to break me. I was thinking about something, but...never mind."

"Jackie?"

Tyson's chest deflated, and he handed back the flyer. "Am I that obvious?"

"Most of the time you're present, but every now and again you go somewhere else in your head. Last night at the restaurant, I had to call your name twice before you noticed the waiter was ready to take your order."

"I hope I'm not spoiling your time here."

They started strolling down the avenue.

"Nah, I'm good. But I understand. Jackie's quite a woman."

"Don't do that shit," Tyson groaned. Kendrick had already teased him several times about Jackie.

Kendrick laughed, a welcomed sound despite the reason for it. The past two weeks, his son had become more relaxed around him. They'd shared plenty of laughs, engaged in thoughtful conversations, and he'd learned more about Kendrick's dream to become an actor. A teacher had initially stoked his interest by pointing out his innate talent, and he'd secretly taken acting classes two years ago to work on his craft. What Tyson had assumed was an impulsive hobby, his son had clearly put a lot of thought into and was very serious about.

"But it's true, she is an amazing woman. Fine, smart as hell in business. Definitely driven. The two of you are alike in that way."

Tyson came to a stop with the other pedestrians waiting to cross the street. "Yeah, she's something," he murmured, thinking back on the night at the beach, when she looked up at him and he saw the promise of a future together in her eyes.

"So what happened? Because it's obvious something is wrong," Kendrick said.

"Let's grab a bite here," Tyson said, pointing. "They're supposed to have great cheesecake."

"So you're not going to tell me?"

Tyson didn't answer right away, but a side glance at Kendrick made it clear that his son expected an answer. "All right, I'll tell you, but let's have a seat first."

They were lucky enough to get a table outside so they could people watch. While they waited for their coffees and cheesecake to arrive, Tyson opened up and told Kendrick about Jackie's adoption plans and the last text he received from her.

By the time he finished talking, they had their food in front of them. Kendrick dived into the New York cheesecake with cherry topping, but Tyson couldn't touch a bite of his strawberry cheesecake.

"I have a question for you," Kendrick said, putting down his fork.

"Shoot." Tyson sat back and readied for an inquisition.

"Do you love Jackie?"

"Yeah, I do. I fucking do." He rubbed both hands over his bald head to stem the pain that overcame him at the thought of losing her again—this time for good.

"So why are you willing to walk away?"

"I'm not willing to."

"You are. You told me—"

"I'm not the type of man she needs. I'm letting her go because I suck at being a parent. Never mind I'm old and set in my ways. I can't raise a kid now."

He watched pedestrians rushing by—some laughing together, others alone, head down or head high as they barreled toward their destination.

In a low voice, he added, "I'll probably mess up her kid and mess up the life she has planned raising her."

"Is that what you're worried about?" Kendrick asked quietly.

Tyson swallowed past the lump in his throat. His chest hurt. He couldn't look at his son right then and kept his eyes on the black coffee in the white cup on his side of the table.

"You and I just started getting along. I don't want to screw up any more kids in this lifetime."

Silence filled the space between them, and Tyson's gut burned with shame. He had a good life now and had finally achieved a life-long dream of financial success, but at what cost? He'd alienated his kids and only established a decent relationship with them as adults.

"I don't have a clue how to be a father. I'm just winging it right now." He lifted his gaze.

"Does any man really *know* how to be a father? I figure every-body's just winging it and hoping for the best. Personally, I think the most important part of being a parent is showing that you care. For the longest, I didn't think you cared, and um...it hurt, you know? That you could just set me aside and focus on whatever you thought was more important—business, women, my sisters. Even Jackie." He swallowed. "Paying for this trip wasn't necessary. Don't get me wrong, it's nice, and I appreciate it. But for me, the best part of this whole trip is that you came with me. You chose to be here when you could be anywhere else in the world doing a million other things. You waited in the lobby for two hours while I went on an audition because you knew I was nervous. You went over my lines with me. You helped me map out my day, and in between all that, hit sightseeing spots. I just wanted your time, Tyson. That's it. If you have time to give to Jackie's kid as her stepdad, then...I think you'll do just fine."

Warmth expanded in Tyson's chest. His kid had dropped some knowledge he could appreciate. "You trying to make me cry or something?"

"No," Kendrick said with a laugh.

"Thanks. I didn't realize it, but I guess I needed to hear that."

"You're welcome." Kendrick picked up his fork and placed a big hunk of cheesecake in his mouth.

"You think you'll ever be able to call me something other than Tyson? Like Dad or Pops or something?" Tyson picked up his fork, too, and waited.

Kendrick finished chewing, and the corners of his lips tipped upward. "Maybe. Let's see how things go."

So that wasn't a *no*. Tyson's mouth curved upward into a smile. "Okay, let's see."

More progress.

16

Jackie froze with her eye against the peephole.

Tyson stood on her doorstep, looking as scrumptious as ever in a dark pullover that clung to his biceps. He'd adhered to the request in her last text, sending a single word later that night—*OK*. She hadn't heard from him since then, and she sent the text seven days ago.

The bell chimed again, and she rested her forehead against the door, biting her upper lip. Could she handle talking to him? Why was he here?

Finally, she smoothed her hands down the front of her denim dress and wondered if she should close the top buttons she'd left undone. Deciding against it, she swiped her tongue across her mouth to moisten her lips before opening the door.

"Hello, Tyson."

"Hello, Jackie. Mind if I come in?"

God, his voice. She hadn't heard him speak in so long, and that deep voice of his had her ready to dump all her reservations, throw herself at him, and beg for a reconciliation.

"Sure, come in," she said, keeping her tone even.

Tyson walked ahead toward the living room, and she indulged in watching him move across the floor with measured steps. Tall, great ass, and his deep brown skin tempting her to run her fingers over his bald head and bare arms.

To keep from whimpering, she bit the inside of her cheek.

"I know you're probably surprised to see me."

"I am. How did you even know I was home?"

"I didn't, but I stopped by the main store first, and they told me you had taken the day off. I hoped you were home and not out somewhere. I got back to San Diego last night and couldn't wait to see you and talk to you. You look great, baby."

As usual, he ate her up with his eyes, gaze spanning the length of her body from top to bottom—on the way down idling for a breath-stopping moment at her bosom, before continuing the descent to her feet and then climbing back up to her face.

Her skin singed wherever his gaze touched, and heat rose to her cheeks. She needed to calm down and keep a straight head, because she could easily lose herself with him.

"Don't do that, please. Say what you came to say and leave."

"I can't pay you compliments anymore?"

"What do you want, Tyson?" she snapped.

His brow furrowed. "We're not enemies, Jackie. Are we?"

She immediately regretted the sharp tone. "I'm sorry, I wasn't expecting you, and I want to get this over with."

"I guess I should be glad you answered the door then."

"I don't hate you, but as I pointed out in my last text, I don't think it's a good idea for us to stay in touch."

She sat down on the sectional and tensed when he sat down a couple feet away.

"I've been doing a lot of thinking about the conversation we had before I left, and I came here to tell you that I changed my mind. I believe there is a future for us—one where we could raise a child together. I love you, Jackie, and I don't want anything to stand in the way of us being together. I screwed up letting you go before, and I can't do that again."

She rubbed her trembling hands together, queasy from the

opposing forces of elation and anxiety that raged a war in her abdomen. "You're saying everything I want to hear, but you and I won't work. You know it and so do I."

"I don't know that," Tyson said quickly.

She stood and faced away from him, assembling her thoughts. When she swung around, he was standing too, but had moved from in front of the sofa.

"Tyson, I know how you feel. Some days I don't want to get out of bed because I miss you so much, but I have responsibilities. Employees, bills to pay. I make myself get up because I have to. I miss you, and I'm a little angry that you made me realize how much my life has been lacking. I've enjoyed the times we've spent together on dates, talking, the general companionship, the sex. But there's something else I've been missing for years, and that's motherhood. I'm not willing to give up being a mom for you."

That's basically what her decision had boiled down to at the basic level. She'd had to make a choice, and she chose motherhood—the same way he'd chosen to sow his wild oats and pursue his dreams of entrepreneurship ten years ago. Once again, their timing was off.

"I'm not saying you should—"

"I wouldn't dream of asking you to be a father again because the last time we were together in this living room, you were very clear. So if you think you can convince me—"

"Woman, would you stop talking for five minutes!"

Tyson walked over and took both of her hands in his. Shocked by his outburst and hypnotized by his warm touch, Jackie fell quiet, focused on his eyes and the impassioned expression within them.

"I love you, and adopting a child is not a deal breaker for me. I was worried because I want to spend the rest of my life with you, and the idea of being a father again scared me."

"Scared you?"

"Yes, scared me. I screwed up big time before, but Kendrick and I talked one night, and he made me realize that I didn't have to be afraid. Kids need love and attention and time, and I can offer that." He brought the back of her hand to his lips. "We can do this, you and me. Raise a little girl. I think about my grandkids and how much I enjoy spending time with them. Kids are precious. They give so much more than they receive, and I'm ready to be a dad, stepdad, whatever you need me to be. I'm still scared as hell, baby, but I'm a different man than I used to be, and I'm looking forward to it."

"Are you sure? I'm going to adopt. I'm not changing my mind."

"I don't want you to, and yes, I'm sure."

His words sank in. "So you're still talking about a future together, and some day getting married?"

"Absolutely."

"And you don't mind being the oldest parent at the PTA meeting?" She grinned.

"Nobody better say shit." Tyson came closer, his black eyes soft, his enticing mouth close enough to kiss.

"Tyson, I'm scared, too," Jackie admitted, whispering as if someone could overhear them. "I've always been an overachiever and been successful at every venture, so I've never felt as if any goal was beyond reach. I simply set my mind to it and worked my butt off. But being a mom is—whew, a nerve-racking concept. My parents think I'm crazy, but they also thought I was crazy for starting my own business."

"And you showed them."

"I sure did."

"And you'll show them again by being the best mother on the west coast. Listen, if nothing else, I can make sure you know what *not* to do as a parent."

She laughed then quickly sobered. "Just so you know, I found a girl I'd like to adopt. She's nine years old, but she has an older brother who's thirteen. I told my caseworker I want to keep them together, so I'm going to adopt them both." She waited for his reaction.

"That's great."

"They've been in the system for a while, and it's possible that one or both of them come with some challenges," she warned. She'd already made up her mind to meet any difficulty head-on and give those kids the most supportive, loving home she could.

"Nothing you can't handle, you and me. Together."

Tension eased out of her muscles. Jackie gave Tyson a hug and rested her head against his chest. He kissed her temple, and she closed her eyes.

"Together."

EPILOGUE

I'm a graduate!

Hand in hand with Hector, Adelaide practically skipped into the restaurant on a cloud of happiness. Located above La Jolla Cove, Beach Dream was a popular spot that offered dining on a large patio overlooking the ocean.

She and Hector took their time through the crowded restaurant, winding past tables toward the back. Murmured conversations filled her ears, and the scent of spices and fresh seafood dishes perfumed the air around her. They walked toward the private dining room, where friends and family awaited their arrival.

At the doorway they stopped, everyone sprang to their feet and started applauding—even the attending servers.

Junior, her eldest, stood tall and handsome in front of her. He stuck two fingers in his mouth and whistled. Beside him, Karen—whom everyone said was Adelaide's twin—yelled, "Yeah, Mom!" Beside her, looking a lot more mature nowadays with a shorter haircut, Daniel grinned while cradling his sleeping son strapped to his chest. In a few weeks he'd be taking over management of Solar Beams III in Carlsbad. Jamie stood beside him, her long blonde hair hanging over one shoulder.

Adelaide walked farther into the room with Hector right beside her. The applause died down as she surveyed the room, grateful to see all the familiar faces.

"I don't know what to say. You all know I'm better one-on-one, instead of having to do a speech in front of a group, so I'll keep this short." She took a deep breath and released it. "First of all, thank you to my wonderful husband, Hector, who has been very supportive during the past year. He's been so patient, giving me room when I needed to study and making me go to bed when I stayed up late stressing about one thing or another. Thank you, honey." She raised up on tiptoe and planted a kiss on his soft lips.

"Aww," the crowd said. Then low chuckles rippled through the group.

"*Te amo.* I'm proud of you," he whispered in her ear.

"I love you, too, honey." She returned her attention to the guests. "I'm not finished! Thank you to my kids and every single one of you who encouraged me. I'm so glad you're here—my goodness, I didn't expect to see so many people!"

She laughed, her heart full, and cleared her throat of emotion. Her eyes searched the room, and she found the two people she was looking for. Renee and Jackie were with Clive and Tyson, seated near a gift table piled high with bags and wrapped boxes.

"A special thank you to my best friends, Renee and Jackie. You wouldn't let me have doubts and insisted I could complete the coursework, even when I didn't believe I could. You're the best friends in the world. I did it!" Adelaide held up her diploma and the group cheered and clapped again.

She visited each table, saying hello to everyone and giving hugs and kisses. Then she finally sat down with Hector, her kids, and Jamie at the front of the room.

The buffet menu offered plenty to drink and eat—seafood salads, shrimp and scallops with pasta, sea bass, chicken dishes, rice, and a potato dish. Adelaide chatted and laughed, sipping wine and savoring the meal as she celebrated with family. At the end of dinner,

with a slice of coconut cake and an espresso before her, Renee and
Jackie came over out of the blue.

Renee placed a hand on Adelaide's shoulder. "Can we borrow the
graduate for a little bit?" she asked the family.

"What's going on?" Adelaide asked, even as she rose to her feet.

"We'll show you in a minute," Jackie replied, placing her hand in
the middle of her back to shove her toward the door. "We won't be
long, and we'll bring her right back," she promised.

They went to Jackie's BMW, and she pulled out a basket and blanket. "We're going to do your favorite thing. Watch the sunset."

"Did I mention you two are the best friends ever?"

"We know," Renee said.

Laughing, they made their way down the steps to the beach.
Adelaide trailed behind her friends, stepping carefully across the
sand as strands of hair blew across her face and the hem of her dress
flapped in the cool breeze.

They settled onto the blanket with Adelaide in the middle, Renee
to her left, and Jackie on the right. Jackie poured them each a glass of
white wine and they sat in silence while sea lions barked nearby and
a group of older teens yelled at each other over the sound of loud pop
music.

Renee finally spoke. "We knew you wouldn't want to miss this."

"Thank you. You know, I was just thinking how much has
changed since last year. This time last year, I couldn't decide if I even
wanted to take the culinary classes." She shook her head.

"And Renee was terrorizing her neighbors," Jackie quipped.

Renee giggled. "I'm going to let you have that, because I'm in a
better place now where I can admit that I was a bit of a bitch. I'm a
new person."

"Thank goodness for Clive. Are you ever going to marry that
man?"

"I haven't decided yet." Renee sipped her wine.

"After a while he'll stop asking," Jackie said.

"No, he won't," Renee said confidently. "And believe me, I know how lucky I am. But for now, I'll wait. We're in no rush, and he's still taking his classes."

"How are those going?" Adelaide asked.

"Really well. He's come a long way, and he even texts me now. I'm so proud of him. But while you're talking about me, Jackie, have you and Tyson picked a date yet?"

A humungous diamond solitaire sparkled on Jackie's left hand.

"No," her friend said with a shake of her head. "We can't decide if we want to wait for the fall or put it off until next year. Right now I'm so busy with the kids, I don't have time to plan a wedding. He's keeping busy, too. He's going to New York to spend time with Kendrick again, and ever since he took JC surfing, he's been obsessed and I swear they're like two fish—always in the water. Brenda loves her martial arts class, so I've enrolled her in classes for the summer, and she mentioned wanting to take dance lessons with her best friend, so that'll be another activity to add along with everything else they get into this summer."

In typical Jackie fashion, she'd cruised into motherhood and didn't need much help—at least now, she didn't. The first few months had been quite an adjustment period for her and the kids, and there had been a few panic-stricken late night phone calls where she didn't know how to handle a temper tantrum or an argument that involved tossed dolls and slammed doors.

Adelaide had calmed her down and reminded Jackie that she was doing a great job and gave advice on how to proceed. Like all families, they still had their moments of friction, but Jackie was better equipped to handle those problems now.

"Next week I'm going to apply for my catering license. Soon I'll officially be in business," Adelaide said.

"I'm sure Eleanor is glad," Renee said.

"She is. She already has me lined up for her big birthday bash coming up next month."

"Get those business cards printed up, because I have a feeling after that party, you're going to be very busy," Jackie said.

"I love that idea."

The sun crept toward the horizon, and the three of them fell quiet.

They sat on the beach, sipping wine, listening to the waves wash up on the shore. The sun continued its descent, splashing the evening sky with red and orange and yellow, before dipping behind the ocean.

ALSO BY DELANEY DIAMOND

More stories with mature couples!

Passion Rekindled (Brooks Family #2). Oscar Brooks has always assumed that his ex-wife hates him, but after an unplanned kiss, he's not so sure. Why does Sylvie Johnson always have such a hostile response to his presence? Is it love, or is it hate? He's determined to find out. (Not available in paperback.)

Still in Love. Cortez Alesini long ago accepted that his music career aided in the demise of his marriage. So he didn't expect that he and Nadine would spend passionate nights together while she's back in his home country of Argentina, causing them to question if they gave up too soon.

Without You (Quicksand #2). Charisse Burrell divorced Terrence after his cheating ways broke her heart one too many times. In a moment of weakness she gives in to her desires and makes a mistake that she soon regrets. Now Terrence wants her to believe that not only has he changed, they should try again. Will her heart give him another chance?

ABOUT THE AUTHOR

Delaney Diamond is the USA Today Bestselling Author of sweet, sensual, passionate romance novels. Originally from the U.S. Virgin Islands, she now lives in Atlanta, Georgia. She reads romance novels, mysteries, thrillers, and a fair amount of nonfiction. When she's not busy reading or writing, she's in the kitchen trying out new recipes, dining at one of her favorite restaurants, or traveling to an interesting locale.

Enjoy free reads and the first chapter of all her novels on her website. Join her mailing list to get sneak peeks, notices of sale prices, and find out about new releases.

Join her mailing list
www.delaneydiamond.com

facebook.com/DelaneyDiamond
twitter.com/DelaneyDiamond
instagram.com/authordelaneydiamond
bookbub.com/authors/delaney-diamond
pinterest.com/delaneydiamond

Made in the USA
Columbia, SC
14 July 2020